The Lightbearers:

A W A K E

Beth Hermes

7/26/12

Carol —
Lightbearers bloom
where they're planted!
Enjoy!
— Beth Hermes

Black Rose Writing

www.blackrosewriting.com

ISBN: 978-1-61296-120-0

PUBLISHED BY BLACK ROSE WRITING

www.blackrosewriting.com

Printed in the United States of America

The Lightbearers: Awake is printed in Times New Roman

For Craig, Abigail and Benjamin.

Acknowledgments

Special thanks to the Shift Sisters: Asha Lightbearer, Carla Flack, Carol Reinlie, Laura Mikszan, Jill Felts, Susan Hoffman and Tonya Joy, who checked in often and kept me focused; especially Asha and Carla, who listened to the premise, read the first draft and offered their encouragement. Thanks, as well, to my writing students and friends who support our independent booksellers, whose kind words and enthusiasm were an enormous source of inspiration; and to Ellen Ward, Jackie Tanase and Karen Schwettman of FoxTale Book Shoppe, who have shared my excitement as this series has come to light.

Thanks, too, to Black Rose Writing, for the opportunity to share the story of *The Lightbearers.*

The art on the cover was created by posi-artist Carla Flack and the cover was designed by artist Carol Reinlie of Hot Biscuit Marketing.

The Lightbearers:

AWAKE

Chapter 1

The sky was an eerie gunmetal blue, seamlessly meeting an ocean of the same color on the distant horizon. Although the wind had barely begun to pick up, the waves already bore the force of the storm churning a day or more off the coast.

Cara closed her eyes and breathed in deeply, luxuriating in the pungent salt-water smell and enjoying the crackles of electricity that seemed to penetrate the air on the beach. She smiled slightly, in spite of herself. She was somehow energized by the storm's intensity, although it had not yet begun to reach its potential. Storms changed everything: the wind, the water, the temperature of the air, even the people in their path.

Inside the hotel room behind her, the television weatherman spewed warnings, his voice brimming with excitement as he indicated maps on the screen behind him and attempted to project the storm's path.

Storms were a reminder, she thought, of the imbalance of power between mankind and nature. No matter how much control a person thought he or she had over the forces of nature, nature always revealed her true power in the end, and it dwarfed that of humans immeasurably. Projecting the path of the storm would be as simple as catching a rainbow in a jar, Cara thought with a smile.

She opened her eyes as she heard the hotel room's glass door slide closed behind her.

"Do you smell that?" Stephan asked as he approached her,

coming to a halt just inches from her elbow.

She turned to look at him. "I do," she said.

"Salt," he said. "And fish."

She cocked an eyebrow and shook her head, turning to face him. "Hopeless," she told him. "It's energy. Don't you feel it?"

He frowned at her and opened his mouth to answer, but turned as a sudden movement caught his attention past her, at the water's edge, and his eyebrows shot up in alarm.

Cara turned to look and gasped as a sudden gust of wind whipped her hair into her eyes. She reached up to brush it away and exhaled impatiently. "Tell me they're not going to do it." Her breath caught in her chest and she moved her hand from her hair to her throat – her expression of sudden anxiety.

Stephan shoved his hands in the pockets of his sweatshirt and shrugged. "Looks that way." He squinted into the wind, watching. His voice was quiet, but Cara recognized his concern – the sudden intensity in his eyes, the working of his jaw.

She shook her head. "Don't they understand?"

He laughed without humor. "Apparently, they don't care."

Cara turned her attention back to the edge of the water. She and Stephan watched as the first of two figures halted and faced the water, a surfboard tucked under one arm. The second figure was more hesitant, struggling to maintain control of on his own board. The first was gesturing to his companion, obviously trying to convince him to take the risk and ride the threatening waves.

"Don't do it," Cara muttered, hoping her will would carry her warning to the hesitant figure on the beach.

Stephan shook his head and bumped his arm against hers. "You can't make them stop. Not from here, anyway."

She looked up at him and frowned. "Do you think they would listen?"

He shrugged. "Worth a shot, isn't it?" A grim, humorless smile stretched his lips as he spoke.

They had barely made their decision to intervene when a cry for help came from the beach in front of them. The hesitant figure had tossed his board aside and was waving his arms frantically, screaming, trying to catch Cara's and Stephan's attention.

"What..." Stephan began.

Cara covered her mouth with one hand and pointed with the other, the blood draining from her face. "Oh, God!"

Stephan's gaze shifted to follow the direction in which she was pointing and Cara felt the energy of his body intensify beside her.

The first man had plunged into the water with his board and was immediately caught by a wave and thrown off into the dangerous surf. The board had flipped over and was being carried back toward the shore, riderless. The man who had held it moments before was nowhere to be seen.

Stephan bolted toward the scene, sand flying from under his tennis shoes. Cara turned away, covering her face. With enormous resolve, she inhaled deeply, pulling salty air into her lungs and loosening the grip of anxiety in her chest, then pulled her hair back and ran after him, muttering under her breath at the stupidity of some people.

The man on the beach was waving his arms wildly as he babbled, his eyes scanning the water for his friend. "I told him..." he blubbered. "He wouldn't..."

"Shh," Cara said, reaching a hand toward him, looking at the water, not at the young man. The scent of fish and salty air grew suddenly stronger and she shuddered.

"There!" Stephan shouted, pointing farther down the beach than Cara and the young man had been searching. They turned to look at the man, who resembled a rag doll as he flailed his arms helplessly against the unseen rip tide.

Stephan hesitated for a moment, then looked at Cara, who felt his body tense in resolve. Her eyes grew wide and she shook her head, grabbing his arms. "No! You can't! The tide is too strong!" The wind and panic combined to make her voice sound shrill, foreign to her own hears.

He frowned and shrugged her off, then turned and scanned the dunes. He paused and pointed. "There's a life preserver!" he shouted, running in the direction of the dunes as he spoke.

Cara's hand came to rest over her heart. "Thank God!" she said, her voice quiet in the rising wind.

The young man looked at her, his eyebrows knitted together. His expression was a mix of pain, frustration, fear and terror, into which anger was now introduced. "What do you mean, 'Thank God'?"

"Sorry," she told him. "We don't need two people lost in the water. The waves may not be high, but the rip tide is fierce strong. Even a strong swimmer can't navigate the water when it's like that."

"Lost?" His face crumbled and Cara thought he was about to cry. "I know!" he said. "That's what I told Kip!"

She opened her mouth as if to speak, but changed her mind. This was no time to admonish him; he was feeling guilty already, and it looked as though Kip might already have been lost to the ocean.

Stephan returned, carrying the life preserver, and handed an end of the rope to Cara and the young man. "Hold onto this and don't let go, whatever you do!" he warned them. "It's not my choice to be a hero, but I really don't have any aspirations of martyrdom. Understand?"

His attempt at brevity may have seemed odd to the young man, but Cara recognized it as a mask for Stephan's fear. He hated the water when it was calm – he had always harbored an irrational fear of sharks. For him to be jumping into a rip tide had to have his stomach in knots.

Cara gulped and handed part of the rope to the young man. "Hold this," she said, "and don't let go!"

"What's this going to do?" the young man asked, his voice cracking. "Kip is way farther out than this!"

With a sudden sick feeling, Cara realized he was right. Either Kip would have to swim to Stephan – which seemed unlikely by this time – or Stephan would have to let go of the life preserver and swim to Kip. Either way, she was sure she'd lose them both. But it was too late to say so. Stephan had already shed his shoes and jacket and splashed into the waves; he was struggling to keep Kip in view.

Cara held on tightly, and she urged the young man into the water up to his calves. "We've got to give them extra rope," she shouted.

"He'll never reach your friend unless we get a little wet!"

The young man gulped and edged his way further into the water. "This tide is strong!" he said unnecessarily. "Why the hell did Kip think he could jump in like that?"

"That's what I was wondering," Cara said. She spoke quietly, but obviously the young man heard her, because he turned toward her and frowned.

Cara stared at him until he looked back out over the waves. When something resembling a smile crossed his face, she felt her heart leap in her chest and she looked out as well. Stephan had somehow managed to wrangle the other man from the tide and drag him to the life preserver. She felt a pull on the rope and struggled to maintain her hold as the two men fought against the tide to maintain their hold on the floating circle. She felt her heart beating in her throat as she watched helplessly, then took a deep breath as Stephan nodded, indicating she and the young man should begin hauling them in toward the shore.

She braced herself, allowing the water to spill sand around her ankles, and she started pulling the rope as hard as she could, shouting orders at the young man to do the same. He was strong, which was a good thing, because a smaller, weaker man would have been useless against the force of the tide beneath the waves.

Finally, with Kip and Stephan thigh-deep in the water, Cara dropped the rope and ran out to help. Kip was slouched somewhat, with his head flopping over his chest. His legs were moving, but he looked like a marionette, and Stephan was the puppet master pulling the strings.

They walked as far as they could past the water line and collapsed on the beach, Kip sputtering and coughing, eventually puking what seemed like a gallon or more of sea water onto the sand.

"What the hell, Kip?" his friend shouted as Kip finally raised himself up on his elbows and wiped his mouth with the back of his hand.

Although he looked a little green around the gills and smatterings of sand were clumped in his hair and on his skin, Kip had the audacity to grin. "That was a trip, man. You should've tried it."

Cara recognized the nervous energy around the young man, which he was trying to cover with his bravado. Kip's companion, however, took the words seriously and kicked his foot angrily, sending sand flying over Kip and Stephan. Cara blinked and spat as some of the sand blew into her face.

"What the hell?" Kip shouted, spitting to expel the sand from his mouth. "That was..."

"Idiotic?" the young man spat. He wore twin blotches of red on his cheeks as the anger that had been suppressed by fear finally surfaced. "Yeah. Well... Now you know how I felt about *you* when you were floating out there without your damned surf board, Kip!"

"Hey, but if I *did* have the board, that would've been, like, the *coolest* ride ever!" Kip said, smiling.

Cara could tell by looking at him that the smile was forced, but apparently Kip's companion couldn't. He dropped to his knees in the sand and began sobbing. "Don't you *ever*, man. Do you hear me? *Ever - do* that again!"

Kip simply looked at Cara and shrugged. "I can't help it. I'm a thrill-junkie."

She could feel the heat in her own cheeks as she frowned at him. "Well, have a thrill with something that's a little less ominous next time. Perhaps you could try jumping out of a plane," she told him, her voice shaking.

He grinned. "Did that. Any other suggestions?"

"Just stay the hell away from hurricane beaches," she said. "They're unpredictable and dangerous!"

"I've ridden them before," he told her.

She shook her head and looked out across the water. "Not like this one."

"What do you mean?" he asked. "The waves aren't even that high yet."

"Not up top," she said. "It's the under water current that will get you. You're a surfer; you should know this stuff."

He shrugged. "What can I say? I told you, I like the thrill of the ride."

She stared at him levelly. "Then go out to California. They have one or the other. You get really big waves but not hurricanes. When you're used to the water out there, you can read it. Here, it changes every time." She raised her eyes to the water as she spoke, invoking the danger of the waves, then looked back at Kip.

He nodded, eyes wide as he hung on her every word.

Cara thought that perhaps she was actually getting through to him, until she realized that Stephan had risen to his knees and was holding onto her elbow, staring at her face. The young man was also staring at her, his red-stained cheeks cartoonish against his wide eyes.

"What?" she asked, but she couldn't hear her own voice. She glanced from side to side, but could find no evidence of a heavy wind that could be responsible for drowning out her voice. She panicked, sucked in a deep breath and pawed furiously at her ears as a humming noise grew louder and louder. Finally, when the volume grew too loud for her to bear, she closed her eyes and felt herself sink to the sand, supported by several hands.

* * * * *

When Cara awoke, she was no longer on the beach. In fact, the weather outside the window seemed balmy rather than threatening, making her wonder if she had dreamt the entire episode. She changed her mind as she looked around and realized that the surroundings were unfamiliar. The bright lights, sanitary smell and hard tile floor told her she was definitely not in their room at the hotel.

Stephan was dozing in a chair by the window, sand still clinging to his brown hair and the ends of his long eyelashes. Cara glanced at him and briefly recalled the scene on the beach, wondering what had become of the young man. Her last memory before losing consciousness was of arguing with him after he had just vomited seawater onto the sand, and of the increasingly bad weather and strong tides – and the humming sound she thought was the wind. The mere thought of that sound made her shudder once more.

She closed her eyes and held her hands to her ears. *Vertigo,* she thought. She'd had it before, when she was pregnant with the twins, but it had been more of a ringing noise. This had been a distinct *hum,* like a swarm of bees, and very, very loud.

She frowned and turned her attention to the television. She searched briefly for the remote and tapped the volume button, trying not to disturb Stephan. She channel-surfed until she came to the Weather Channel, and squinted at the screen. The swirling graphic that represented a hurricane was hovering somewhere east of Puerto Rico, and the weatherman was saying that it would likely bounce off the eastern United States before drifting harmlessly out to sea.

Cara shook her head. Somehow, she knew this wasn't the case, but she wasn't sure how she knew. After a brief infatuation with the idea of becoming a meteorologist (The clothes! The lights! Those cool green screens with the maps!), she realized she had no desire to spend her career racing into storm zones with a microphone and a logo-emblazoned rain slicker – not to mention receiving hate mail from prospective brides, athletes and folks who had scheduled vacations. No, instead she had gone into accounting, so that folks only despised her *en masse* for a short time every year.

Something hummed and she stiffened, remembering the noise that had resonated inside her head just before everything went black. She relaxed when she realized it was a man-made, electronic noise, and not that of the ocean talking to her.

Stephan stirred in his chair and reached into his pocket for a cell phone, turning off the buzzing sound without so much as opening his eyes. He shifted his position in the chair, frowned in his sleep, then settled in with his mouth slightly open and began snoring softly.

She laughed quietly to herself and watched him sleep, feeling the protective instinct rise within her. He had risked his life to save a stranger – and an idiotic stranger, at that! What if something had happened to him? He was like the brother she'd always wished for, and she didn't know what she would do without him.

She sighed and turned her attention back to the television, where the live-action radar was now displayed on the screen. It showed an enormous mass of clouds hovering over the Atlantic, blocking most of the tiny Caribbean islands from view.

"Damn, that's big," she said.

"Huh?" Stephan stirred again. His eyebrows drew together as he squinted at her through barely open lids and smiled lazily. "Hey, you're awake." His voice was rusty with sleep and seawater.

"Captain Obvious!" Cara said, smiling.

Stephan rubbed his face with one hand, grimacing as he smeared sand down his cheek, tiny granules making impossibly loud noises as they pinged off the tile floor. "Gross," he said. "I need a shower."

She shrugged and nodded in agreement. "That's what you get for sleeping in the same clothes you swam in," she said, smiling.

He raised an eyebrow. "That wasn't exactly by choice."

"I know," she said. "I'm grateful, even though you did scare me to death."

"No worries. I survived," he said. "How are you feeling?"

She shrugged. "Fit as a fiddle," she told him. Her forehead creased as she recognized the dull throbbing inside her head as the beginning of a migraine. "Well, maybe a bass fiddle," she amended. "That was really weird!"

"Yeah. Tell me what happened. One minute you were helping me and that kid Travis haul Kip out of the water, and the next minute they were helping me haul you off the beach to the hospital. It was really bizarre," he said.

"Travis. Was that his name? I didn't even think to ask," she said.

Stephan nodded and Cara continued. "What did the doctor say?" she asked.

He pushed himself up, stretching his long arms over his head as he yawned, then shaking his head. "You've got them stumped. All the tests they did came back completely normal."

She slumped down against the pillows. "That's going to cost me a pretty penny."

"I thought you had insurance."

She sighed and wrinkled her nose. "They kind of like it when you pay them on a regular basis," she said. "I've not exactly been their ideal client."

"You didn't let it lapse, did you?" he asked. "I mean, I assume they checked before they ran all those tests." He frowned and peered at her closely. "Besides, I thought Brandon was supposed to keep those bills paid."

She shrugged again, ignoring his comment about her estranged husband. "No matter," she told him. "I just have to get home and get back to work. No more play time for me."

Cara reached over to the bedside table and picked up a pen and pad of paper and began scribbling notes, pausing every few lines to gather her thoughts before scribbling some more.

"What are you doing?" Stephan asked.

She peeked over the note pad and held up a finger and finished her thought. She put the pad down and looked at him, smiling. "Working," she said.

"You're in the hospital!" he said. "Can't you give yourself one minute's rest?" He frowned, then added, "You don't have anyone's accounts here. How the hell are you working?"

She shook her head and shrugged. "When did they say I could leave?"

"They haven't figured out what's wrong with you," he said. "You may not be able to leave."

"Oh, I have to," she told him. She picked up the remote and searched for the Call button. "If they can't find anything wrong, they can't keep me here, right?"

He opened his mouth to speak, but thought better of it. He had known her long enough to realize that he couldn't change her mind once she'd made a decision. And in Cara's mind, the absence of symptoms meant she was healed – or hadn't been ill to begin with.

She pressed the button and heard a buzz somewhere down the hall. The noise gave her a moment of anxiety and she felt a flush rise in her cheeks, but she forced a smile when the nurse knocked on the door and came in. "Hi," the woman said. "You look better!"

"Yup. And I'm ready to go," she said, which garnered a doubtful expression from both the nurse and from Stephan.

The nurse carried a clipboard with her, which she placed on the tray next to the wall. Reaching for a supply cart, she pressed a button and withdrew a thermometer attached to a long, blue spiral cord. "Open up," she told Cara, and popped the thermometer into her mouth. "Now just stay quiet for a minute while I get your temperature, okay?"

Cara nodded and tightened her lips around the thermometer, watching the digital readout flashing on the display. When it beeped, she opened her mouth and glanced at the display. "I'm normal. Can I go now?"

The nurse raised an eyebrow. "Your temperature is normal. But the doctor thinks you had a seizure. She really doesn't want you to go anywhere." She removed a blood-pressure cuff from the cart and peeled the Velcro loudly, making Cara flinch.

"You okay?" the woman asked.

Cara nodded. "I can't stand Velcro. That noise is worse than fingernails on a blackboard, don't you think?"

The nurse shrugged and glanced at Stephan, but he had turned away from them and was staring intently at the television mounted on the wall above his head. She took Cara's blood pressure, which was 110/70. "Pretty good," she commented. "Much better than when you arrived."

"Would've been better than that if you hadn't just ripped that Velcro and scared me to death," Cara said, rubbing her arm. "I *really* hate that stuff!"

The nurse frowned, glanced down to make a note on the paper attached to the clipboard, then clicked her pen and returned it to the pocket of her flower-patterned scrubs. "Dr. Findlay wanted to see you when you woke up. Just sit tight and I'll let her know you're awake."

"And ready to go," Cara added, drawing another skeptical look from the nurse.

"I'm Jackie. Just let me know if you need anything," the woman said over her shoulder as she disappeared through the door.

Cara sighed with frustration as the door slowly swung shut. "Nurse Jackie. How cliché!" she said and sighed. "I really just want to go home."

Stephan frowned at her and put one hand on his forehead in frustration. "Keep your voice down. You don't want to make an enemy of the nurse. She carries needles!" he said. He stood up, walked to the window and opened the blinds. The sun was shining, but there were patches of heavy gray clouds gathered in the distance.

"Is that the ocean?" she inclined her head toward the window, indicating the clouds.

Stephan nodded. "The storm's not gone yet."

"What happened to that kid?" she asked. "You said his name was Kip?"

He folded his arms and continued to stare out the window. "He went home."

She snorted. "He's the one who needs his head examined, not me."

"How do you figure?" Stephan asked, unfolding his arms, which sent more granules of sand bouncing to the tile floor.

"I didn't go jumping into a tsunami-level rip tide with a surf board." she said.

"He didn't black out on the beach complaining of organ music," Stephan snapped back.

"Is that what I said?" she asked, surprised. "*Organ music?*"

He shook his head. "No. You said it was a hum."

"Not organ music," she said, and he shook his head. "Did *you* hear organ music?" she asked him.

He opened his mouth, then closed it again, shaking his head unconvincingly, and turning away from her as the door swung open and the doctor walked in, staring at the paper on the clipboard she carried.

She looked up and smiled. "Well, hello!" She scribbled something on the paper then clicked the pen shut, setting both items on the table and making eye contact with her patient. "I'm Patricia Findlay. How are you feeling?"

"I told Nurse Jackie, I'm fine," Cara said, trying to hide the irritation in her voice. She didn't like being confined; she preferred to be busy.

"Well, you seem to have suffered a seizure. We'd really like to figure out why," Dr. Findlay said. Her syrupy tone was one which Cara would have used to reason with her boys, and she didn't care for it one bit.

"I don't think it was a seizure," Cara told her, struggling to keep the irritation out of her voice.

Dr. Findlay cocked her head to one side and crinkled the corners of her eyes. "Oh? From your friend's account, it sure sounded like one." She pulled up a chair and sat down. "Now that you're awake, why don't you tell me what happened?" She tilted her head to other side and forced a smile.

Cara sighed, impatient with being treated like a child. "Well, I think it was more from the, uh, commotion, you know? I mean, we had just pulled that guy..."

"Kip," Stephan supplied.

Cara shot him a look and Dr. Findlay glanced at him as well. "Right. Kip," Cara continued. "We had just pulled him out of the water and I watched him throw up on the sand." She shrugged and made a face that she hoped would garner some sympathy. "I really don't handle that kind of thing well, you know?"

The doctor folded her arms across her chest. "Which part?"

"Well, all of it," Cara told her. "I mean, I live a pretty humdrum life. Boring. Predictable. I'm an accountant, you see. Numbers make other people sick, but not me. They don't bleed and they don't vomit, and I like not having to see body fluids, you know? So the adrenalin probably kicked in or something. Or maybe it was the smell. I don't know..."

Dr. Findlay nodded, and raised her chin skeptically. "Mm-hmm. Go on."

Cara sighed and rolled her eyes. "And then when he – Kip – threw up, well, I've never been able to tolerate someone else's being sick. Always turns my own stomach. I give you a lot of credit. You probably see people throwing up all the time."

The doctor chuckled at this. "Well, that's true." She turned and

19

picked up the clipboard from the table, and clicked the pen open. "Has this ever happened to you before?"

Cara shook her head. "No." She paused and frowned. "Well, yes," she admitted.

Dr. Findlay paused and looked at her patient.

"I had vertigo when I was pregnant. Twins. My doctor told me it was probably stress and hormones," Cara said.

"Are you pregnant now?" the doctor asked, even though she had the answer in front of her from Cara's blood work.

"God, no!" Cara said. "That would be something, wouldn't it?" She turned to Stephan. "An immaculate conception, for sure!"

Dr. Findlay laughed and scribbled something else on the chart. "Okay," she said, flipping to another page and making yet another note before looking directly at Cara once more. "Did you have anything to eat before you went out on the beach?"

She shook her head again. "No. Well, I had coffee..."

The doctor raised an eyebrow. "Coffee is *not* food."

"Right. I know that," Cara said.

She scribbled some more notes on the chart. "History of a heart condition?"

Cara shook her head.

"High blood pressure?"

"No."

"Anyone in your family ever have a seizure?"

"Not that I know of," she sat up a little straighter. "Look. This is really nothing, I'm sure of it."

"What do you do for a living?"

"Um..." Cara paused, frustrated. Hadn't she just finished telling the doctor that she worked with numbers? "I'm an accountant, remember? What does that have to do with it?"

"Environmental toxins sometimes cause a reaction," Dr. Findlay said.

"Yeah. I don't think so," Cara said. "I told you. I make sure people's balance sheets are, well, *balanced*. Not too many environmental toxins in that profession. Unless you count printer ink and the acid stuff they put in paper."

The doctor squinted at her.

"I clean up other people's messes," she said. "Just not those of the vomit variety. Although, the way some people bring their stuff to me makes me sick to my stomach sometimes. You can tell a lot about a person by the way they treat their money."

"Is that so?" the doctor asked, cocking her head.

Cara nodded. "Yes. Well, some people are really organized and bring me paper-clipped stacks of receipts and spreadsheets, all in nice, neat manila folders. Other people bring me shoe boxes full of wrinkled receipts that I have to sort out the best I can. You wouldn't believe some of the nasty things I find in those boxes!"

"Really?" Dr. Findlay asked.

Cara waved a hand in front of her face. "Yes. But nothing as nasty as vomit," she said and peered over the edge of the clipboard at the doctor's notes. "Can I go now?"

Smiling and shaking her head, Dr. Findlay lifted the clipboard away from her patient and scribbled one last note on her chart before clicking the pen shut. She exhaled and stood up abruptly, fixing Cara with a tight smile. "Well, Miss Porter, I can't find any reason to keep you here. Your vitals are all completely normal, you haven't shown any signs of being at risk for another episode." She shrugged. "This is a mystery to me."

Cara sighed and cast a mischievous glance at the doctor. "I guess that's why they say medicine's a *practice*, right?"

Dr. Findlay forced a laugh, although she did not look amused. "Right, then. You can get dressed. I'll have the nurse bring your discharge papers in a few minutes." She turned and left the room, her shoulders squared against the insult Cara had dealt her.

"Probably not the best idea, to tick off the doctor," Stephan said, fixing her with a disapproving stare.

"What? It's on all the paperwork they make you sign – 'the practice of medicine is not an exact science,' and all that jazz. You have to pay them even if they have no effing idea what's wrong with you." She laughed and looked at Stephan. "Do you think I could get away with that in my business? 'Sorry, Mr. Smith. I have no earthly idea what's going on with your finances. I recommend you just let that nice examiner from the IRS hang out with you for a few days and check out your paperwork from the last three or four years to see if any of that new code they've passed in secret has anything to do with your audit. That will be four hundred dollars, please!'"

He shook his head. "You're a mess."

"I know. And you're covered in sand," she said. "Now, get out of here so I can get dressed. If it wasn't for the surfing freaks, we'd have been on the road hours ago."

"And if you'd had a seizure in the car, we'd have been up a creek," Stephan said.

She frowned and looked up at him. "You know something? I don't think I'd have had that little episode if we were in the car." She refused to give it the title of *seizure,* as if bestowing it with the title would make it so. "I think it only happened because we were on the beach."

"What, so you think you're allergic to the beach?" he asked. "Let me get the doctor back in here for that official diagnosis."

"Ha-ha." She shook her head. "I can't explain it. It was like the air and the water were trying to talk really loud, like the storm was making them send a message."

Stephan clapped his hands over his ears and started toward the door. "I did not just hear that," he said. "And if I were you, I wouldn't repeat that kind of thing in here, or they'll forget about calling it a seizure and start examining the inner workings of your brain!"

She shrugged. "I'm not crazy. I just don't know how to say it any other way." Pulling the sheet back, she turned and lowered her feet to the freezing tile floor. "I'll be out in a minute," she told Stephan, and grabbed her clothes from the hangers on the bathroom door.

* * * * *

Stephan insisted on driving the entire six hours back to Atlanta, telling Cara she should rest so she wouldn't have another seizure.

"*Episode,*" she corrected. "And I'm not tired," she told him, ignoring the dull headache that was fighting to take up residence inside her skull. "In fact, I'm kind of wired."

"You're like that John Travolta character in that movie," Stephan said. When Cara looked confused, he added, "You know, the guy who thinks he was struck by an alien ship or something and he gets really smart?"

She frowned and shook her head. "Never seen it. What happens?"

"Turns out he had a stroke or a tumor or something that was pushing on the intelligence part of his brain," Stephan told her.

"Are you saying you think the hum in my head was a stroke?" she asked, then grinned. "It was not a tumor," she added in a poor imitation of Arnold Schwarzenegger.

He laughed and shook his head. "No, no. They would have found that," he assured her. "I'm just saying it's weird that you went through all of that and you aren't tired. Makes me wonder if the guy who wrote the movie went through something like that." He glanced at Cara and added, "or lived with somebody who did."

"Hm," she said, and grinned. "Do you think I'll get really smart?"

He laughed. "Right. I don't think so," he said, which earned him a punch in the arm. "Watch it! I'm driving!"

"What did you mean by that – *I don't think so*?" she asked.

Stephan shook his head and grinned. "You are so high maintenance, you know that?"

She made a face and looked out the window. The farther north they drove, the less ominous the storm clouds looked. In fact, the sun was peeking through the clouds ahead, and although the wind was stronger, the skies had been bright with occasional patches of blue since they left the hospital.

They rode without talking for nearly an hour, until the radio offered more static than music. Cara straightened the hospital discharge papers she still held on her lap and stashed them in the glove box, then began turning the dial on the radio, trying to find something other than country music. Finally, she gave up and pressed the button to turn it off.

She turned to look at Stephan. "Are you getting tired yet?"

He shook his head. "No, I'm fine," he said. "Are you?"

"No. I took a pretty good nap in that incredibly comfortable hospital bed. You should be the one resting," she told him. "After all, it was you who decided to take a little swim this morning."

He laughed. "Yeah. That's what I decided to do – take a refreshing dip in an angry ocean." He shook his head. "I took a nap while I was waiting for you to wake up. The chair was really comfortable, too." He still wore a smile, but that changed as he turned to her and saw her face, drained of color. "What's wrong? It's not happening again, is it?"

She felt cold, and gooseflesh rose on her arms and her neck. "No. It's what you just said about the ocean being angry. That's what I was trying to explain to you, back at the hospital. But it wasn't just the ocean. It was like the ocean and the wind were, I don't know, *alive* or something, and they were trying to tell me something."

Stephan gulped then turned his attention toward the road. He nodded and glanced at Cara. "There's a couple of restaurants at the next exit," he told her. "I think we need to stop and get something to eat."

She glared at him and crossed her arms. "Fine," she told him. "But I'm not crazy."

"No, but your blood sugar must be low or something. You didn't eat anything this morning."

"Now you sound like Dr. Findlay," she said, turning her head to stare out the window once more, adding in a lower voice, "I know what I heard. And apparently, so did you."

Stephan reached over and patted her knee. "You need to get out more, away from those damned spreadsheets," he said, then turned on his blinker and steered the car down the exit ramp.

They ate a leisurely lunch at the Cracker Barrel that overlooked the interstate, and Cara took her time wandering through the gift shop while Stephan paid the bill and used the restroom. When they climbed back into the car, she opened the magazine that she had left on the floor board and began leafing through the pages, stopping every so often to read an article or blurb.

Not long after they passed through Macon, Cara paused and frowned at the image on one of the pages.

"What is it?" Stephan asked. His voice was rusty, making her do a double-take.

She shook her head. "Strange picture, that's all." She held up the page for him to see – the image of a woman dressed in ribbons, floating in a swirl of water.

He shrugged. "It's an ad for a washing machine, I think," he told her. "You've never seen it before?"

"Of course I have," she told him. "I've just never really looked at it before."

"You in the market for a washing machine?" he joked.

Cara rolled her eyes. "Give me a break. It's just..."

"Don't tell me the picture is *speaking* to you."

She frowned. "No," she said, then hesitated. "Well, not really. But it just... I don't know... struck a chord with me this time."

"It's a *washing machine*, Cara," Stephan said. He gripped the steering wheel with both hands. "Did Dr. Findlay tell you to follow up with your doctor at home?"

"God, Stephan! Yes, she did. But I'm not crazy. I'm telling you, I just feel like I'm..." she squeezed her eyes shut and snapped her fingers, struggling to find the right word. "Aware? Awake? Yes – that's it! I feel like I'm waking up! Like when you smell coffee brewing in the kitchen and it kind of takes a little while to drift through your senses and pull you out of sleep?"

"So, a washing machine ad is making you wake up and notice that the ocean is alive and talking to you?" he said, fighting the urge to laugh.

"Don't mock me, Stephan!"

He held up his hands for a split second then returned them to the wheel, trying to hide a smile. "No, no! Just trying to piece together what you're telling me, that's all." He couldn't keep the humor out of his voice.

She slumped in the passenger seat, the magazine still open to the picture of the ribbon-clad woman. "I guess it does sound a little... how

25

does my mom say it? 'Woo-woo'."

He laughed. "Yeah. It does."

She traced her fingers along the pattern of the ribbon in the photo, deep in thought. After several minutes, she nodded as if making a decision, and turned to Stephan. "So, you only smelled fish and sea water, huh?"

He glanced at her and she saw his Adam's apple bob up and down as he swallowed. He'd been caught.

Chapter 2.

Hurricanes don't usually reach Atlanta, Georgia, in the traditional sense, although they tend to spawn other weather events like thunderstorms, floods and tornadoes.

Although she didn't plan to, Cara followed up with her regular doctor when she returned home, if only to find relief for the cluster of migraine headaches she'd suffered since the episode on the beach. She had a brief love affair with Imitrex that lasted the entire month of September and into October, before the headaches stopped suddenly and didn't return.

"Do you think it had something to do with the sei... uh – *episode* you had at the beach, Cara?" Stephan asked her one unseasonably warm and sunny October afternoon. He had been traveling with his band since he and Cara returned from the beach, and although he called to check on her every day, they hadn't spent time together.

"Yeah, probably," she told him regretfully, then stood in front of the open window, taking deep breaths. "Ahh, that feels good!"

"What?"

"Fresh air," she told him. "Between the headaches and the weather, I've been cooped up in this house for so long I feel like I'm coming out of a cocoon."

Stephan, who had been slicing an apple at the kitchen counter, stopped, put down his knife and cocked his head, considering her words carefully.

When he didn't respond, she turned around to find him deep in thought. "Okay, so now you're freaking me out," she said, laughing. "Did you cut yourself?"

"Hm? Oh, no. You just said something interesting, that's all," he said.

She rolled her eyes. "Wow. I'm glad I don't do that very often, if this is the effect it has on you!"

He shook his head. "Ha-ha. You said 'the headaches and the weather,' right?"

She nodded. "Yeah. So?"

"Okay. Think about this for a minute." He wiped his hands on the kitchen towel and walked slowly toward her, his brows knitted in concentration and his voice taking on the tone of a college professor – or a trial lawyer. "What happened when you had your seizure?"

"It wasn't a seizure," she said.

"Whatever," he said, gesturing impatiently with his hands. "Just answer the question."

She sighed and folded her arms across her chest, cocking her head to one side. "It wasn't..."

"Fine," he said, inhaling deeply and staring at the ceiling before he turned toward her, his face red with frustration.

"Um, excuse me," she said. "*You* were swimming and pulling that guy out of the water..."

"No. Before that." He moved his hand in a circular motion, like he was rewinding something, making Cara laugh.

"It wasn't a seizure," she said again, shaking her head. "Man, you are like a dog on a bone about this, aren't you?"

"Yeah, well, I was a little worried that the doctors couldn't find anything wrong with you," he said, annoyed that she wasn't getting the point. "Listen. It was a big storm, right?"

"Gee, you could say that." She raised her hands to her face and began to massage her temples, a habit which had developed over the several weeks when she was experiencing excruciating pain. "But it didn't make landfall – at least, not in Florida. Not that day."

"Ah, but it *did* make landfall in South Carolina. And it *did* mess up the tides along the coast of Florida." Stephan wore a smug grin and held one finger in the air, as if convincing the jury of his point.

Cara un-crossed her arms and stuck out her chin. "I feel like I'm being cross-examined," she told him. "I assume there's a point to all of this?"

He nodded. "Yes. Migraine headaches are often associated with extreme drops in barometric pressure."

She cocked her head to the side and raised her eyebrow. "So?"

"Extreme drops in barometric pressure," he repeated. "Like what happens during a hurricane."

"Okay, so why do I get headaches here in Atlanta? You've already said that the only effect to our weather this summer was a bunch of floods and..." she paused and looked at him.

He was nodding, a wide grin on his face. "Yes! Flooding, thunderstorms and tornadoes. You know how the weather people are always talking about a drop in the barometric pressure."

Her eyebrows were knitted together and she was tapping her chin with her finger. "Yes. That must be it. Because we haven't had any significant storms for about two weeks, and that's about the time when my headaches started to go away." She looked at him and smiled. "Stephan? You're a genius!"

He shrugged coyly. "Really, Cara. It was just a matter of finding a scientific reason for your being sick."

She laughed. "I wonder if the doctors will give me a refund when I tell them my friend is the one who figured out what was wrong with me."

"I doubt it," Stephan said.

Cara waved her hand. "I've just gotten rid of one kind of headache. Believe me, I'm not planning to go after some big medical company or anything. I don't think my worthless, high-rent insurance policy covers medical-professional-induced illnesses."

"You never know," he said.

"Trust me. This, I know!" she said. "I happen to do the books for a family practice office over in Crabapple. Cheapskate doctor, but a really nice guy. Cycles through surly office worker after surly office worker because he can't afford to bring in someone who stays a long time and has a decent personality."

"Your point?"

"Ahem," she said, raising an eyebrow. "My *point* is that I'd be going to him if his office staff were any good, because he actually listens to me when I tell him one of my off-the-wall theories. But he's not on my insurance, and I can't afford to go out of network. He *does* agree, though, that a lot of the folks who graduated from medical school know even less than we do about our own bodies. They just can't admit that because they'd lose patients." She paused, looked at Stephan and chuckled at her own pun.

"Well," he said, returning to the task of cutting his apple in the kitchen, "You'll be pleasantly surprised when you get *my* bill." He paused a moment then added, "Insurance? Did they take you back?"

She punched him in the arm and nodded. "Yes. I figured it would cost less to pay that than some monstrosity of an emergency room bill." She grimaced. "Took a bit of fighting with Brandon, though. The asshole," she muttered.

"It cost him less this way, though," Stephan said. "Isn't that why he has insurance?" He tapped his head with his index finger and waggled his eyebrows. "Takes a genius to figure that out, eh?"

"Maybe that's what I got when I had that *episode*," she said, drawing a blank look from Stephan. "You said it made John Travolta smart, remember?" She shook her head and continued, "Okay, Mister Genius. Let's stay focused here for a minute. I can accept that the storms and the barometric pressure are causing my headaches. That kind of makes sense. But how do you explain the noise?"

"You mean the sound of the ocean talking to you?"

"Yelling at me, is more like it. But, yeah. How do you explain that?"

"The migraine made your hearing hyper-sensitive?" he suggested.

"Maybe." She walked over to the counter and crossed her arms, bracing herself before revealing her hand.

He popped an apple slice into his mouth and offered her one. She shook her head and took a deep breath. "So, would the same theory apply to other senses, do you think?"

He shrugged and rinsed the paring knife under the running water, then dried it with the dish towel. "I guess it's possible. Why? Was there something else you didn't tell me about?"

"I didn't have to. It was all yours," she said, a sly grin spreading across her features.

His jaw froze in mid-chew. "What do you mean?"

"Fish and sea water, my ass, Mister."

He shook his head. "Really. That was it."

"But that wasn't it," she continued. "It was really strong, right?"

His moved his shoulders as if he was trying to loosen his shirt. From the flush rising in his cheeks, Cara could tell it wasn't working, that her questioning was having more of an effect on him than the temperature in the room.

"Every time we go there, you say how refreshing the smell of the ocean is to you. This time it repulsed you. Why is that, Stephan?" Now she was the trial lawyer, and she was enjoying the sense of power.

He frowned and swallowed his apple without looking at her. After an uncomfortable silence, he took a deep breath and stared at her. "I thought maybe the tide was so strong that it pulled stuff up from the bottom of the sea that shouldn't have come to the surface."

"Like..." Cara stared at him, challenging him with her eyes.

"Damn," he whispered, and began cleaning up the remnants of apple.

"Steph..."

Stephan dumped the seeds and core into the trash and turned to look at her. "Like, I don't know, those one-eyed fish that glow in the dark and have big teeth? You've seen those, right?"

"Have you?"

"Yeah. On the Discovery Channel!"

"So you didn't see them on the beach, but you automatically assumed that there was some sort of creature..."

"What do you think, Cara? You seem to have some sort of answer that you're not telling me." His face was still red, revealing to her that he was bluffing.

She glanced at the clock above the stove and realized she didn't have time for any more drilling. "You have to go," she said. "My boys are going to be home any minute."

He tossed the sponge into the sink and put his hands in the air as she pushed him playfully toward the front door. "Fine," he said, and the door swung shut behind him.

Cara heard his car start and pull away, but she didn't go to the window to watch. She cleaned up the dishes from their lunch and put them into the dishwasher, then went to the laundry room to load the dryer. She was folding the last of the towels when she heard a car door slam in the driveway, and she walked to the front door in time to see the twins lifting their backpacks and suitcases out of the hatch of Brandon's SUV.

Her soon-to-be ex-husband didn't get out of the car – didn't even un-fasten his seatbelt. Cara opened the front door and waved, but he looked away, shouting something to the boys.

"Okay, Dad," Dylan said.

"See you Thursday!" Ryan chimed in.

They rolled their suitcases onto the walkway and turned to watch Brandon back down the driveway. He tooted the horn in response to their waving, but Cara could see from the awkward position of his head that the cell phone was already attached to his ear.

"Hi, guys! How was your time with your dad?" She forced her voice to sound bright to fight back the threatening tears. Things between them didn't work out; he didn't have to take it out on their boys.

Dylan turned around first, dropped his backpack and threw his arms around Cara's waist. "I missed you!" he announced.

She tousled his hair and bent to give him a kiss on the top of his unruly mop. "I missed you, too." Cara was surprised by his display of affection and squeezed him once more before he pulled away.

Straightening, she cleared her throat and addressed Ryan. "Did you do anything fun, Ry?"

He shook his head and turned slowly towards her, reaching absently for the handle to his rolling backpack. "Not really," he said. "Dad made us do homework."

"Well, that's good," she said. "It's not going to get done if you ignore it."

"I don't like doing homework at Dad's house. He's always on the phone and he doesn't help with anything." Ryan looked as if he would cry at any moment. At eight, he was still very much affected by his parents' split, and he had never been close to Brandon to begin with.

Cara put her arm around him and walked with him toward the front door. "Well, you know he has to work so you can do fun stuff later, right?"

Ryan looked up at her with his big, brown puppy-dog eyes and nodded sadly. "Yeah. I know," he said.

"But what if he works and works and forgets about the fun stuff?"

"Geez, Ry," Dylan said. "He took us to see Ironman."

"On a school night?" Cara asked, surprised.

"Yeah. He said it would be okay as long as we finished our homework," Dylan told her.

"Well, then, I guess you did it, since he took you to the movie," Cara said.

Dylan shook his head. "Ryan said he was finished, so Dad thought that meant both of us. I still have to finish my spelling words."

"Me, too," Ryan said.

"I'll help you, if you like," Cara offered.

Ryan smiled up at her sadly and nodded. "Okay," he said, so softly that she barely saw his lips move.

"Do you need me to help you finish, Dyl?"

Dylan nodded, making his hair fall into his eyes. Cara moved to brush it out of his face, but he pulled away. "Just leave it. I like it that way," he snapped.

"Did Dad feed you sugar?" she asked, drawing her hand back.

"Maybe." He brushed past her and deposited his suitcase in the laundry room. "I'm going to take a shower."

"A shower?" she asked, eyebrows raised.

"Yeah. Dad says we're too old for baths."

"Hm. Well, I'm a lot older than you, and I still take baths," she told him. "I rather like the water. Calms me down, you know?"

Dylan rolled his eyes. "That's different. You're a lady. Ladies are supposed to take baths."

"And men are supposed to stink?" she asked, trying to get him to smile.

Instead, he made a face. "No. We shower."

"Do you use soap and shampoo in this shower? Or do you just stand there and let the stink kind of run off of you?"

Dylan was fighting a smile. Cara felt a moment of triumph when she noticed the dimple appear and disappear as he fought to maintain his aloof manner. Instead, he turned and walked to his room. "You can sniff me when I'm done," he said over his shoulder, then slammed the door.

"Can't wait!" she said, and laughed. Turning to Ryan, she asked, "And what about you? Do you need a shower tonight?"

His eyes grew wide and he shook his head. His hair was a darker blond, almost brown, and his glasses kept his hair from blocking his face. "No, ma'am," he said. "I still like baths."

"But your dad says you're too old for that."

"Dylan's older than me," he said.

"By about two minutes, Ry," Cara told him. She put her arm around him and gave him a squeeze. "That's okay, though. You don't have to take a shower. I know grown men who like to take baths and there's nothing wrong with that."

He nodded slowly and pressed himself closer to his mother.

She put her arms around him and kissed the top of his head. "Is something bothering you, Ry? You seem awfully quiet."

He shrugged.

"What is it?"

He looked up at her, his eyes bright with unshed tears. "I know me and Dylan are brothers, but sometimes I don't feel like Dad is my dad. I think my dad must be somebody else."

Cara felt a lump rise in her throat and she hugged him closer. "Oh, sweetheart! Why would you say that?"

"I just don't think he understands me, that's all," Ryan said quietly. "And I watch Dylan with him and it doesn't seem like I'm even from the same family."

Cara sighed. "I kind of felt like that around your dad, too," she admitted.

"Is that why you aren't married anymore?" Ryan asked her, his voice muffled by her arms around him.

She released him from the tight embrace, held him at arms length and nodded. "It's for the best. Really, it is."

"My dad likes me," Ryan said, his voice suddenly stronger.

"Of course he does. He loves you. He just finds it hard to show that sometimes."

"No," Ryan shook his head. "I'm not talking about Dylan's dad. I'm talking about mine."

Cara frowned. "You're twins, honey. You have the same dad."

Ryan looked at her and she was taken aback by the depth of knowledge in his eyes. He wasn't her meek, timid little boy; in mere minutes he had somehow acquired the self-assurance of a much older person, and his gaze unsettled her.

He sighed and the look was gone. He shook his head. "Never mind. He said you might not understand."

Cara felt the hairs raise on her neck and arms. "Who?"

"My real dad."

She put her hands on his shoulders and looked him in the eye. "Ryan, does your Dad know you've been talking to strangers?"

The boy frowned. "No. But..."

"Where did this person come from? Does your dad know him?"

"I doubt it," Ryan said. "He's from..." He frowned, confused, then looked back up at his mother. "I'm not really sure where he's from. But I know he isn't from here."

"Where did you meet him, honey?" she asked.

"I was walking. I was, like, on the beach or something. Really, Mom, I don't remember."

Now Cara was confused. "Dad took you to the movies, honey, not the beach." She stood up straight and crossed her arms, her forehead creased in thought. "Your dad hates the beach. When did you guys go there?"

"We didn't go with Dad," Ryan said.

"So, you were with me when you met this man?" Cara asked, struggling to keep her voice calm.

He shook his head again. "No."

Cara exhaled impatiently, frustrated with her son. He wasn't one to make up stories – that was usually Dylan's department. Ryan was the one she came to when she needed to figure out the truth. "Ryan, you have me a little worried, honey. If you met this man on the beach, and you weren't at the beach with me or your dad, then maybe it was..." she had to be careful; Ryan was very sensitive.

"It wasn't a dream, Mom," he said calmly. "I was there, but it wasn't now." His eight-year-old words were insufficient and he shook his head in frustration. "Forget it." In a more Dylan-like display, he put his hand up and walked down the hall, dragging his now-empty suitcase, leaving Cara standing alone in the kitchen hugging herself and rubbing her arms against the sudden chill.

She stared after Ryan, even after he had turned to go into his bedroom. This wasn't like him. He was her go-to. Although she had a good relationship with both her boys, she had always joked with friends that she was glad she had twins: Dylan related better to Brandon and she had Ryan. Dylan was the one who could push her buttons. He was the one who socialized too much in school, excelled in sports and couldn't care less about his academic subjects.

Dylan also was closer with Brandon, having a similar personality to the man. They understood each other, enjoyed the same things and often excluded Ryan simply because they were consumed with a sporting event on television, or the discussion of one. Following Brandon's example, Dylan often found fault with the way Cara did things, never hesitated to voice his disappointment of her and rarely apologized.

Ryan, on the other hand, was more sweet-tempered. He was the younger twin, but he acted more responsible, taking on chores to help her at home and choosing school work over both athletics and socializing. He had friends, but where Dylan was usually surrounded by a pack of boys, Ryan tended to have one or two friends at a time.

Although the quiet twin, Ryan was fiercely protective of his mother. He rarely stood up for himself against Dylan's mistreatment of him, but he would often demand his brother's silence during one of his tirades against Cara – which happened most often after a weekend with their father.

Having Ryan at odds with her was unsettling. She expected opposition from Dylan, but she could feel her energy being sapped at the mere thought of having two defiant boys at home. She put her hand to her temple, expecting the twinge of a migraine, and was relieved when she realized there was no dull ache, although there was plenty of time before the twins went to bed.

Cara sighed. She supposed it was inevitable, having both boys pull away from her and assert their independence. It meant she was doing her job as their mother. Still, it concerned her that Ryan seemed intent on pulling away into a make-believe world.

She closed her eyes and exhaled, then went into the kitchen to start dinner.

The shower finally stopped and Dylan stepped into the hallway wearing a towel, steam billowing out behind him.

"Don't drip on the floor, Dyl!" Cara called.

"I'll clean it up!" he shouted back. She heard his bedroom door slam and looked down the hallway at the trail of watery footprints on the hardwood floor.

Ryan emerged from his bedroom dragging a towel and mopped up the mess. Cara pretended she didn't see him, but she wondered how long he had been covering his brother's tracks – literally.

He quietly tossed the towel into the pile in the laundry room and appeared in the doorway to the kitchen and smiled. "What's for dinner?" he asked.

"Chicken. Broccoli. Potatoes." She glanced at him, relieved that his pleasant disposition had returned. "Sound good?"

He shrugged. "Yeah. I guess. When do we eat? I'm starving?" He climbed up onto the bar stool to watch her, dragging the copy of the local newspaper from the recycling pile in front of him and scanning the front page. Judging from the slightly discolored look of the paper,

Cara judged that it was likely several weeks old. When she didn't answer, Ryan looked up from his paper and raised his eyebrows hopefully.

Cara laughed. "About ten more minutes, little man," she said. "Anything interesting in there?"

"Looks like the tornado made a mess," he said, turning the page to look at the photo gallery inside. "This was right around here, wasn't it? I think I know that house."

She nodded. "Yup. The wind was pretty bad. Thanks to the remnants of that hurricane."

"But don't hurricanes happen in the ocean?" he asked.

"They do, but they're huge," she said, enjoying the opportunity for a science lesson and her first love, meteorology. Ryan was always interested in knowing how things worked, and she was happy to indulge his curiosity. She flipped the page back and pointed to a black-and-white satellite photo of the hurricane. "See that?" she asked, pointing to the dark circle in the center of the storm.

Ryan bent closer to the paper and nodded.

"That's the middle of the hurricane. It's called the 'eye.' The winds turn really fast right there around the middle, but then all the clouds and everything that spin out from the middle can go for miles and miles. And the winds are pretty strong, so sometimes they run into another bit of moving air and there's a struggle and they wind up making tornadoes, far away from the middle of the main storm."

He thought about that for a minute, then looked up at his mother. "So, what you're saying is, the middle of the storm is where the energy is, but it can reach far away, right?"

She smiled. "That's right."

"What about other things?" he asked, sitting back on the stool.

She stabbed the potatoes with a fork and frowned. "What do you mean?"

He chewed his lip for a moment and thought about what he was trying to say. "Well," he said, finally, "I mean, do you think that other things with energy can make things happen far away?"

The hair began to prickle at the back of her neck. "Sure," she answered slowly. "I mean, I suppose."

He nodded, still chewing his lip.

"Do you have something in mind?"

Ryan shrugged. "I don't know. I mean, water from far away can come to the land, like on waves at the beach, right?"

"Right."

"Like, water near Africa can travel all the way over here," he said, more telling her than asking.

"Sure, but that's not..."

"And when that big wave happened when I was little..."

"The tsunami?" Cara suggested.

"Is that the one that was all over the news?" he asked.

"A few years ago, yes," Cara said. "You were really small. I didn't think you'd remember that."

Ryan nodded thoughtfully. "It wasn't the water, though. Right?"

"What do you mean?" she asked.

"The water didn't just all of a sudden become a big wave," he said. "There was something else, something *under* the water that made that happen, right?"

"Right. In that case, there was an earthquake and it made the waves," she said.

"Like when I'm in the bathtub and I fart?" He smiled.

Cara laughed, feeling as if she had been played. "Is that what this is all about? You taking baths?"

He shook his head. "No. Not really," he said, his voice once again taking on a more serious tone. "I was just thinking. Do you think that maybe there were other times when big waves happened like that? What did you call them?"

"Tsunamis."

"Yeah. Tsunamis." When she didn't answer right away, he looked at her, his eyebrows raised. "Well? Do you?"

She shrugged. "I suppose so," she answered slowly. "In fact, I'm sure of it, since there were things written about them before this one happened."

"How long ago?" he asked.

"Geez, Ryan, I have no idea," she said, stirring the water in the pot before dumping the broccoli into it. "Why do you ask?"

He sighed. "Well, didn't the animals hear the tsunami and get away?"

"Long ago?" she asked.

He shook his head. "No. That one when I was little. Didn't the animals know the wave was coming?"

Cara frowned, placed the lid on the boiling pot of broccoli and turned the temperature down on the stove before turning to answer her son. "I seem to remember reading something like that, yes."

"How come the people didn't hear it?" he asked.

"I don't think people have hearing like that," she told him. "It's kind of like dogs. You know they can hear things a lot farther away than we can. That's why they howl when there's a siren, even before we can hear it."

He nodded. "But what if people can hear things, but they don't want to, or they just don't know what the noises mean?"

"Wow, Ryan," she said. "You've given this a lot of thought, haven't you?" She tousled his hair, grateful that their conversation had turned to a science lesson and away from his believing another man was his father, although there was something in his line of questioning that left her senses on high alert.

He grew quiet, flipping through the pages of the newspaper, and Cara assumed the conversation had ended. She opened the oven and checked the meat, then closed it again. "Want something to drink, sweetie?"

Ryan shook his head and turned toward the empty hallway. Cara turned, following the direction of his gaze. "What is it?" she asked.

"Dylan," he said. "He's doing something he isn't supposed to."

"What?" Cara asked, frowning.

"He brought his video game home from Dad's. Dad told him to leave it. He's in his room playing it," Ryan said. He glanced at her briefly, then turned his attention back to the paper.

Cara put the glass of water she had been drinking down on the counter and frowned at Ryan. "I don't hear anything."

Ryan shrugged without looking up. "Just sayin'."

"Did you see him bring it home?" she asked.

He shook his head. "No. I hear the buttons clicking. And there's a weird hum."

"A hum?" she asked, feeling a little apprehensive.

He nodded. "Yeah."

Cara sighed, trying to convince herself that he was bluffing. "Ryan. If you're trying to use this whole discussion to get your brother in trouble..."

"No, Mom," he said. "Really. I hear it. Don't you?"

She paused for a moment and cocked her head. She did hear a slight noise, almost like something vibrating, but she assumed it was the refrigerator running, or maybe the dryer. At least, she hoped that's all it was.

She started down the hallway, Ryan looking after her from his seat at the counter. She knocked on Dylan's bedroom door and heard scuffling noises inside. "Yeah?"

"Dyl? What are you doing, honey? Are you getting dressed?" She jiggled the door handle, but it was locked.

She heard more thumping and scraping noises, then the sound of Dylan jumping up and coming toward the door. "Huh?" he asked, opening the door wide.

Cara raised one eyebrow. The boy was definitely hiding something. "The door was locked," she said, keeping her voice low. "What are you up to?"

He looked around and shrugged, his wet hair dripping on his pajama shirt. "Nothing."

She stepped inside the room and bent to pick up his wet towel, but he lunged for it. "I'll get that!" he said.

She frowned. "Oh. Okay." She crossed her arms. "Do you have something here that you're not supposed to?"

He coughed. "Um. Like what?" Color stained his neck and was rising to his cheeks, like it often did when he was lying to her.

She shook her head. "I don't know. But you're acting kind of like you're hiding something."

"Me? No, Mom. That's silly." Then he frowned and crossed his arms. "Did Ryan try to tattle or something?"

"Why would he do that, Dyl? What does he have to tattle about?"

"Damn!" the boy whispered.

"Dylan!"

"Sorry. I just..." he hung his head and sighed. "I'm sorry, Mom." Dylan bent to pick up the towel and Cara noticed the video game hidden underneath.

"Oh. So you brought that back from your Dad's, eh?"

Dylan sighed. "Ry told on me, didn't he?"

Cara didn't appreciate the murderous look in her son's eye. She crossed her arms and leaned against the door frame. "No. He didn't."

"That sucks," he said, squinting at her in anger.

"Dylan Waters, I've had just about enough!" she said, raising her voice despite her best efforts.

"I wish I was back at Dad's. He doesn't treat me like a baby."

"No. He treats you like you can do no wrong. But you are eight years old, not eighteen, and you are not allowed to cuss at your mother or lie to me or steal from your father..."

"It's not stealing! It's mine!"

"It's yours when you're at your dad's house. Now, I want you to call him right this minute..."

"No!"

"Dylan!" she shouted, but he was already slinking past her and running down the hallway. She heard, "You're a tattle-tale baby, Ryan! You know that, right?" followed by a slamming door.

"Dylan!" Cara shouted again, leaning out the door.

"He won't go far. He's just doing this to tick you off," Ryan said, without looking up from the paper.

Cara turned around, having seen Dylan hiding behind her car. She knew he'd only be outside a short time before he came back inside. He'd be too embarrassed to go far, wearing his pajamas – and he wasn't wearing any shoes. Besides, she knew he had likely eaten whatever junk food he wanted at his father's all weekend. His growing body needed something nutritious, then he'd return to his normal surly behavior, instead of this surly-on-overdrive.

She sighed as she returned to the broccoli, boiling away to mush in the pan. Turning to Ryan, she said, "You knew he had it, didn't you."

Ryan sat at the counter with his head down, staring at the paper.

"Ry?"

He nodded ever so slightly. "Yes, ma'am."

"Did you see him take it?"

Ryan shook his head and slowly raised it to look at her. "No, ma'am. I told you. I heard it."

"Your hearing isn't that good, Ry."

"Sometimes it is," he told her. "I don't know how to explain it. Maybe I got it from my father."

"Brandon Waters has never heard a thing anyone has said in his whole life," she said, exasperated. She closed her eyes and raised her chin, trying to get a hold of herself. She counted to ten, sighed and looked at her son seated at the counter. "Sorry. You didn't deserve that. The problems between me and your father should not be your problems."

Ryan shrugged. "It's okay. He doesn't hear me, either."

The door opened and both of them turned to see Dylan come inside. His eyes were red and his face was blotchy from crying, but he still wore a defiant look. He glanced back and forth between the two of them and walked to the counter, pulling the video game from behind his back. "Here," he said to Cara. "You can hold onto this until I go back to Dad's."

She shook her head. "Thank you. But you really should call him and tell him that it's here."

He sighed and nodded, his lips a thin line in his red face. He looked up and asked, "So, are you both going to punish me?"

Cara shrugged. "Depends."

He looked as if he would start crying again at any moment, then turned to lift the telephone handset from the base. He pressed "2" on the speed dial and waited with the phone pressed against his cheek. When he heard the click of the phone on the other end and his father's

43

voice, he rounded the doorway and went to sit in the dark dining room.

Cara closed her eyes, pressed the heels of her hands against her lids and groaned. "Ohh, what am I going to do about this? You can't stand going to your dad's house, and Dylan can't stand being with me."

"So split us up," Ryan suggested.

She lowered her hands and snapped her head to attention. "Excuse me?"

"Yeah. Makes sense, right? I mean, Dad doesn't understand me," Ryan said. "I think I kind of scare him. Dad and Dylan are way more alike."

"I couldn't do that, honey," Cara said. "I love the both of you."

"So does Dad."

"I'm sorry that you had to hear me vent. It isn't your problem. Really, it isn't."

Ryan shrugged. "You're a part of all of it, but Dad and Dylan..." he bit his lower lip and leaned closer to his mother. "I mean. Everyone is a part of it. But they aren't like us."

Cara clapped her hands together and rolled her eyes. "Okay. What are you talking about, Ryan? I am really confused."

"No, Mom," Ryan said. "You're just not listening."

"Listening? I always listen to you, honey. But right now, the only thing I'm not doing is understanding."

Ryan shook his head. "You were listening at the beach," he said. "I should have been there."

Her blood went cold and she stared at him. She hadn't told him anything about the incident at the beach. She hoped Stephan hadn't either.

"What about the beach?" she asked him quietly. She could hear Dylan still talking quietly to his father in the other room, and she moved closer to Ryan.

"You got sick," he said, then shook his head. "No. That's not right. You felt sick, but you weren't sick. You just didn't know what happened."

She considered him for a moment, frowning. "Did you talk to Stephan?"

He shook his head. "No, Mom. I saw you. You were on the beach and you heard it. You know you heard it, but you weren't ready to hear it."

"Heard what, honey?" She was covered in goose flesh and wrapped her arms around herself to try and calm herself. "What did I hear?"

"The hum," he said.

Cara coughed. "Wow. Did I talk in my sleep or something?"

Ryan shook his head. "No. It was my father. You heard him, but you weren't ready."

"Your father wasn't at the beach, honey. You were with him, camping, remember?"

"Not him, Mom. The one from the sea."

Movement from the doorway caught Cara's eye and she turned to see Dylan enter the room, the phone held toward her in his outstretched hand. "He wants to talk to you," he said.

She nodded and took the phone, still feeling cold. "You two behave, okay?" she warned before she took the phone down the hall to her bedroom.

"You shouldn't have told on me," Dylan said quietly to his brother.

Ryan shrugged without looking at his twin.

"I got in trouble," Dylan told him.

"I know," Ryan said.

"Why'd you do it?"

"I don't know. I was mad, I guess, because you took yours and I left mine. I didn't think it was fair."

"I would have shared," Dylan said.

Ryan shook his head. "No you wouldn't."

Dylan smiled and gave his brother a friendly punch. "Yeah. You're right. I probably wouldn't have."

Cara came back into the kitchen, replaced the handset in its base and tried to salvage what she could of their dinner. "Well, the chicken's a little burned and the broccoli's a little mushy, but the potatoes look good. It's tough to ruin potatoes."

"Amazing," Dylan said, unenthusiastically, but Cara was relieved that at least he was being somewhat pleasant. He brightened and suggested, "We could order a pizza!" to which Cara and Ryan both shot annoyed looks.

"It smells good," Ryan added, elbowing his brother and shaking his head. "Thanks for cooking, Mom. You always did like to burn things."

"What are you talking about, doofus?" Dylan asked. "Mom doesn't burn stuff. Dad does." Cara raised her eyebrows in surprise. Dylan was *defending* her?

"I'm not talking about food, Dyl," Ryan said, and hopped down from the stool to go wash his hands.

Dylan looked at Cara with a frown, hiking a thumb toward Ryan's back. "What's he talking about?"

Cara shook her head. "I don't have any idea." She looked toward the bathroom and made sure the door was closed before turning back to Dylan and whispering, "Did Ryan and Dad have a fight?"

Dylan shrugged. "I don't think so. Why?"

"Just wondering," she said, straightening up and draining the green water from the pot of broccoli. "He's been acting strange since he came home."

He shook his head. "No. He was like that at Dad's, too," Dylan told her. "But it's been like that every time we've gone to Dad's since the camping trip."

"Did something happen when you guys were camping?" she asked. She thought that perhaps that was where Ryan had met the man at the beach. Although their campsite was at a lake, there was water nearby.

Dylan hopped down from the stool and walked to the kitchen sink to wash his hands. "No," he said, then frowned and cocked his head to one side. "Well, come to think of it..."

"What?"

"He had a nightmare the last night we were there. He kept yelling that there was a fire, and he kept shouting for Dad."

"Really?" She made a face that she hoped Dylan didn't see as she added servings of mushy green mess to each of their plates.

Dylan nodded and turned off the water. Reaching for a towel, he said, "When Dad woke him up, it was like he didn't know who he was. Dad, I mean. Ryan looked at him like he didn't know him. He said to take him back to the water."

"Did you go to the lake that day?" she asked.

"Yeah, of course," Dylan said. "But it was like Ryan was still asleep when he was talking. Then when Dad asked him if he left something on the boat, it was like he woke up and didn't remember what he was saying. It was like everything was fine."

"And was it?"

"Yeah, it was," Ryan said, startling both of them. "I didn't have a nightmare, Dyl. Don't you remember? I told you what happened."

Dylan sighed and looked at his mother. "He said he saw you by the water and you were covering your ears. He said you were sick and he needed to help you."

Cara felt the blood drain from her face.

"What is it, Mom?" Dylan asked, uncharacteristically concerned by his mother's reaction.

"Mom did get sick at the beach, Dyl," Ryan told him, in a voice that sounded much older than his eight years.

"You did?" Dylan's eyebrows shot up. "Man! Ryan was freaking out the whole way home from camping. Dad was really pis- I mean, Dad was mad because Ryan was so upset."

"I tried to call you on Dad's cell phone, but you wouldn't answer," Ryan said.

Cara rubbed his arm and made soft shushing noises. "Well, I'm here and I'm fine and that was a long time ago."

"Not that long," Ryan said, his lip poked out defiantly.

"Give it a rest, Ryan," Dylan said. "Mom's good."

"Mom would be better if she listened," Ryan said.

Dylan looked at his mother. "Are you going to punish him, Mom? I mean, you'd punish me for saying that!"

She gave Dylan a sharp look, then turned to face his brother. "You keep saying that I'm not listening. What do you mean, Ryan?" she asked, trying to keep her voice calm.

"They're trying to tell you something and you need to listen," Ryan told her.

"Who?"

"Your people," he said, then shook his head and frowned. "No. That's not right. They aren't people."

Dylan laughed. "If they're calling her from the water, maybe they're mermaids!"

"It's not funny, Dylan!" Ryan said, raising his voice for the first time all evening. He was usually so mild-mannered that his outburst startled both Dylan and Cara.

"Whoa! Okay!" Dylan held his hands in front of him and backed away, carrying his plate over to his seat at the breakfast room table.

"You must be hungry," Cara said, trying to change the subject. "Maybe that's why you got upset. Let's sit down and eat and we can talk more about this later, okay? And maybe you can tell me what happened on the camping trip."

She handed a plate to Ryan, who rolled his eyes and sat down at the table.

Cara brought a can of peaches from the kitchen, and added a serving to each of their plates. Both boys looked at their plates, then at their mother, eyes wide. She shrugged. "It's the least I could do, since I messed up the other stuff."

When she sat down, Dylan lowered his head and folded his hands, then said the blessing without being prompted.

"Amen," all three said in unison, and Cara laid her napkin in her lap.

"I'm glad you're home," she said. "I missed you." She looked pointedly at Dylan and said, "Both of you."

Dylan took a bite of his chicken and forced a smile. "I missed you, too, Mom," he said. It was silent while he chewed, then he added. "I'm sorry I was rude to you when I got home."

Ryan looked across the table at his brother and made a slight movement with his head. When Dylan didn't say anything, Ryan opened his eyes wider. Cara looked from one twin to the other, confused. Finally, she put down her fork and folded her hands. "Okay. What's going on?"

Dylan put his fork down and sighed. "Dad was talking to some lady while we were with him this weekend," he said.

"Was it Claudia?" Cara asked, her voice flat.

Dylan frowned. "You know about her?"

She smiled. "Yes. Your dad and I have talked about it, and I'm happy for him. Happy for both of them, actually. Claudia seems to enjoy being with someone who works a lot and..." She cleared her throat, then stabbed a piece of chicken with her fork. "What about her? What did they say?"

"Well, I think that Claudia is moving away," Dylan said.

"That's too bad," Cara said, fighting to keep the amusement from her voice. "Is your dad upset about it?"

Dylan sat statue-like, staring at Ryan. Finally, Ryan spoke. "I think Dad wants to move away with her."

"Well, he hasn't said anything to me," she said. "And he'd have to..."

"He wants us to go and live with him," Dylan blurted.

Cara exhaled, frowning, her fork clattering on the side of her plate. "Alright, listen. If your dad is moving across town or across the country, he and I have to discuss it. And we haven't discussed anything, so as far as I'm concerned, there's nothing going on." She turned to Ryan. "As for you, Ry, I want to know what happened when you were camping that got you so upset." She paused to take a breath, then addressed them both. "And I want to know who told you I got sick while I was at the beach. Because I wasn't sick, I just got dizzy."

Dylan frowned, then his eyes grew wide as he looked at his mother. "You really were sick at the beach?" He turned his head back and forth, between Ryan and Cara. "Ry? You said..."

"I told you she was dizzy, Dyl. She heard the same thing I did."

Cara, who had been sitting in her chair with her arms folded, waiting for the boys to quit their arguing, sat up and stared at Ryan.

She took a deep breath to calm her rapidly beating heart, then turned to Ryan.

"You forgot to tell me that part, Ry," she said as calmly as she could.

The boy cleared his throat and sat up straighter in his chair. "I didn't want to scare you. And I though you'd get mad."

"No, Ryan. I'm not mad," Cara assured him. "What I am, though, is a little bit concerned. You didn't get dizzy, did you?"

He shrugged, looking more like her son and less like the older stranger who seemed to be inhabiting Ryan's body moments earlier.

"Does your dad know about this?" She looked back and forth between the boys. "Well?"

Dylan leaned forward. "He told Dad something was wrong with you. It was when you went away with... uh, your friend. You know – Stephan? Dad calls him your friend, and he said if something was wrong, your friend would call and let us know."

She closed her eyes and shook her hands on either side of her head, as if trying to clear her thoughts. She didn't know they knew she'd gone with Stephan, and it would be worse if Brandon thought something was going on, or made it seem that way to her boys. She couldn't explain it to them right now. There was enough to deal with already.

"Let's start at the beginning, shall we?" she asked, regaining her composure.

The boys nodded, looking at one another – Dylan was wary, Ryan was composed – completely the opposite of their usual demeanors.

Dylan spoke first. "Well, you know when we stayed at Dad's. It wasn't good. Dad was supposed to be away and he didn't go and he had to take us last-minute."

"Which is why I went to the beach," Cara said, mentally chastising herself for offering some sort of apology to the boys. She was an adult, and Brandon was their father.

Brandon had shirked enough responsibility over the last two years. Cara had planned to take the boys to the beach before school started, but the divorce papers were delivered the day before, and

Brandon had called to say he wanted to take the boys camping to give Cara some "time alone, to think." Brandon had never been fond of the outdoors, so she assumed that taking the boys camping was his way of apologizing for using them as pawns for so long, and she agreed to forgo taking them to the beach. Thanks goodness Stephan had been in town and agreed to go with her instead - her options of either staying home or traveling alone were equally unbearable.

She looked at Dylan and nodded. "Sorry I interrupted. Go on, please."

He glanced nervously at Ryan and raised his eyebrows. Ryan shook his head slightly and sneaked a sideways peek at his mother before moving his chin, encouraging Dylan to go on.

Cara watched the whole interaction with some interest. She propped her elbow on the table and perched her chin atop her hand. "Please, somebody say something. I'm really interested in what may have happened to make you two switch places like you have."

Both boys looked at her: Ryan's eyebrows were up, lost somewhere in the heavy hair that flopped over his forehead, and his mouth made a perfect "O." Dylan, on the other hand, sighed and resigned himself to the telling of the story. Finally, Cara thought, they'd regained their usual positions.

Dylan cleared his throat and shook his hair out of his eyes. "Well, anyway, like I said," he said, stalling, "We told Dad something was wrong and he got all pis... uh, mad because he thought we were calling you. We told him we didn't have our cell phones and he punished us because he thought we were using his phone and costing him more money..."

Cara felt her face grow hot. "He said that to you?"

Dylan nodded. "Yes, ma'am."

She closed her eyes and pinched the bridge of her nose. When she opened her eyes again, she looked right at Dylan, forced a smile and nodded for him to go on.

"Yeah. So me and Ryan got in trouble and Dad sent us to bed early and I was all mad at Ryan all night because Dad doesn't usually punish us..."

51

Cara closed her eyes and shook her head. "No, Dyl. He usually doesn't punish *you*."

He smiled at her sheepishly. "Yeah."

She frowned. "But I didn't get any calls from you while I was away."

Dylan shook his head. "We didn't *actually* call."

"So why did you get in trouble?"

"We did *try* to call," Ryan said. "Mom didn't answer before Dad took the phone away."

Dylan frowned, then nodded. "Yeah. I remember." He inhaled, then looked back at his mother. "Ryan got all mad at Dad and started yelling at him because he said something was wrong with you and Dad wouldn't let us check on you. And Dad said if something was wrong you had his phone number and Ryan said if you couldn't call then how would we ever know. That's when he said your friend – Stephan – could find the number if it was really an emergency." Dylan's cheeks were red and splotchy from the exertion of telling his story. He looked up at Cara. "But you were okay, right?"

She shrugged. "I'm okay."

"And you came back, so Dad told Ryan his feeling about something being wrong with you was all wonky and..."

Cara laughed. "Your dad actually used that word? *Wonky*?"

Dylan smiled and nodded slightly. "Yeah. He did. If he wasn't so mad, me and Ryan would have laughed at him. But we were already in enough trouble."

She looked over at Ryan, who had been noticeably quiet throughout the exchange. He was sitting on his chair with his hands clasped together between his knees, his head bent down in thought. His shoulders were leaning forward, but they were straight, as if he was in control, not rounded like when he was trying to make himself into a ball and escape. She would have put her arm around him, but he seemed far away, and she didn't want to startle him.

Dylan's gaze followed Cara's, and the pair of them sat staring at Ryan until the quiet became its own presence in the room. Ryan, interrupted more by the overwhelming quiet than he had been by the noise, slowly raised his head. The deep, knowing look in his eyes sent a feeling like an electric shock through Cara, who struggled to keep from shivering.

Ryan sighed.

"Are you okay, honey?" Cara asked tentatively.

He nodded.

"Did your dad hurt your feelings? Is that why you said he wasn't your father?"

Ryan closed his eyes, took a few deep breaths, then opened them again. He looked at Dylan, then at Cara and shook his head. "No. I mean... I can't really tell you what I mean. When I try to tell you, it doesn't come out right."

Cara leaned forward with her hands on her knees. "Try, honey," she said. "Try again. Maybe I wasn't listening right last time."

He smiled, then cocked his head as if listening to someone. His smile grew and he nodded, then looked back at his mother. "He told me that was what you would say. But when you knew that was the problem, you could make it go away and it would be easier for me to tell you."

Dylan frowned and looked up at his mother. "Mom?" he whispered. "What does he mean?"

Cara held up a hand, not taking her eyes off Ryan. "Just listen, honey," she said quietly. "Ryan lets you do most of the talking most of the time, but when he has something to say, it's important."

Ryan sighed in relief. "Well," he began, his brows knitting together as he sought the words. "I had a dream." He shook his head, frustrated. "But it wasn't a dream, because I wasn't asleep." He looked at her, his palms up. "See? It's so hard..."

She reached out and held one of his hands. "It's okay. Just go slow. We have all the time in the world."

His eyes grew wide and he shook his head. "No. You see? That's the problem. I'm just a little kid, so I can't tell you what I need to tell you. But you need to know. It's important. And we might not have time."

Both his mother and his brother wore nearly identical looks of confusion, but neither said anything, waiting for him to continue.

Ryan looked at his brother, who usually handled all of the talking, hoping he had understood and would help him explain. When he saw that Dylan didn't seem any more clear than Cara, he squared his shoulders and continued. "Okay. I was at the beach and I heard the same thing you did, Mom."

Cara felt a chill that rose from her bones, and she shivered. Frowning, she asked, "are you boys cold? I keep shivering. Dylan – go check the air conditioner."

Ryan held up his hand. "No, Mom. It's not that. When you hear something you know, but you just don't know that you know it, you feel cold." He shook his head and leaned closer. "See? It's so hard! That sounded stupid, even though I know what I want to say. It just doesn't come out right."

Cara hugged her arms and ran her hands up and down, trying to fight the chill. "It's okay, honey. Take your time," she said again. She wished she could understand; he seemed so frustrated, but all she could do was listen.

He shook his head and was quiet for a moment, gathering his thoughts. "Okay. Remember when Grandma Lu said she'd get cold and say a goose was walking on her grave?"

They both nodded. "I always thought that was a funny thing to say," Dylan said.

Ryan smiled, relieved that his brother didn't look quite so scared anymore. "Well, it's kind of like that," he said. "It's like when you know something, not in your head, but in your... oh, what's the word?"

"In your soul?" Dylan suggested.

"Spirit?" Cara said.

Ryan shrugged. "Sort of. I mean, it's inside, but not part of your body - at least not a part that they teach us in science class. But that's close enough, I guess." He took a deep breath. "Well, okay, it's like you know something in there, and you shiver when you hear it. It's like your – spirit?" he said, trying out the word, then nodding to himself before continuing, "Yeah. Like your spirit is trying to tell you that it's something true."

"Like a detective's clue?" Dylan asked.

Ryan nodded, smiling. "Exactly!"

Dylan smiled, proud that he had understood what his brother was saying.

Cara frowned. "I think I've heard something like that before, when I went on a ghost walk in Roswell."

The boys looked at her blankly and she smiled. "I think it was before you were born. Or maybe you were really little. You weren't with me. But it was really cool."

"What happened?" Ryan asked.

"Well, we were walking through the town at night," Cara said, struggling to keep the ghost-story quality out of her voice.

"Eeww. Creepy," Dylan said. "Do ghosts really only come out at night?"

She laughed. "I'm sure they are there all the time, Dyl. But it's easier to get people to do a ghost walk at night."

"Good point," he said, nodding.

She laughed and continued. "So we got to the cemetery..."

"There's a cemetery in Roswell?" Dylan asked.

"Lots of them," Cara told him. "But this one is really old."

"Cool!" both boys said in unison.

Ryan shot his brother a look, then turned his attention back to his mother.

"Anyway." She shook her head. "I can't believe I'm sharing this story with my eight-year-old twins."

"It's okay, Mom," Ryan said. "We want to hear it. It's not scary."

"No. But it's embarrassing," she said.

"Why?" Ryan asked.

She shook her head and waved her hand. "Never mind that." She sighed and continued. "So we got to the cemetery and somebody asked if there were ghosts there."

"Were there?" Dylan asked, his eyes wide.

She nodded and held up her index finger. In spite of herself, she lowered her voice and leaned in closer to the boys as she spoke. "The ghost walk lady told us that there were lots of ghosts that inhabited the buildings and cemeteries in Roswell, but they didn't always appear to the people on the walk. And then somebody else said they smelled something funny, like rotten eggs, and the tour lady said that's one of the signs that a ghost is nearby."

"Rotten eggs?" Dylan asked, wrinkling his nose. He looked at Ryan. "That's weird."

"Not just that," Cara said. "Sometimes you can smell other things, like somebody's perfume or smoke. And sometimes you see smoke."

"But I'm not talking about ghosts, Mom," Ryan said.

She smiled. "But the guide said that one of the surest signs that a spirit was present was feeling chills or goose bumps."

"Like a goose walking on your grave!" Dylan said, smiling, although his face was a bit drained of color.

"Right!" Cara said.

"But it's not ghosts, Mom," Ryan repeated.

"I know, honey, but I'm trying to relate it to something I've heard before – as much for Dylan as for me to be able to understand."

Ryan nodded. "Okay. So did you feel goose bumps?"

"At the cemetery?" she asked.

He shook his head.

"Well, I did at the cemetery," she told him. "But I think that was because it was October and it was night time and it was chilly." She frowned a little, looked at Ryan with an embarrassed smile and added, "At least that's what I told myself at the time."

"I don't mean at the cemetery, Mom," Ryan said. "I meant the other time..."

"On the beach?" she asked, and Ryan nodded.

She frowned and thought for a moment. "You know what? I really don't remember. But I do remember feeling like the air pressure changed suddenly. I got light-headed. Dizzy," she told them.

"What's the word you used when you were talking to Dad?" Dylan asked.

"Vertigo."

Dylan nodded, smiling. "That's a cool word."

"Not a cool feeling, unfortunately," Cara said. "It made me feel sick to my stomach, even though I didn't have anything except coffee that morning. And I blacked out. That's why Ste... um, that's why I had to go to see the doctor."

"It's okay that Stephan was with you," Ryan said. "He's our friend, too, Mom. It's okay."

"He is just a friend," she blurted, then shut her mouth, aggravated with herself for feeling she had to explain her relationship with Stephan to her boys. Brandon certainly didn't hide his relationship with Claudia. And there was nothing romantic between herself and Stephan, and she was sure her boys knew it.

"We know, Mom. We like him," Ryan said.

Dylan nodded in agreement. "He's cool. And he isn't like Claudia, who acts all goofy when she's around Dad. She's gross," he said, wrinkling his nose.

"Gross?" Cara laughed. "How so?"

"Well, you know, she has to hang all over him and stuff. Like she has to show us how much she likes him. Like we wouldn't approve or something," Dylan said.

"We don't," Ryan said. "Approve, I mean. She doesn't like it when Dad pays attention to us."

"Well, that's just too bad, isn't it?" Cara said, not sure how they had come to the topic of their father's girlfriend.

As if sensing her discomfort with the direction of the conversation, Ryan cleared his throat. "Anyway. About the thing you heard at the beach..."

"How did you know about that, Ry?" she asked, interrupting him.

He shrugged. "I just did. I don't really know how. But I told you my father lets me know things when he thinks I should. I guess he just needed me to know that about you, so I would be able to know I could talk to you."

"Of course you can talk to me, Ry," she said, leaning forward a little. "Don't ever think you can't."

Ryan shook his head. "For a long time I couldn't. Not about stuff like that. You weren't ready. You wouldn't understand," he told her. "But after the thing that happened to you at the beach – the noise you heard – I knew after that that I could talk to you and you wouldn't think I was just being weird or something, even if I can't talk about it very well."

She felt a shiver up her spine and the little hairs rose on the back of her neck as he spoke. "So I can understand now, Ry?" she asked him.

He nodded. "I think so. You're starting to, anyway."

"What about me?" Dylan asked.

Ryan raised his eyebrows and looked at his brother apologetically. "Sorry, Dyl. I don't think you're awake yet."

Goose bumps rose instantly on Cara's arms and she shot up straight in her chair. "What did you say?"

Ryan turned his head toward his mother. "About what?"

"About being awake," she said.

He smiled. "Yeah. You know when you're really tired and you hear things but they sound far away so you don't really listen?"

She nodded slowly. Dylan returned a blank look.

Ryan sighed. "Or when you go in a pool and you sit on the bottom and you can hear somebody talking but you can't make out the words?"

Dylan nodded and his expression brightened. "Yeah. That's fun. I played that with Alex Parker over at Dad's pool."

"Huh?" Ryan frowned. "Oh – I wasn't really talking about the pool game, Dyl. I mean that's what stuff sounds like when you aren't awake."

Dylan's shoulders slumped and he nodded. "Yeah. You know what? I don't think I hear anything when I'm asleep." He smiled and added, "I have had dreams in color, though. That's kind of cool, isn't it? I heard most people don't do that."

Ryan looked pleadingly at his mother. "That is cool, Dyl," she said and patted his knee before turning her attention back to Ryan. She folded her hands, trying to compose herself, although her entire body felt like it was hooked up to a car battery with bolts of energy shooting up and down her spine and her limbs, a feeling she betrayed only by the slight bouncing motion of her right leg.

58

"So, Ryan, you said you told Dad that I was sick and he didn't believe you." She paused, then looked at her son again. "Is your dad, um, *awake*?"

Ryan shook his head solemnly. "And I don't think he will be. I haven't seen him." He glanced nervously at Dylan, then focused on Cara again. "Just you," he added, his voice almost a whisper.

Dylan sat up straighter in his seat, his red face contorted. "What? I'm not in your dream, Ry? We're twins!" Dylan said, his voice quivering. But he didn't seem angry; rather, he was hurt that his twin brother, to whom he had dished out plenty of bullying and unkind words in their short lives, didn't choose to include him in what appeared to be a big adventure - even if it was in Ryan's imagination.

Ryan shrugged. "It's not my choice, Dyl," he said. "Sorry."

"Who do I talk to? Can't I wake up, too?" Dylan asked, although he sounded as if he didn't believe what his brother was saying.

Ryan smiled. "Maybe it's just not your time yet," he said, but Cara could tell he was just trying to be kind. Instinctively, she knew that Dylan and Brandon were not a part of the bigger picture – at least not the same one to which she and Ryan belonged.

At least not yet.

She reached out and put her hand on Dylan's shoulder, and he spun his head toward her. "Mom! Make him do something!" he demanded.

She shrugged. "What would you like me to do, Dyl? Reach into his dream and plop you into it?" She felt the tingling sensation again as she spoke, but fought it. "Sometimes we don't get to make choices, honey. Sometimes, choices are made for us."

Dylan crossed his arms and stuck out his lower lip in a pout, glaring at his brother. Cara patted his knee and turned once more to face Ryan.

Ryan's shoulders sagged a little and he smiled up at her, his exhaustion evident on his face. "You believe me, then," he said. It was a statement, not a question.

Cara hesitated, then nodded her head slowly. "There are things I don't completely understand that you seem to be able to answer for me, Ryan," she told him. "Now, I don't want you going around and thinking you can boss your mom around."

"No way," he said, smiling. "I know better."

"She wouldn't do anything to you," Dylan said crossly.

"She has before," Ryan said. "I know what she can do, and I don't want her mad at me."

Cara laughed. "Oh, sure. I've been a big, mean mom before, is that what you're saying?"

Ryan raised an eyebrow and Cara realized that wasn't what he meant.

Dylan huffed. "I don't think she's so tough. I'm more scared of Dad."

Ryan shook his head. "Nope. Mom loses her cool and '*poof!*' Things can go really wonky."

"*Poof?*" Cara asked, her eyebrows raised.

"Oh, yeah," Ryan said, nodding. "People are scared of you. You're pretty tough when you want to be."

Dylan put his hands up and huffed. "This is too weird! It sounds like a movie."

Ryan laughed. "Yeah, well sometimes people try to put messages in movies."

"Really?" Cara asked, tingling again. "Hopefully not all of them are messages. I'd hate to think that some of the scarier things are anything more than a figment of someone's imagination."

Ryan considered her with a raised eyebrow and the shiver grew stronger, like a current coursing through her body. "Not everything, of course," he said. "But, you know, sometimes people don't listen. You have to put a story into something so they get it, even if they don't know they get it."

"Another hidden message?" she asked.

He nodded. "Why not?"

She shivered again and rubbed her arms, then looked at the half-eaten plates of food on the table in front of her. The three of them had been so engrossed in their conversation that the food had grown cold, and she doubted that any of them would eat any more.

She raised her eyebrows at both of the boys. Ryan looked away, and Dylan pushed his plate toward her in response.

Cara sat forward in her chair, picked up her dinner plate and began scraping the scraps onto Dylan's plate. She picked up Ryan's plate and did the same, then stacked all three plates together on the table and glanced between the boys. "Whose night is it to clear the table?"

The twins looked at each other and Dylan rose from his chair with a heavy sigh. "It's mine," he said, his chair scraping the floor as he slid back from the table.

"I'll help you, Dyl," Ryan said, and he stood up to take the serving bowls into the kitchen.

Cara sat alone with her thoughts in the dining room with her elbows on the table, the heels of her hands pressed against her eyelids until she saw stars. Surely there must be some way to make sense of all of Ryan's stories. Surely, her son wasn't delusional.

She sat up suddenly, her eyes blurry from pressing on them. She blinked a few times, then smiled. Of course, she thought. Her friend Marlene had been telling her for some time that Cara had a "very prominent aura," but Cara had dismissed it as one of her dear friend's idiosyncrasies.

Marlene had served as a key member of Cara's support system during her separation and the impending divorce from Brandon, and had kept her "freaky-talk" to a minimum.

"That's okay, sweetie," Marlene had told her. "You'll come around when the time is right."

Cara pushed her chair back and rose from the table, thinking that it might be the right time to get together with Marlene for a cup of coffee and engage in a little of her "freaky-talk."

Chapter 3

The boys had stayed up a little late the night before; Ryan was in a rare talkative mood and Dylan was sufficiently spooked by the thought of his mother and twin brother being so involved in science fiction talk. Despite having the air conditioner running to keep the humidity at bay, Cara had fixed hot cocoa with tiny marshmallows, and they had sat around the living room simply enjoying each other's company.

She let them sleep until 7:30, then fixed a hearty breakfast of turkey bacon and eggs and the English muffins with strawberry jam that Dylan loved so much, then drove them to school in time for the first bell. Then she wrestled the morning traffic to meet Marlene at Jitter Beans in Crabapple.

Cara sat in the coffee shop, staring out the window and waiting for her friend to arrive. She had her hands wrapped around the white ceramic coffee mug; she hadn't been able to get warm since she and Ryan had discussed "waking up." Although it wasn't threatening to return, the mere memory of the migraine-like symptoms she experienced at the beach - and during the turbulent weather patterns in the weeks that followed - made her jumpy, and she felt as if electric jolts were careening off her bones all through her body.

The hum she had first heard at the ocean seemed to have taken up residence within her brain as something of a curiosity, rather than an annoyance. It wasn't constant, but rather something she became aware of when she thought about her conversations with Ryan.

And those conversations had certainly sparked some wild

thoughts. She recalled dreams that seemed too vivid, coincidences that felt as if they had meaning. Ideas, thoughts -*memories?* - circled throughout her brain. She felt as if she had answered a telephone but had a poor connection – she knew there was someone at the other end, but couldn't tell who it was or what they were trying to say.

She glanced at her watch, then at the cars in the parking lot, watching for Marlene. She was eager to meet with her quirky friend, and wondered what was keeping her. She sat in an overstuffed armchair near the window that afforded her a view of the cars pulling off the main road into the parking lot. Her right leg was crossed over her left and her right foot was bobbing up and down like an over-sprung wind-up toy. Despite having drunk very little of her coffee - her mug was still nearly full – and sleeping fitfully the night before, she felt energized.

Her mind had raced all night, conjuring images she didn't understand but somehow recognized. *Deja vu.* It didn't frighten her, exactly, but she wanted to make sense of it; perhaps that would help her control the jolts. She was hoping Marlene would help her uncover some answers. She had a feeling, in fact, that was exactly what Marlene was planning to do.

She took sip of her coffee and lowered the cup, concentrating on the tiny chip on the rim above the handle. Turning the cup, she noticed a faint gray line that began at the chip and traversed the entire side of the mug, disappearing below the base, and her forehead creased into a frown. Even that crack in the cup seemed significant.

The bell over the door rang, shaking her from her trance, and she heard Marlene's melodic voice greet the barista. "Karen! Darling, how *are* you?" she asked, leaning over the counter and hooking the woman's neck in the crook of her arm.

Karen smiled and patted Marlene on the back. "Marley, sweetie, where have you *been?* Book club just isn't the same without you!"

Marlene released Karen from her grip and waved both her hands, revealing multiple rings, including a new one on her left thumb. "Oh, honey. I wanted to come, really I did. But I..." she paused, her mouth open and pointed to Karen's neck. "That one's new, isn't it?" she asked, pointing to a dragon tattoo behind the barista's left ear.

Karen smiled and pulled her hair back, turning her head to one side to give Marlene a better view. "Yup. You like it?"

Marlene nodded. "I do. That one's a beauty. Usually I'm not into neck art, but that's very classy."

Karen beamed. "Thanks. She's a guardian. She had to be visible."

Cara felt the chills run up through her core and shivered at the word "guardian," and she uncrossed her legs and sat up straighter in her chair.

Karen picked up a large ceramic mug and turned to look at Marlene over her shoulder. "The usual?"

"Of course!" Marlene said. "Do you have any honey?"

"Of course!" Karen replied, laughing. "Fresh, too." She leaned over the counter, raised her hand to her mouth and whispered, "it's from the apiary not too far from here. Lois Bertram, do you know her?"

Marlene shook her head but smiled. "That's wonderful! I've been hearing about more and more woman beekeepers. When they said the bees were disappearing, I just thought the news people weren't looking in the right places, is all!"

Karen nodded and dunked a teabag into the hot water with which she had filled Marlene's mug. She handed her the bottle of honey with a wooden dipper and looked around. "This is just for my special customers," she told Marlene. "I don't think the Health Department would approve."

Marlene waved her hand again. "What the hell do they know?" She watched the amber liquid drip into the water and sink to the bottom, then replaced the dipper in the jar and handed it back to the barista.

"I agree," Karen said as she put the jar into a corner cabinet. "This unregulated stuff is better for your health than the honey that's shipped here from freakin' Washington State or somewhere. Pssh!" she said, closing the cabinet and turning back toward the counter. "Want me to heat the muffin?"

"Sounds good," Marlene told her, handing her the plate.

Karen nodded. "Go sit with your friend. I'll have it out for you in a minute."

"Thanks, precious!" Marlene said, blowing her an air-kiss.

She walked over to Cara's table, set the mug of tea on the wooden block that served as a bistro table, and bent over to give her a hug. Despite her tiny size, Marlene had a very strong grip and a presence that filled an entire room. Her melodic voice made heads turn, even when she spoke quietly – which, Cara had to admit, was rare. There was no ignoring Marlene Luzell.

"And how is my favorite ostrich?" she asked as she sat down in a large green chair across from Cara at the small bistro table. "Still thinking I'm all 'freaky-talk' now?" Her bright red lips stretched into a grin and she dunked her tea bag several times before removing it with the spoon and squeezing out the excess liquid. She placed the spoon and the bag on a napkin, then sat eyeing her friend with a single raised eyebrow.

Cara blushed and ran her thumb along the handle of her ceramic mug. "Jury's still out, Mar," she said. "But I don't think you're certifiable, if that's what you mean."

Marlene raised her eyes dramatically and smiled. "Thank Heaven for small favors! And I *do* mean small. You say Ryan is your little lampholder?"

Cara closed her eyes and shook her head at the reference, then took a sip of her coffee and nodded. "Apparently. He didn't say anything to me at the time, but I guess he knew what happened to me when Steph and I went to Amelia Island back in September."

"Your little earthquake?" Marlene asked. Both eyebrows went up in question over the rim of her mug as she sipped her tea. "Ooh. Hot!" She dabbed her lip with a napkin and held it away to inspect the lipstick stain left behind.

"Is that what you're calling it?" Cara asked, rolling her eyes and snorting. "Geez, Mar, you're subtle, aren't you?"

Karen emerged from behind the counter and laughed as she put the plate with a steaming cranberry-orange-nut muffin in front of Marlene. "Her? Subtle?" She looked at Marlene and snorted. "I thought you two have known each other for a long time!"

Marlene raised a single eyebrow at Karen. "We have. But some people live in *denial* a lot longer than others. This one," she said, hiking a thumb toward Cara, "must've thought she was freakin' Cleopatra or something!"

Karen laughed at Marlene's clever word play and reached over to pick up the discarded spoon and tea bag, which she deposited in the pocket of her apron.

"Hey, now," Cara said, leaning across the table. She looked around to make sure no one overheard, then whispered, "I'm still not sure about all this stuff. But Ryan has said a lot of things that sounded like what you believe, and I know the two of you haven't talked." She shrugged. "I'm on a fact-finding mission. That's all."

Marlene looked up at Karen. "Sounds real official, doesn't it?"

Karen nodded, still smiling, and turned her gaze from Marlene to Cara. "Who's Ryan?"

"Her son," Marlene said. "He's, what, *eight?*"

Cara nodded and Karen smiled. "Good for you, to listen to your kid," Karen said. "Most parents tell their kids they're too old for make-believe friends, or that the stuff they believe doesn't fit in with whatever the family believes. They discourage their kids, so the kids bury the stuff away and become frustrated adults." She shrugged and patted Cara's shoulder. "She's good, you know," she added, nodding toward Marlene. "Knows her stuff. But if what she has said about you is true, there will be no stopping you once you know what's what."

Cara frowned. "What? You talk about me?"

Marlene waved her hands and shook her head. "Don't flatter yourself, honey," she said. "I'm not talking about you, *per se*. Not the way you are now, anyway. But Karen's right. Once you get going, things are going to move very fast in this world. You just wait and see."

"Shifts and all that," Karen added. "Cool stuff."

"Really? *Shifts?*" Cara asked, then closed her eyes and waved her hands in front of her. "I'm just curious. That's all."

Marlene laughed. "Uh-huh." She peered over her shoulder and hooked a thumb toward the counter. "You've got *male*," she told

Karen, indicating a gentleman who had approached the counter for a refill.

Karen looked toward the counter, then back to the two ladies seated before her. "Oh! Excuse me," she said to Cara while pretending to straighten her hair. "Nice talking to you!"

"Same here. I'm sure we'll catch up again soon," Cara called after her.

"No doubt," Marlene said after Karen left. "Karen is one of the reasons I love this coffee shop. She's very enlightened."

"Enlightened," Cara repeated. "As in, she has had an experience like mine or Ryan's?"

Marlene shook her head. "No. Well, sort of." She shrugged and took another sip of her tea.

Cara frowned. "Sort of. What does that mean?"

She put her cup back on the saucer, pulled off a bite of muffin and popped it into her mouth. She chewed slowly, swallowed, thought for a moment, and said, "A lot of people have been open to certain beliefs for a long time, but not everyone is a leader." She inclined her head to one side and smiled at Cara. "Sometimes even very strong souls take a while to shake off everything they've learned in this life and figure out that they are part of something bigger."

"Are you saying that I'm part of something bigger?" Cara asked.

Marlene burst out laughing, which made several patrons turn their heads and stare. After a moment, her laughter died down and she waited for the people to return to their business before continuing. "Oh, honey, you have no idea!"

Cara sat back in her chair and folded her arms, fixing Marlene with a stare that included one eyebrow raised. "Alright. So, how long have you known about me?"

Undeterred by the stare, Marlene took another bite of the muffin. "Ooh. Cranberry!" She wore a smile while she chewed and returned Cara's look with one of her own, but didn't answer.

"Well?"

"Cara, honey. You haven't learned anything in all this time," Marlene said. Despite their being nearly the same age, Marlene's tone was one of a mother scolding her child. She shook her head. "You can't get what you want by blustering and pushing. You have to be patient. Everything in its time."

"But I thought you said it *was* time."

Marlene shrugged and sipped her tea, smiling as the liquid hit her tongue. "Oh, my. Have you tried that honey? Those bees did a good job this year, I can tell you."

"No shortage?"

"What? Of honey?" Marlene frowned and waved her hand. "The idiots on the news just didn't know where to look. They see a few hives die off or move away and they have to make some big to-do about it – tie it into their *global warming* thing." She waved a hand in dismissal of the idea.

"So what happened?"

"The hum changed," Marlene said, without missing a beat. She didn't look at Cara, but took another bite of the muffin and closed her eyes to savor the taste.

Cara laughed. "The what?"

"The hum," she repeated, then opened her eyes and stared at Cara sharply. "Don't act like you don't know what I'm talking about. You've heard it, even if you want to pretend you haven't."

Cara opened her mouth to protest, then frowned and closed her mouth again. She thought for a moment and took a sip of her coffee. "You mean the beach?" she asked.

Marlene nodded. "Well, that's one example. Yes."

"What else?"

"I don't know the specifics in your life. You do, though. Think about it – it will come to you." Marlene popped the last bite of muffin into her mouth, moved the plate to the side and brushed the crumbs from her lap.

"I swear, Mar, I don't know how you stay so tiny. Just looking at that muffin, I feel like I'm popping out of my clothes!"

Marlene laughed and waved her hand again. "Silly girl!" she said. "You need to relax and enjoy things. Enjoy the world around you. If you think too hard about controlling everything, you'll miss some of the best things that will come your way – people, too, come to think about it."

"But I thought you told me I had to pay attention. That's controlling my thoughts, isn't it?"

"Not hardly," Marlene said. "For example, in the morning, what's the first thing you do?"

"Turn off the damned alarm clock and get the boys ready for school."

"Okay. What about waking up five minutes earlier so you can relax and ease into your day?" Marlene suggested.

"Oh, and let the stupid woodpecker outside my house help me start my day with gritted teeth?" Cara said.

Marlene cocked her head to one side. "Woodpecker?"

Cara nodded.

"Maybe the woodpecker is trying to tell you something," Marlene suggested. "Have you thought of that?"

"Yeah, like I have termites or something in the side of my house!"

"Cara," Marlene said, intoning her motherly voice once more.

"I suppose you know what it means?"

Marlene nodded. "How long has the woodpecker been creating a racket outside your window?"

Cara shrugged. "I don't know. Off and on for about six months or so, I guess. Since the spring."

Marlene's eyes grew wide as she stared at her friend, patting her chest to keep from coughing on the crumbs from the muffin. "That long? And you haven't paid attention?" The volume of the woman's voice caused a few people in the coffee shop to turn around and stare. She took another long sip of honey-infused tea while she waited for the results of her disruption to go back to their business. "Sorry," she said, shaking her head. "You always have been stubborn."

"Why am I just finding this out now?" Cara asked.

"No matter. You'll figure it out when the time comes."

"The woodpecker?"

"Oh. It's very cryptic, honey," Marlene said.

"Really?"

"No, of course not!" Marlene said. "It means that something is right in front of your nose and you're not paying attention."

"Wow. That's really tough to decipher," Cara said.

"So why haven't you?" Marlene asked. "Hm?"

Cara shrugged. "I guess I was just waiting for him to get bored with my house and fly off to destroy somebody else's."

Marlene shook her head. "Not going to happen until you listen."

"So what is it trying to say?" Cara asked. "Am I supposed to go outside and have a conversation with a woodpecker? Brandon would love that. He'd have me locked up!"

"Birds don't talk, silly girl!" Marlene said.

"Oh. That's a relief!"

"Seriously, Cara. Woodpeckers mean that you have let things get out of balance, and you need to do something to get them back into balance," Marlene told her.

"But isn't that playing into my control-freak tendency? I thought that's what I was trying to get away from," Cara said.

"No, no. You can create balance without pulling the strings on everything and everyone around you," Marlene explained. "All you have to do is pay attention to what your soul is trying to pay attention to. Your eyes and your energy are not necessarily looking for the same things, although your energy needs your physical eyes to process what's going on."

"I have to listen to my soul? My energy? That sounds complicated," Cara said.

"It really isn't," Marlene said, leaning forward in her seat. "Think of all the unhappy people in the world who are the way they are because they're doing something to make money instead of satisfying their souls."

"I think I know a few of those," Cara said.

"Don't wallow. Just listen," Marlene scolded. "We've become so shut-off to the world around us that we stay in the same rut, even when our energy is instructing us to move elsewhere."

"Like the bees?" Cara asked.

Marlene nodded, smiling. "Now you're getting somewhere."

"Okay, so if I listen then maybe my woodpecker will go away and bother somebody else?" Cara asked.

"Maybe."

"No guarantees, then."

"Nope."

"This just keeps getting better and better," Cara said, pouting. She sighed heavily, then took another sip of her coffee, making a face as she took in a mouthful of the unexpectedly chilly beverage.

Marlene grew quiet and looked out the window over Cara's shoulder. After a moment, she nodded and said, "Yes. That, too." She focused her attention back on Cara and said, "woodpeckers also remind us that we have to be careful what we say."

"Wow. Little bird, big message. Are you sure you're not talking about a carrier pigeon?"

"Focus, Cara," Marlene said.

"Sorry."

"You tend to speak before you think, and that gets you into trouble," Marlene said. "It has many times, and you haven't learned that lesson yet."

"Thick-skulled," Cara said.

"Obviously."

Cara frowned and twisted her lips, thinking about how to phrase what was bothering her. Finally, she looked up at Marlene and took a deep breath. "You keep saying that I've done things many times, or for a long time. We're not talking about since 1967, are we?"

Marlene's face relaxed into a smile, and she shook her head. "No. Not hardly."

"How long are we talking, may I ask?"

Marlene shrugged. "A long, long time."

"A couple of lifetimes?"

Marlene raised her tea to her lips and took a long sip, her eyes considering Cara over the rim of the mug. When she put the cup down on the table once more, she leaned back and propped her elbow on the chair, then leaned her face on her hand. "More than a couple," she said.

"Many more?"

Marlene smiled. "You tell me. You know already, but you have to accept it."

Cara nodded and rubbed her arms, which were covered in chill bumps. She reached for her cup, but changed her mind, as it had gone cold, and she considered a refill to help warm her from the inside.

But Marlene shook her head. "It won't help," she said. "You aren't cold. You're getting a message."

Cara snorted. "Goose bumps: the fax machine of the energetic world."

Marlene laughed and shook her head. "Hopeless!" she said.

The two sat quietly for several minutes before Cara stood up, grabbed her coffee mug and took it to Karen for a refill.

"Sure thing, honey," Karen said. "You can go sit. I'll bring it out to you."

Cara made her way back to her seat and was surprised to find Marlene sitting with her eyes closed, a smile on her face. She opened them as Cara took her seat, then put her hands together and made a "steeple" with her forefingers, waiting for Cara to begin the conversation again.

Karen brought the coffee over to the table and waved her hand as Cara tried to pay her. "Free refills, as long as you're sitting in here," she said, and hurried back to the counter to wait on another customer.

Cara dumped some flavored creamer into the cup and stirred it around, taking a sip before speaking. She put the cup on the table and sat back to face Marlene with raised eyebrows. "You've been doing this stuff for as long as I've known you," Cara said.

Marlene nodded. "There's a reason you've kept me around, even though you had a hard time accepting who you are."

Cara rolled her eyes. "A lot of that was Brandon," she said. "What a mistake that was!" She took another sip of coffee and sat back, holding the mug in her hands.

"Not a mistake," Marlene said. "Necessary. You got your boys out of that union."

Cara tilted her head to one side. "About that," she said. "Ryan seems to be very... what's the word?"

"Intuitive?" Marlene suggested.

"Right. Intuitive," Cara said. "He just says what he thinks, without worrying about what anyone else thinks about it."

"But he wasn't always like that," Marlene said.

Cara shook her head. "No. He's the younger twin. Dylan kind of overshadows him. I used to think he was bullying Ryan, but now I see it more that he's protecting him."

Marlene shook her head. "This is not the first time they've been together. But it is the first time that Dylan is taking his job seriously."

"What do you mean? They've been brothers before?"

"Maybe. I'm not sure about that," Marlene said. "But he has seen things happen to Ryan in the past and he hasn't done anything to stop them. This time, he is here to make sure that Ryan is as safe as he can be."

Cara felt cold. "Ryan says he knows things, but Dylan doesn't."

Marlene shook her head again. "No. Dylan is not truly a part of this. Well, he is, but... He isn't an active participant, per se. Ryan is."

"Ryan told me that he doesn't feel like Brandon is his father," Cara said. "I've always thought it was because he's more like me, and Dylan and Brandon are so much alike."

"Ryan is like you," Marlene said. "You'll have to watch Dylan. He is going to be jealous of Ryan, if he isn't already. He wants to know things, and he's a little afraid of his brother, because he knows what Ryan is saying isn't just make-believe."

"So you're saying that when Ryan tells me that he has spoken to his father, he really doesn't mean Brandon?"

Marlene nodded. "You know it, too."

"Who is his father?"

Marlene sighed. "I'm going to leave it up to Ryan to share that with you when he's ready." She picked up her tea, closed her eyes and took a long sip. "He may not be sure himself yet."

Cara was frustrated. "You haven't told me anything," she said. "I thought you were going to help me."

"You know what they say, honey," Marlene said.

"About what?"

"Giving a man a fish or teaching him." She cocked her head to one side and squinted. "You know more than you want to admit. You're just in denial." She laughed. "I'm just handing you the fishing pole, honey, not filling your basket for you!"

Anxiety filled Cara's chest. "So all this stuff I've been dreaming about doesn't mean I'm crazy."

Marlene shook her head. "It's not dreaming, hon."

"It's not?"

"Mm-mm," Marlene shook her head slowly.

"So what is it? I mean, it's the stuff I think about when I'm in deep sleep and my eyes are closed. Obviously, I'm dreaming."

"Dreams are funny things, honey," Marlene said. "Sometimes they are just little re-caps of your day, sometimes they mean nothing more than you ate something that didn't agree with you too late at night."

"But that's not what this is?"

Marlene raised an eyebrow. "How much stock do you place in psycho-babble these days?"

"You mean like Freud and stuff?"

She nodded.

Cara shrugged. "Depends, I guess. I mean, there's some merit to the theories. Dreams have to mean something, after all. And with all the studies done on REM sleep and..."

Marlene put up a hand. "Stop. What do you believe?"

Cara thought for a moment. "Well, I had a dream awhile back that I remember vividly. It was when Brandon and I were still together but I kind of knew what was coming. He was traveling and it was just me and the boys at home – that happened a lot. But I had a dream that I was flying and I went over this hotel in the town where he was staying for work and I saw a rental car in the parking lot and I knew, somehow, that it was his."

Marlene nodded.

Cara sighed. "So, anyway, I sort of flew up by the window of this one room and I saw Brandon in there with this woman." She laughed and shook her head. "Take that back. It was a *girl* he was with, and she was all giggly and not at all like what he said he expected of me. And when Brandon got home from his trip I was all pissed off at him and he asked me why and I asked him if she was at least legal age."

"Wow!" Marlene said. "I've never heard this part of the story."

Cara shook her head. "Well, Brandon turned white and at first he denied everything, but I just kept fighting with him, even though I knew it was irrational to be angry with him over something I dreamed about." She shrugged and rubbed her knees with her hands. "I just couldn't let it go."

"But it was true, wasn't it?"

Cara nodded. "About a month later, Brandon said he was not happy, that he wanted out of our marriage, and he moved out. The first time I met Claudia – I guess it was about six months later – I about fell out."

"It was her, wasn't it?"

"Yup," she said. "And she's just like in my dream, all giggly and needy. It kind of freaked me out a little bit, to tell the truth."

"You weren't dreaming, Cara," Marlene said.

"I woke up in a sweat, Mar," Cara said.

"You were traveling."

Cara closed her mouth and sat straight up, defiant. "That's ridiculous!"

"Is it?"

"I've seen movies about this kind of stuff. Purely science fiction."

"How do you explain Claudia?" Marlene asked.

Cara shrugged. "Maybe I smelled perfume on his clothes when he got back from his trip. Maybe it smelled like what someone at the grocery store was wearing and she resembled Claudia, and my subconscious mind put it together in a dream."

Marlene cocked her head to one side. "You've put a lot of thought into that excuse, haven't you?"

Cara snorted and turned away in disgust.

Marlene raised her eyebrow and lowered her chin. "Really? Is that what you believe?"

"Sure, it is. It's the only rational explanation for all of this."

"Rational? Based on what?"

"Reality, Marlene," Cara said. "People don't travel outside their bodies."

"They don't?"

Cara frowned. "Of course not! It's physically impossible."

"With your physical body, yes. I agree," Marlene said. "But your physical body isn't all that you are. In fact, you've had a whole lot of them. Your spirit, your soul, whatever you want to call it, understands that it is only confined to that physical body when you're awake. At night, it can do whatever it wants, go wherever it needs to go."

"You're serious?" Cara asked, lowering her voice. "You really believe that is a possibility?"

"I know it is."

"You've done it?"

Marlene nodded. "You have, too. You remember, as you've just told me."

"So I can go anywhere."

"Within reason."

"I've been other places?"

Marlene nodded again.

"Okay, so how did I get this ability?"

Marlene laughed. "You've always had it. You were born with it – all of us were. Well, *most* of us. But the physical world doesn't take kindly to souls just floating around and being aware of their power. Could you imagine? It would be like all the airplanes in the world flying around without an air traffic controller!"

Cara shook her head, frowning, trying to grasp what Marlene was telling her. "The physical world? You mean, the planet has some sort of..."

"No, no. The earth is connected to us, surely. But there are other..." she frowned. "This part is where I don't know how to explain it."

"What are we?" Cara asked.

"Oh, we are what we think we are," Marlene told her. "We're

people, living day to day in relationships with one another. Some people are perfectly content to stay asleep throughout their entire incarnation and deny that they've ever been here or anywhere else before. Others, well..." she spread her arms wide and smiled. "Others of us want answers."

"Answers."

Marlene nodded. "You know there's something else. Everybody feels that they're part of something bigger, but sometimes it's easier to just deny it than to embrace it. The physical world here tells us that certain things are impossible, and it's easier for us to believe that and simply exist than to dig a little deeper and truly understand why we're here."

"Why are we here?"

"To get it right."

"What?"

Marlene shrugged. "We're interconnected. Energy attracts energy, but it also repels. Ideally, we should act in harmony, but ego gets in the way. So we keep trying to get it right, without our egos getting in the way, to react in a way that our vibration is in harmony."

Cara's eyebrows went up and she suddenly felt a chill. "Vibration?"

"Yes."

"Like what happened at the beach?" Cara asked, her voice barely a whisper.

Marlene smiled. "Now we're getting somewhere."

"What was that?" Cara asked. "At the beach? What was it that I heard?"

"To put it into terms you'd understand, that was your alarm clock," Marlene told her.

"My alarm clock," Cara repeated. "You mean, I wasn't paying attention to the messages – the woodpecker, the dreams - so the vibration gods, or whatever, decided that putting me in the hospital might get my attention?"

Marlene laughed. "Silly girl! That's your ego talking!"

"What?"

"There are no 'vibration gods' or higher power, per se. The power comes from all of us who are alike working together. It's what we want to do."

Cara frowned. "I don't really understand."

"Why do you think being in sync is referred to as 'working in harmony'?" Marlene asked.

"Hmm. I never thought of it that way," Cara said.

"You've been to a concert before when one of the musical instruments is out of tune, right?"

"Yeah," Cara made a face. "It's awful! Hurts my ears."

"It's because the instruments are vibrating on different levels. They aren't working together."

"Distortion?" Cara asked.

Marlene nodded and clapped her hands together. "Exactly!"

"So, what does this have to do with the beach? I've had mild vertigo before, but that was horrid!"

"That was the hurricane, most likely," Marlene said. "Extreme weather can really wreak havoc on our energy."

"So the earth does have something to do with us," Cara said.

Marlene nodded noncommittally. "Sort of. The earth itself isn't a living thing – not like you and me, anyway - but it helps to channel our energy. It acts as a conductor of sorts. And if someone's vibration isn't in accord with the others, it can cause a bit of..."

"Distortion," Cara said again.

"Right."

"Surely, one person can't be so out of whack that they make a hurricane," Cara said.

"Of course not," Marlene said. "But when that one person is supposed to influence a lot of others, and those others are swirling around searching for their placement, then things can become a little chaotic."

"Oh, come on," Cara said. "How could a single leader create that kind of dissonance?"

"Ego," Marlene said. "A good leader has to have enough of it to draw others to him or her."

"But I thought you said that ego was a bad thing," Cara said.

"It is, when it works against the group."

Cara put her hands up near her face and began massaging her temples with her fingers. "I don't think I quite understand."

Marlene drained the last of her tea and leaned toward Cara. "It's not hard if you accept it for what it is," she said. "It's when you try to apply the rules of this lifetime to the whole that it becomes confusing. Take the blinders off. Open your eyes – your spiritual eyes. It's all right there in front of you."

She opened her eyes and concentrated on Marlene. "And Ryan already gets it?"

Marlene smiled and nodded. "He doesn't have thirty-some-odd years of rules to overcome."

"He is young," Cara said.

"Not really," Marlene said. "You've heard of the term 'old soul,' I assume?"

"Is that what Ryan is?"

Marlene nodded. "You know that. It's one of the reasons you relate to him better than you do Dylan."

"Dylan isn't an old soul?"

She shrugged. "Who knows? Not in the same sense as Ryan, and you, and me, and..." She waved her hand in front of her face and shook her head. "Well..."

"What? Are there others?" Cara demanded.

"Of course there are!" Marlene told her. "Some of them you already know. Others, you'll recognize when the time is right."

"The vertigo, then? My alarm clock?"

"Well, honey, I guess the time is right," Marlene said, and she smiled.

Cara took a deep breath, considered the chill bumps that covered her arms and the butterfly feeling inside her chest and smiled back.

Chapter 4

Brandon dropped the boys off at Cara's house on Sunday night – late, as usual. They were in a particularly edgy mood, having eaten a diet of fast food and sugary treats with their father all weekend, and Cara was agitated with her ex-husband's lackadaisical attitude toward his sons' well-being.

"Take a shower, please, Dylan," Cara said as she emptied the contents of his rolling suitcase and found burrs all in his clothes. She wrinkled her nose as the smell of dried sweat and mud filled her nostrils, and she held the clothing at arm's length. "Where did your dad take you this weekend, anyway?"

Dylan brushed past her with a scowl on his face. "Kennesaw Mountain," he said.

She raised her eyebrows in surprise. Brandon was not exactly the "outdoorsy" type, but the recent camping trip, and now Kennesaw Mountain, made it seem as if her was making an effort to spend more time outside with the boys. She wondered if he had taken his cell phone with him.

"Did he take you hiking?" she asked.

The bathroom door slammed shut and Dylan shouted through it. "Yeah!"

"Did you enjoy yourself?"

The door opened again and he stuck his head through, still scowling. "No!" he shouted, before slamming the door shut once more.

Cara rolled her eyes and sighed, picking the burrs from his sweatshirt and dropping them into the trash can in the laundry room. "Sounds like it should have been fun," she said to herself.

Ryan rolled around the doorway and leaned his head and shoulder against the door jamb. "It was fun, sort of," he said, struggling to drag his suitcase into the laundry room with one hand as he held the other behind his back.

She held a hand to her chest and gasped. "God, Ryan! You scared me!"

He smiled. "Yeah. I know. That was funny!" He tilted the suitcase so it was lying on its side and undid the zipper – again with one hand.

A raised eyebrow indicated she didn't agree with his idea of humor, and she continued pulling burrs from the older twin's clothes. "You may want to start on your stuff so I can get this laundry washed tonight."

Ryan shrugged and pushed himself away from the door. He pulled a red Blow Pop from behind his back and stuck it into his mouth, then bent over his suitcase and began sorting his clothes.

"What? No burrs?" Cara asked.

He shook his head, keeping it low so she wouldn't see the candy.

"Ry? Didn't you go to the park with your dad and brother?"

He nodded and Cara frowned. She bent down and saw the stick to the sucker protruding from his mouth and frowned. "Really?"

Ryan shrugged, straightened and took another few licks from the sucker before wrapping it in the paper he pulled from his pocket and tossing it into the trash can. He smiled at Cara, his lips an unnatural shade of red.

She made a face and shook her head. "Didn't you have enough of that with your dad?" she asked.

He wrinkled his nose and shook his head. "I didn't eat mine at Dad's," he said.

"Oh? Why not?"

He smiled. "It kind of pisses him off when I get on my soap box about sugary treats. I asked him to buy carrots!"

"Oh, Ry!" Cara said, shaking her head. "You are going to be the

81

death of your father. You know that, don't you?" She mock-scowled at him. "And watch your language. You know I don't like that," she scolded.

"Sorry," he said, shrugging. "I figure I can get Dad to eat better if I just keep on him, like you do on me and Dylan." He grinned and added, "even if we cheat once in a while." He bent down and picked up a pair of blue jeans, shook them out and examined them before tossing them into the wash pile. "You tell us we are what we eat, right? Well, I figure I can tell Dad that if he feeds us junk, he gets junk!"

She laughed and tousled his hair. "Wow. That must have really set him off. I think part of the reason we got divorced was because I refused to cook hot dogs on Friday nights!"

"Really?" Ryan asked, straightening to look at his mother.

"No. Not really. But I didn't like that stuff, even way back when." She patted her midsection. "Always made me feel bad afterward."

Ryan wrinkled his nose and nodded. "Yeah. Me, too." He picked up a t-shirt and tossed it into the pile of laundry. "But I think a Blow Pop is okay once in a while. Don't you?"

"No. Not really," she said. "Have you seen the color of your lips?"

He shook his head and stuck out his tongue. "Nud abud dah?"

"Disgusting!" she said. "Bright red, like a clown's nose!"

He shrugged. "Oh, well. It tasted good!" He picked up his socks and unrolled them, then tossed them into the pile.

"The sugar could explain Dylan's lovely mood, then, heh?" she asked.

Ryan shrugged and nodded noncommittally as he continued pulling clothes from his case.

Cara watched him and frowned. "Wait a minute. Didn't you say you went with Dad and Dylan to the mountain?"

Ryan nodded.

"So, why are Dylan's clothes all covered in burrs and yours don't have a thing on them?" she asked again. "You didn't answer me."

Ryan shrugged and pulled a sweatshirt out of his bag. "He went the wrong way, I guess," he said.

"Did you not stay on the paths?" she asked.

He shook his head and handed his shirt to her. "Dylan and Dad did. But there was one part where they cut through to see some sign or something. I didn't go there."

"Why not? That's a history lesson," she said.

He shrugged. "I found a bee hive and I thought that was more cool to look at than reading some sign."

Cara felt chill bumps rise on her arms and a tingling sensation at the base of her neck. She gulped to steady her voice, then asked, "A bee hive? Really? This late in the season?" She was surprised, as they had already had several cool nights. "Are you sure it wasn't yellow jackets?"

He shook his head. "It was bees," he said. "But they weren't out flying around or anything. I just heard them in there, buzzing a little bit." He paused and bit his lip, a frown creasing his brow. "It was kind of warm yesterday."

"I guess. But I would have thought they'd be hibernating already, or whatever it is bees do," she said.

"Guess not," he told her, tossing the last of his laundry into the wash pile on the floor beside her. "What's for dinner? I'm starving!"

She looked at the clock that hung in the kitchen, just down the hall. "It's eight o'clock. Your dad didn't feed you dinner?" she asked, her agitation with Brandon growing.

Ryan shook his head. "We didn't have time, I guess."

"You surely didn't spend the whole day hiking – I think I know your dad a little better than that. What the heck was he doing with you today, then?" she asked, struggling to keep the annoyance from her voice.

"Packing up his stuff," Ryan said.

"What?"

"He's moving out of his apartment," Ryan said. "He said he already talked to you about it."

She put her hands on her hips and sighed. "He told me he was *thinking* about moving. I didn't think it was set in stone."

Ryan made a face and put his hands up in an "I-don't-know" gesture.

"Where is he moving to?" she asked. "And when?" Her mind was already racing, trying to figure out what it might do to their visitation schedule if Brandon moved too far away. Or maybe he was moving closer? If he got a place in the school district, that would save them both a lot of headache, especially on the weekends.

"Don't know, and don't know," Ryan said, although his voice hinted otherwise. "But I guess it's soon, because everything at Dad's was in boxes."

"That explains why he took you guys hiking, I guess," she said. "You probably had nothing to do inside."

Ryan shook his head. "Nope. It was kind of boring, actually."

She exhaled and forced a smile as she changed the subject. "So, did you enjoy your hike?"

"I did," he said. "I don't think Dylan and Dad did, though. They are both kind of out of shape, you know?"

Cara laughed. "I know your dad doesn't exercise, but I think Dylan does pretty well."

"Not hiking up a mountain," Ryan said. He glanced toward the door and lowered his voice. "It wasn't pretty. He got all sweaty and his face was red."

"Really?" Cara glanced at the bathroom door as well. The water was still running in the shower. She made a mental note to drill Dylan more thoroughly about his experience when he came out and got dressed.

"Did you know that you can see the clouds moving from up there?" Ryan asked her.

"Really? On top of the mountain, you mean?" She measured the liquid laundry soap and dumped it into the dispenser, then switched the temperature on the machine to "hot" and pressed the "start" button. *That ought to make Dylan cut his shower short!* she thought.

Ryan nodded. "I mean, there weren't too many clouds, but the ones that were there were moving pretty good."

She frowned. Kennesaw mountain was barely worthy of the designation – it didn't rise up so high that there was a significant altitude change. Certainly not one that would place her son at cloud

84

level. "You're telling me stories, Ry," she said.

He looked hurt. "No. Really! It was when I heard the bees buzzing. I looked around and I saw the clouds. So I turned around, and that was when I saw the fox."

Her eyebrows shot up and she felt the goose bumps rise on her forearms again. "A fox? You have to be careful, Ry. They carry rabies."

Ryan laughed. "I didn't go pick him up, Mom," he said. "He was hunting something. When I looked at him, he stopped and turned his head to me. He looked right at me. It was so cool! He ran off when Dad yelled for me."

"Did Dylan see him?" she asked.

"Who? The fox?" Ryan shook his head. "No. But I told him about it. He looked mad that he had to go look at the sign and I saw something like that." He smiled at her. "We did find some poop, though."

Cara wrinkled her nose. "Oh? Lucky you!"

He smiled. "Yeah. It was pretty cool. I think it was coyote poop or something. Dad said it was too small to be from a bear." He wrinkled his nose and tilted his head, a slight smile crossing his face, and he added, "Unless it was a *baby* bear."

Cara raised her eyebrows and tossed a rolled-up sock at her son, who ducked and giggled. "Yikes!" she said. "Well, either way, I'm glad all you found was its poop!"

Ryan laughed.

Cara tilted her head and said, "from the smell of his clothes, I think your brother may have rolled in the poop!"

He laughed harder, but put his hands over his mouth to muffle the sound as he realized his brother might be able to hear him and would wonder what was going on. Dylan didn't like being made fun of, although he dished it out pretty well.

The water stopped running in the bathroom and they heard a pair of wet feet hit the floor. The cabinet door under the sink squeaked open and slammed shut, followed by the muffled mumblings of a disgruntled eight-year-old boy. Steam poured out of the crack in the door as Dylan leaned his head out into the hallway. "Mom?"

Ryan ducked into the laundry room, hidden from his brother's view. He was doubled over, holding both hands over his mouth, still laughing.

Cara peeked her head into the hallway. "Yes?"

"Can you get me a towel?"

"Sure," she said, and pulled a clean one from the basket on top of the washer and handed it to Ryan, who placed it into the hand protruding through the barely opened bathroom door.

"Thanks," he said and closed the door again. He emerged a few minutes later with the towel wrapped around his middle, his hair still dripping wet. Despite the shower, his face still seemed blotchy.

"You okay, Dyl?" Cara asked.

He pressed his lips into a thin line and nodded.

"Don't get cold," she warned, and handed him a t-shirt and pajama pants from the freshly folded stack in the basket on the floor beside her. She turned back to Ryan. "Is he okay?" she whispered as Dylan, still clutching the towel, carried the clothes to his bedroom and shut the door.

"I don't think so," Ryan said, swallowing the last of his laughter. "He really hates it when there isn't a towel in the bathroom."

Cara frowned. "Yeah, I don't think that was it," she said. "Did Dylan and Dad have a fight?"

"Sort of," Ryan said. "Dad got mad at Dylan for getting mud all over his floor mats."

"In that old junker of his? You're kidding, right? That's why people get SUVs!"

Ryan shrugged again, then grew serious. "Mom?"

She had opened the dryer and was folding some of her own clothes, but the tone of his voice made her turn and look. He was pale, and his eyes looked huge against his pale skin.

"Are you okay?" she asked as she dropped the blouse she'd been folding. "You look like you're going to be sick!"

"I'm good," he said. "But I'm worried. Remember what I told you about Dad when we came back last week?"

She cocked her head to one side. "About..."

"About, well..." Ryan looked nervous and glanced over his shoulder at his brother's bedroom door. He lowered his voice to a whisper. "About him not being my real dad?"

Cara felt a sense of relief. She hadn't wanted to bring anything up with Ryan, having decided after her conversation with Marlene that it would be better for him to tell her things at his own pace. "I remember," she said.

"Well, I said something to Dad," he said.

"Oh, no, Ry," she said. "He didn't take it well, did he?"

Ryan shook his head. "No. And I think he took it out more on Dylan than on me."

"Why would he do that?"

He looked up at her sheepishly and wrinkled his nose. "I think he's kind of afraid of me."

Cara leaned over to pick up the blouse she had dropped, but turned her head to acknowledge what he had said. As she straightened, she shook her head. "No. I don't think that at all, honey," she said. "He knows he's your father. Maybe it just hurt his feelings that you said something."

"He and Dylan are kind of the same, you know?"

She nodded.

"They even look the same," Ryan said.

"I guess they do," she said.

"But not me. And we're twins," he said. "Aren't we supposed to look the same if we're twins?"

Cara shook her head. "That's not always how it happens, Ry," she said. "You and Dylan are *fraternal* twins, which means you were born at the same time, but you can look very different from each other."

"Why did you have twins?" he asked, cocking his head to one side.

She laughed. "I don't know," she said. "It just happens sometimes."

"There's a reason," Ryan said. His voice had changed, and Cara felt cold just hearing it.

"What do you think that reason is, Ry?" she asked, suppressing a shiver.

He looked up at her with a look of very old wisdom. "Because I know things and Dylan doesn't, and this way Dad gets one of us and you get one of us."

"Interesting idea," she said, fighting the feeling of chill bumps rising on her arms and neck.

"No, Mom. It's real," Ryan insisted.

She nodded. "Okay. So, what is it that you know that your dad and Dylan don't?"

"About the water," he said. "And about you."

She shivered again and rubbed her arms. Taking a deep breath, she looked straight at her son. "The water, Ryan?"

"You were in the water, and so was I," he said in a tone that suggested she understood what he was saying. "Dad and Dylan weren't there." He frowned. "Or, maybe they were, but they don't want to remember." He looked up at her. "Some people are like that, you know?"

"I know," she told him, with a sense of pride mingled with sadness at his newfound maturity. His words made her nervous, though. She wasn't quite sure what he was saying, that they were *in the water*.

He frowned again and shook his head. "Maybe they were there, but I really don't think so. Most of the people who were are starting to remember."

She opened her mouth to ask him about that, but stopped as Dylan's bedroom door opened once more. He padded down the hall wearing his pajama pants and an Atlanta Falcons sweatshirt. "What are you talking about?"

"You know..." Ryan said.

"Oh." His face wore a mask of disappointment. He tossed his wet towel onto the heap of dirty clothes and he looked up at his mother. "Why can't I remember anything like Ryan does, Mom? Wasn't I in the water, too?"

She moved toward him on her knees and put her hand on his shoulder. "I don't know, sweetheart," she said. "Maybe you were someplace else?"

He frowned and looked over at his brother. "But we're twins."

"Now we are," Ryan said. "Remember, I told you that we might not have been related before. Maybe that's why you don't remember." He looked up at Cara. "Isn't that right, Mom?"

"I suppose," she said. Her entire body began tingling and she felt light-headed.

"Are you okay, Mom?" Dylan asked, as Cara leaned heavily against him.

She nodded, but felt the color drain from her face as she sat back on her heels. Her fingers were numb and her lips felt cold. "Let's stop talking about this for a minute, okay?" she suggested. Her voice sounded very far away, like she was speaking in a tunnel.

"Mom?" Ryan's voice also sounded far away, and then everything was dark.

When she opened her eyes, she was lying on the laundry room floor with a wet towel under her head. Dylan was holding her hand and crying, while Ryan had a wet washcloth that he was using to lay across her forehead. When she looked around, Ryan smiled at her. "You okay?" he asked.

Cara nodded and put her elbow under herself to push up to a sitting position. "What happened?" she asked, taking a mental inventory of any aches or bruised areas. Finding none, she smiled at the boys, making light of her episode. "I guess I'm a little hungry, huh? I don't remember eating anything today; I was trying to get all of my housework done before you boys got home, and now it's kind of late."

"You fainted, Mom," Dylan said, his voice trembling. He sounded so small. She leaned over, put an arm around him and kissed the top of his head. "It scared me. You're not sick, are you?" he asked.

Cara smiled wearily and shook her head. "I'm fine, honey," she said.

"Is that the same kind of thing that happened to you at the beach?" Ryan asked.,

Dylan turned on him with tears streaming down his face. "Stop saying that! You weren't there! You don't know that she got sick at the beach!"

"Dyl, it's okay. Calm down," she said, stroking his hair.

Dylan's face was blotchy. "Are you dying, Mom? Because I don't want you to die."

"Oh, honey! No!" she said. Her heart felt like it was breaking into a thousand tiny pieces. "Don't worry, Dylan. I'm not going anywhere. I'm fine. I'm right here." She looked around at Ryan. "What did you say to him, Ry?"

"Nothing, Mom," he said, but the look in his eyes was wary, as if he were hiding something.

Cara raised her eyebrows and lowered her chin in her best "Mom" look.

He took a deep breath and leveled a similar gaze in her direction.

They sat staring at one another for what seemed an eternity, until Dylan hiccuped, trying to stifle a sob. "He said... He said..."

"What, baby?" she asked, rubbing the side of his wet head.

"I told him you were starting to remember what happened before," Ryan told her.

She felt the chills again, like her entire body was covered in goose flesh. "What are you talking about, honey?" She felt almost ridiculous, asking her son about a past life. She wondered what Brandon would think of this conversation, or her mother. Neither one put much stock in her strange dreams or her ability to sense things that were about to happen. She thought perhaps it was a little far-fetched, which is why she had kept the feelings to herself for so long, and tried to ignore them. "What happened before?"

"The explosion," he said.

Cara frowned. "I don't remember any explosion, Ry," she said. "You must be mistaken."

"He scares me when he talks like that, Mom," Dylan said. "What is he talking about? Do you know something about an explosion?"

She shushed him and continued to stroke his hair absently while she looked at Ryan.

"You know, Mom. It's why you don't really want to remember. It was... well..." He frowned and bit his lip. "Sometimes, I think I know what happened, but other times it's really confusing."

She reached over to him and pulled him close, and the three of them sat there on the laundry room floor, which is where Stephan found them when he let himself in.

"Hi, Steph," Ryan said, smiling up at him.

"Hey, buddy! How's everything?" He frowned as he took in the gathering in the laundry room. "We having a tea party in here or something? I don't see any little cups or board games..."

Dylan laughed and wiped his sleeve across his face. "Nah. We were helping Mom with the laundry and she kind of fell down."

A look of panic crossed over Stephan's face as he looked at Cara, but she smiled and shook her head. "I'm fine," she told him. "I promise. Just a little dizzy, that's all."

"The weather's been nice, Cara," he said, frowning, then he held up a reusable grocery bag. "Have you eaten? I brought some veggie burgers over, in case you hadn't gotten to the store today."

"Sounds good!" the boys said in unison.

"You're a life saver!" she said, laughing. "I just told the boys I hadn't eaten anything today. I got busy cleaning and it got kind of late, so I didn't leave. I didn't want Brandon to get here and find me gone."

"Did he get here on time?" Stephan asked.

Cara made a face. "Are you kidding?" She took Stephan's hand as he helped her up from the floor. "At least he was only two hours late today. It's better than the last four weeks."

Stephan shook his head and looked at the boys. "Sorry, guys." Then, to Cara, he said, "That ex-husband of yours. Was he a cable repairman at some point? He has the punctuality of someone used to giving people a four-hour window."

"Cute," she said. "No. He's just... Brandon."

"It pisses Mom off, though. That's one of the reasons they got divorced," Dylan said.

"That, and that he eats like crap," Ryan added.

Cara's head whipped around. "Language! Both of you!" She shook her head then turned back to Stephan with a warning look. "Let's not talk about their dad anymore, okay?"

Stephan nodded. "I understand. Didn't mean any harm."

They walked into the kitchen where Stephan began preparing the pan for the veggie burgers. While Cara and the boys often cooked theirs in the microwave, Stephan preferred a skillet, complete with garlic and onions sautéed in. The result was a vegetarian dinner that tasted almost like a beef burger – and they preferred it.

"I'm like the Chick-fil-A commercial," Dylan said after swallowing a bite of burger. "I like a no-cow zone."

Ryan laughed, his cheek full of food. "Since when?"

"Since I got home," Dylan told him.

"Yeah. Because at Dad's you were like, all about the hot dogs and stuff!" Ryan said.

Dylan shot an angry glance at his brother and his ears turned red with embarrassment. He didn't like being ridiculed.

"No fighting," Cara warned. She looked at Stephan. "Thanks. These are really good."

"Claudia doesn't do stuff like this at Dad's," Dylan said as he swallowed a bite of burger.

"She was there this weekend?" Cara asked.

Ryan nodded. "She's there every weekend. She was helping him pack."

Cara raised her eyebrows, then folded her hands on the table in front of her, took a deep breath and looked up at the boys. Keeping her voice steady, she asked, "Do you ever go to Claudia's apartment?" She already knew the answer.

Both boys nodded, although Ryan did so with less enthusiasm.

"She lives in a house now, Mom," Dylan said.

"A house? Really?" Cara swallowed the bite of burger and forced a smile. "I guess that means Dad's staying in town, then, huh?"

Both of the boys shrugged. "I guess," Ryan said.

" And she has a dog!" Dylan said. He had been begging for a dog for as long as Cara could remember.

"A dog? Wow. That should go over well with..." she stopped herself, disliking the bitter tone in her voice.

"Well, not really a *dog* dog," Ryan said, wrinkling his nose. "A *dog* dog could, like, catch a tennis ball or wrestle on the floor with us. Claudia's dog wears clothes and has a place at the table."

"Really?" Cara asked, suppressing a grin. Brandon had always hated the idea of animals in the house. It was one of the reasons they had never gotten the dog Dylan longed for.

Ryan caught her expression and laughed. "Yeah. It's kind of funny. She says she doesn't like kids, but she lets the dog eat off her plate!"

"Gross!" Cara said. Her grin faded and she forced herself to laugh. Inside, she was seething, and she looked to Stephan for moral support. He just shrugged and took the last bite of his veggie burger.

A tapping noise out back made Cara turn her head. "Darn bird is back again, eating up my siding!" she said, running out to the back yard. She slammed the door, expecting the bird to fly away, but it stayed there, staring at her. Every so often it tilted its head to one side, as if trying to get a better view of her – *or to convey a message*, she thought.

She stood on the patio for a long time with her hands on her hips, staring down the brazen bird. Finally, he turned his head, swallowed an insect and flew off. "About time," she said to herself, feeling silly for being involved in a battle of wills with a tiny bird.

As she turned to go back inside, she felt the hair on the back of her neck prickle and she turned around slowly. The woodpecker had landed in the large tree that separated her yard from the next-door neighbor's, and was looking down on her from his perch way above her head. She shook off the chills and noticed a chipmunk gathering acorns below the tree, stuffing them into his already full cheeks. Curiously, she stepped forward to get a closer look at the little animal. It sat upright and twitched its tail a few times before darting off into a small hole under the roots of the tree.

"I'm going crazy," she said. "I feel like Cinderella, talking to birds and rodents."

"You don't look like her," Stephan said, startling her.

"Gee, thanks, friend!" she told him as she caught her breath, holding her hand at the base of her throat. "You scared me half to death!"

Stephan laughed. "The boys sent me out here to make sure you

93

hadn't fainted again. I guess they were afraid of having to pick you up if you were lying sprawled on the porch," he said.

"I almost was, thanks to you," she said, glaring at him.

His smile faded and he raised an eyebrow at her. "You didn't tell me you had fainted. You told me you were dizzy."

"My loving children," she said, smiling. "Or should I call them my little traitors?" She raised her hand to her face and lifted a stray piece of hair that had dropped over her eye, tucked it back behind her ear and shrugged. "I don't know what happened. I hope this isn't the start of some sort of trend. If I have seizures or something, I won't be able to drive."

Stephan shook his head. "It isn't seizures," he said.

She frowned at his change of tune and he backed up, leaned against the porch railing and shoved his hands into the pockets of his jeans. He took a deep breath and squinted at something over Cara's shoulders, then laughed. "Is that the little pecker that's been bothering you?" he asked.

She turned around to look, then nodded. "Yeah. I think I showed him who's boss, though. He flew away after a couple of minutes."

"Did you talk to your friend, Marlene, about it?" he asked.

"About the bird?" Cara rolled her eyes. "Yeah. But she said it just means I have to be on the lookout for things. It's trying to get my attention." She laughed. "Not a very smart way to get my attention, if you asked me. The damned bird was literally banging on the side of my house." She frowned and said, "woodpeckers are fairly common in Georgia. If someone really wanted to get my attention, they'd send an elephant or something! Now *that* would get my attention!"

He looked down and shook his head, still smiling. When he looked back up at her, his smile was gone and his voice was serious. "Look, Cara. I know you think all this stuff is crazy, and that I don't believe you. But I want you to know that I do. This is all real. You're..." he closed his eyes and raised his head, thinking. When he looked at her again, he squinted, as if trying to bore his message into her. "You're *waking up*, do you hear?"

She felt cold. "That's what Marlene told me, too. And Ryan, come to think of it."

He shrugged. "It must be true, then."

"You haven't talked to her, have you?" she asked.

"I don't believe I've ever met *Marlene*, Cara," he said, although she noticed a slight hesitation in his voice as he spoke her name.

"Right," she said in a whisper. She looked past him to check on the boys, who had moved their dinner dishes aside and were playing a card game at the dining room table. "Wow!" she said. "What did you do to them?"

Stephan turned around to peek inside. "Nothing," he told her. "They were worried about you. They don't like the idea that you might not be able to be here for them." He looked back at her.

Her eyes grew wide. "That's not going to happen!" she said. "I'll always be here for my boys."

"I'm sure you will, if you can. But sometimes things happen that are beyond our control," he said, then pushed himself away from the porch rail and pulled up a metal deck chair. He swept the leaves from the seat and sat down.

"Stephan! That's a terrible thing to say!" Cara said. "You don't know something I don't, do you? Am I, like, *dying* or something?"

"No. Don't worry," he said. "I shouldn't have said that. It was stupid. But I do wish you'd stop blacking out. You need to learn to manage that."

"Hm. Would be nice," she said, folding her arms crossly as she leaned against the porch rail.

He closed his eyes and felt the slight breeze on his face, then opened his eyes and looked around. "Someone's burning leaves," he said. "Do you smell it?"

She sniffed the air and made a face. "I do."

Stephan smiled mischievously. "You know, some people say that when you smell smoke, it indicates that a ghost is nearby."

"Oh?" She looked around, spied the smoke a few yards over, and glared back at him. "And what would those same people say if you could see the house two doors down where the neighbor is standing next to a pile of burning leaves with a garden hose?"

He laughed. "Maybe they're trying to smudge out the ghost?"

"Ha-ha." She shifted her weight, put her hands against the small of her back and stretched. When she straightened, she walked over to the metal deck chair across the table from Stephan and sat down. "Are you one of those people who believes in ghosts?"

He reached across the table and picked up a leaf, twirling it around in his fingers. "I wouldn't say *ghost*, exactly," he told her. "Ghosts, like in horror movies? No. Spirits? Absolutely."

"Really."

He nodded and dropped the leaf, looking at her as if to challenge her to say something.

"So, when we were at the beach, did you feel the presence of any particular spirits that were trying to... oh, I don't know, *contact* me?" she asked.

He smiled. "You confronted me about that while you were in the hospital, remember?"

"And you told me you didn't hear anything," she said. "But that's because I asked if you heard a weird noise. I don't think I asked the right question, did I?"

Half his mouth curled up into a smile. "Maybe not."

"Damn, Stephan!" she said, looking away. The chipmunk was back. He had emptied his cheeks and was perched on the porch rail about six feet away, sitting upright, his thin tail twitching. "Do you see that?"

Stephan turned. "The chipmunk? Yeah. I see it."

"Good. Then I asked the right question," she said.

"You're learning."

"What did you *experience* at the beach?" she asked, raising an eyebrow.

He inhaled deeply through his nose and picked up the leaf once more, pinching the stem between his fingers and squinting as he examined the pattern of the veins that criss-crossed its surface. "It's hard to explain," he told her. "I guess the only way to describe it is a *sensory disturbance.*"

"Geez. That's not cryptic!" She laughed and raised an eyebrow. "I don't suppose you'd care to elaborate?"

He was quiet for a moment, looking past her over her shoulder, thinking. Finally, he nodded, as if he had made a decision. When he looked at her again, his eyes were bright with excitement and something she couldn't quite put her finger on. "Okay. I saw the color of the clouds, just like you did. I smelled fish and ocean water, but there was something else I can't quite describe."

He paused for a moment, frowning at the leaf in his hand, watching it as it was caught by a breeze and skidded across the porch. He looked up at her again, his brows knitted together. "Kind of like lightning?" he said, inclining his head and squinting at her, shrugging one shoulder, and she nodded, encouraging him to go on, although every nerve ending in her body was crackling.

"Are you okay?" he asked.

She nodded again. "I'm fine," she said.

"You're not going to faint, are you?" he asked.

She shook her head and leaned closer to him. "I want to hear more."

"Okay. So, there was also a chill, but not cold." He frowned again. "I don't know if that even makes sense."

She nodded again. "It does. Go on."

"That's it," he said, slapping his knees with his hands.

"That's it? You didn't hear anything at all?" she asked.

He shook his head. "The waves were crashing. The wind was whistling a little bit, and I heard the flags snapping in the wind. And those guys shouting. That was pretty much it." He frowned. "Why? What did you hear?"

"Well, I kind of had a similar experience as you with the lightning smell." She laughed. "Actually, when you took me to the hospital, I was a little nervous. I've heard that when you imagine a burning smell like that, it doesn't mean there's a ghost nearby; it means you're having a stroke."

Stephan shook his head. "Nope. That's not what it means in this case, I don't think."

"Good. Because that would suck."

He laughed. "You have such a way with words," he told her. "You always have."

The hair rose on her arms and she froze. "What did you say?"

"You heard me," he replied quietly.

"Marlene told me I knew some others," she said.

He shook his head. "Not others."

She frowned. "No?"

"Mm-mm. We've been together before," he said.

"We have?" She felt the color rising in her cheeks.

Stephan laughed. "Not like that. We've been like this." He pointed to her then back at himself - their present relationship.

"Well, what are we, exactly?" she asked.

"Two halves of the same whole, I guess," he said, without a moment's hesitation.

"You've obviously given this a lot of thought," she said. Her face was hot.

"I have."

"We've just met, though. I mean, in the grand scheme," she said.

He shook his head slowly. "This time around, yes. But in the grand scheme? We've known each other for a long time."

"So, how does this work, exactly?" she asked him.

"You seem to want to know a lot of things 'exactly,' but that's not how I can explain it," he told her. "There isn't an exactly, because no one has been here the whole time – remembering - to be able to say how it works. In fact, there are those who try to keep us from embracing what we are. We can go entire lifetimes without ever truly waking up."

"Really?"

He nodded. "Entire generations of us have to hide who we really are."

"Like the witch burnings?"

"Sort of. I think some of those were simply idiots who were afraid of women," he said.

"Hm."

"There are entire groups of... well, *others*, who use fear to keep folks from understanding that their earthly bodies are simply temporary vessels, and that their souls aren't bound to just Earth and Heaven," Stephan said. He shook his head, frowning. "In fact, I think there are those who are particularly skilled at returning time and again with that end in mind. The ego is a powerful thing."

"So the Catholic church... ?" she asked, raising her eyebrows. It wasn't a question, really; it was more of wishing for confirmation of something she already knew somehow.

Stephan nodded. "Sure. But not just them. They seem to have a lot of things right, in fact," he told her.

"There are a lot of other religions, political movements, the works, that ego-driven people are drawn to. A lot of them remember things, but the ideas get warped somehow. Pretty much any time one person or group is trying to control another group, there's a pretty powerful egomaniacal energy involved."

"Are these controlling people *awake?*" she asked.

Stephan frowned. "Not always. Some of them are. Some of them never will be – not like you and me, anyway. Sometimes, they're just power-hungry. It's easier to control the masses if the masses aren't aware of what's being done to them."

Cara made a face. "Sounds like our politicians!"

Stephen raised an eyebrow and lowered his chin, gazing at her levelly.

"You're kidding," she said.

"Not all of them. But a lot of folks will run for office, thinking they know something that nobody else does," he told her.

"Why don't we hear about this kind of stuff?" she asked, making a fist.

"We do, but the media makes them out to be whack-jobs," he said. "Actually, a lot of people aren't willing to accept the truth, and the media just feeds their fears." He paused, tapping his chin with his forefinger, then looked back at Cara. "Remember what happened when Nancy Reagan used to bring her psychic to the White House?"

She rolled her eyes. "There were a lot of people who thought that she was a little *woo-woo*," Cara said. "My mother was one of those."

Stephan nodded.

"Point taken," she said. She thought for a moment, biting her lip in deep thought. "Has it always been this way?"

He shrugged. "Pretty much, as far as I can tell. Like I said, there hasn't been anyone inhabiting the same physical body for the length of history, and it's kind of hard to take information from one life to the next."

"Can it be done, do you think?" she asked.

He shrugged.

"Reincarnation?" she asked.

"In a way," he said, but frowned. "But not exactly. Reincarnation is one way people try to explain it, but it's more complicated than that. Your energy exists all the time as part of the whole. It never dies; it just moves from one place to another, inhabiting different vessels, or just inhabiting the ethos. But it chooses to inhabit a body... *somewhere*, at various times and places, when it feels it has a job to do."

She nodded. "How many times have we been here?"

"No telling, really." He turned to look at the chipmunk, still perched on the porch rail. "A lot, that's all I'm sure about."

"And we've never..."

He shook his head, still looking away. When he finally turned back to face her, he said, "Never."

She laughed. "That is *so* not like me."

"Tell me about it," he said, folding his hands across his lap and tilting his head back.

She laughed at his impression of a therapist. "Tell you about what?"

He sighed. "You've always been sort of impetuous." He chuckled. "It's gotten you into some trouble before."

"So I've always been this way?" she asked. "In every incarnation?"

He nodded. "The ones I know about, anyway."

"Good. I'll have to tell my mother it's not her fault!" She smiled and cocked her head to one side, gazing at the boys over Stephan's shoulder. They were still playing cards at the table, and getting along rather well.

She nodded and made the decision to ask him about Ryan's remark. "Is my impetuous nature what made me blow things up?" she asked.

Stephan's eyebrows shot up in surprise. "Really? You remember that?"

She felt a lump in her throat and shook her head. Raising a hand to her throat, she took several breaths to compose herself, then said, "no. But I guess I asked the right question." She frowned. "Ryan said I tended to do that. I don't remember anything about that at all. I was hoping you could enlighten me."

Stephan shook his head. "I don't think so," he said. "Not my territory."

"You were there, though. Weren't you?" she asked.

He nodded, but said nothing, and Cara noticed the muscle clenching in his jaw.

"I have to remember this stuff on my own?"

He nodded again. "I think that would be best."

"Hm," she said, biting her lip. After a moment she said, "Maybe I'll ask Marlene."

Stephan leaned forward in his chair, making the sides squeak a little under his shifting weight. "I don't think that's a good idea, either," he said. "Marlene has some interesting theories..."

"I thought you didn't know each other," Cara said.

He froze, and his Adam's apple bobbed up and down in his throat. Finally, he sighed. "Like I told you, I've never met *Marlene*," he said.

"Ah," Cara whispered, nodding. "I see."

"Do you?"

She shrugged. "Doesn't matter, does it? Neither one of you will tell me what I want to know – even if I ask the right questions. You both want me to *remember*."

Stephan sat back in his seat and re-folded his hands in his lap, making a pyramid of his thumbs as he stared down at his hands.

Cara watched him and felt a shiver of recognition at the shape. Whereas she had been feeling light-headed and chilly all day, she suddenly felt warm and empowered. She closed her eyes, took a deep breath and held it, then exhaled slowly, a smile spreading across her face. When she opened her eyes, Stephen was staring at her.

"What?" she asked.

He shook his head. "You." He rested his head on his hand, his elbow propped on the armrest of the deck chair. "You look different, somehow."

"Really?" She frowned. "How do you mean?"

"You're... I don't know how to explain it. You're *you*, now," he told her.

She laughed. "I kind of feel a little different. Bigger, somehow."

"Don't let it go to your head," he told her. "Take it slow. Figure things out. Let it come to you. You don't need to get so empowered that you go passing out again!"

She made a face and cocked her head to one side. "You know what? I feel like I've been doing this for a long time."

"You have."

She shook her head. "I don't mean *before*. I mean, now. Like, in this life." She laughed and looked away. The chipmunk was perched on its hind legs, watching her, its tail twitching. "This is so weird."

"Not really," he said. "You'll get used to it."

"So, who am I? Or, who *was* I?" she asked him. She held her hands out in front of her and examined them, first the backs, then turning them over and looking at her palms, bending her fingers toward herself, one by one, examining herself as if with new eyes: The small scars that left white marks on her wrists and forearms were so faded, she hardly remembered how she had gotten them; the one errant freckle on her left hand that was larger than the rest; and the darker patch of skin on her right palm that looked almost as if she had been burned, her mother had told her was a birthmark...

He was quiet, watching her. She looked up at him and, seeing his expression, she laughed. "What's so funny?"

He shook his head. "You," he said. "I think this is the first time I've been awake before you." He smiled. "To tell you the truth, I'm kind of enjoying it."

"Great," she said, lowering her hands to her lap.

Out of the corner of her eye, she watched the chipmunk scamper off the porch rail, and she noticed Ryan and Dylan at the back door. Ryan pulled the door open and poked his head outside. "Are you okay, Mom?" he asked.

She nodded. "Fine, honey. Are you finished with your dinner?"

"And dessert," he said, grinning at her mischievously.

Cara raised an eyebrow. "Didn't you have enough junk with your father?"

He laughed out loud. "Me and Dylan split an apple!"

"Oh. Good!" she said. She looked around, then realized it was nearly dark. "What time is it, Ry?"

"Nine-*ish*," he said, smiling.

She raised an eyebrow and looked at the sky, noticing the inky blackness dotted with stars. She was sure it was on the later side of "nine-ish," and probably closer to ten, but she smiled at the boys. They were getting on so well, she didn't want to ruin the moment. "Okay. Well, you and Dylan can stay up for a little while longer. No TV, though, okay?" she said.

"Can we come out there with you and Stephan?" Dylan asked, poking out his lower lip for emphasis.

She paused and raised an eyebrow toward Stephan, who nodded.

"Sure. Just make sure you don't catch a chill," Cara said.

The boys bounded out, sending the chipmunk scurrying into his hole beneath the tree roots. The woodpecker, however, remained perched sideways on the heavy bark, ten feet above their heads, cocking his head to one side as if trying to gain a better view. Cara thought it odd that the bird was still alert so close to dark.

She hitched a thumb toward the bird and asked Stephan, "doesn't that thing have a nest to go to?"

He shrugged and laughed at her. "Who knows?"

"Cool!" Ryan said, pointing to the bird. "It has a red head!"

"That's a big bird!" Dylan said. "Is that the one that's been making all that noise by your room, Mom?"

She glanced over her shoulder and rolled her eyes. "I think so," she said. The bird shifted closer toward them, as if in response. Cara looked back at the boys. "He certainly got my attention."

Ryan smiled at his mother and shoved his hands in the front pocket of his sweatshirt. He nodded and said, "me, too."

"You heard him?" she asked.

Ryan's eyes grew wide. "Well, yeah! How could I not?"

Cara looked at Dylan. "What about you?"

He shook his head. "Nope. I guess my room is too far away," he said.

Ryan cocked his head to one side as he looked at Cara. It looked as if he was imitating the bird, but he looked so serious she grew concerned. "What's the matter, honey?" she asked.

He pursed his lips and frowned. "I don't know, exactly." He looked at Dylan, then back at his mother. "You look different, somehow." He looked back at Dylan. "Don't you think so, Dyl?"

Dylan squinted, turned his head one way, then the other, then shrugged and shook his head. "She looks like Mom to me," he said.

Cara looked at Stephen, who raised his eyebrows and held his hands up in response. "Not my call."

She took one last look at the bird over her shoulder, then clapped her hands and stood up from her seat. "Okay, boys, it's time for game night! What'll it be? Cards or board game?"

"Cards!" Dylan shouted. He drew the deck he and his brother had been using from the pocket of his sweatshirt and smiled.

Ryan smiled, looked at Cara and shrugged. "Fine by me," he said.

The four of them went into the house. Cara turned around and looked once more up at the tree, where the woodpecker seemed content to watch over them. Apparently, whatever she was supposed to be awakened to hadn't reached her awareness yet. Either that, she thought, or she had some very tasty insects that were living in the siding above her bedroom window!

Chapter 5

Brandon moved into Claudia's new house, which put the boys' father in their school district for the first time since he and Cara had separated. They were able to take the bus home to his house on his designated days, allowing Cara to handle some later appointments than she had before.

Even though her business was going well, she felt herself growing restless. She was good at number-crunching, but since her experience on the beach and the subsequent bouts of goose bumps, dizzy spells and feelings of empowerment, she felt she had a different calling. She just wasn't sure what it was.

"Mom? What's wrong?" Ryan asked her one afternoon when it was just the two of them. His notebook was open, along with several textbooks, and his space at the table was littered with worksheets and old tests that he was trying to sort through as he cleaned out his notebook.

Cara had a client's paperwork strewn across the dining room table and was trying to figure out which of the receipts in the plastic shoe box matched the scribbled and smudged lines on the worksheet on her laptop screen. Her eyes were watering and she felt as if a rock band had taken up residence inside her skull. She didn't even bother to lift her head from her hand when she turned to look at Ryan. "What did you say?" she croaked.

"Geez, Mom! Your eyes are all red and puffy! Have you been crying?" He scooted his chair back from the table, his eyes wide with concern as he hurried to stand beside his mother.

She forced a smile and straightened in her chair. Reaching to hug him, she said, "No. But I'd like to. This paperwork is driving me out of my mind!"

The boy glanced at the piles on the table and raised his eyebrows. Swallowing audibly, he wrinkled his nose and said, "I'm glad I'm not good at math. This doesn't look like fun."

Cara closed her eyes and rubbed them with the heels of her hands. When she looked back at Ryan, her mascara had smudged, and he laughed.

"What's so funny?"

"You look like a raccoon!" he told her, stifling a giggle.

Sighing, Cara forced herself up from the table and limped into the bathroom to wash her face. She had been sitting at the table for so long that her right foot had fallen asleep and was tingling. When she reached the bathroom, she lowered herself to the side of the tub and reached down to massage her foot, sighing in ecstasy as the blood rushed back into her toes.

Rising from the tub, she turned on the faucet and paused as she caught a glimpse of her reflection in the mirror. She grimaced at her pale reflection, then bent down and splashed water on her face, taking special care to rub the mascara smudges away. When she stood up, Ryan was beside her with his hands behind his back, a worried expression on his face.

Cara raised her eyebrows, then brought the towel to her face, muffling her voice as she said, "better?"

He was smiling when she removed the towel, and he nodded. "This is kind of cool, isn't it, Mom?"

With a quizzical look, she put a hand on his shoulder and ushered him out of the bathroom, turning off the light as they moved toward her bed and lay down on the piles of pillows. "What? You getting to watch me transform from raccoon back to mother?" she asked him, flexing her foot.

He shook his head. "No, silly!"

Cara slapped her hand against her forehead in mock realization.

"Oh! You must mean you and me, here at home!"

He nodded. "Yeah. Without Dylan." He shook his head and waved his hands. "Not that I don't like having him around. He's my brother. But it's kind of nice to just have you-and-me time."

She smiled and rubbed his arm. "Yup. It is," she said, and ruffled his hair with her hand. She sucked in her breath as she continued to rub her leg from the knee to the arch of her foot and back again, shivering against the tingling sensation of her foot waking up from its massage. She wiggled her toes and frowned, an idea or bit of knowledge floating around the outer recesses of her brain, but she couldn't catch it and she shook her head as she continued to move her fingers over her skin.

The woodpecker was shuffling around on the siding outside Cara's window – she saw the bright white feathers of its underbelly and the darker feathers of its tail scoot past the window out of the corner of her eye. She frowned. "Damn bird!" she said under her breath.

"Five cents, please," Ryan said.

"'Damn' isn't a cuss-word," she said.

"Does that mean I can say it and you won't get mad?" he asked, raising his eyebrows.

Cara sighed and Ryan grinned. He knew he had her there, and he held out his hand. She patted her pockets and gave him the evil eye. "Does it look like I have money anywhere around here?"

Ryan glanced around the room and shrugged. "I'll take an IOU," he told her.

Cara laughed and reach out to ruffle his hair again, but he ducked past her. "You may not like numbers, but you're a good hustler," she said. She stretched her arms over her head and yawned, then opened her eyes and looked back at him. "What do you want for dinner?"

Ryan put his finger on his chin and stared at the ceiling for a moment. Then he smiled and said, "breakfast?"

She nodded and rose from the bed, testing her foot on the floor as she stood. "Sounds good to me!" she said.

Feeling confident that her leg wouldn't give out beneath her, she nudged him out of her room and the two of them padded down the hallway to the kitchen. Ryan pulled two heavy cast-iron pans from the cabinet and laid them noisily on the stove while Cara rummaged in the refrigerator for eggs, bacon and butter. She peered over the door, just her eyes and nose visible to Ryan. "Toast or English muffins?"

He grinned. "English muffins!"

"You got it, buddy." She handed the package of store-brand cinnamon-raisin muffins to him and he pried the plastic clip from the bag and pulled out two. "Dark?" he asked.

Cara nodded, then cracked four eggs into a large bowl and began whisking them until the entire mixture was yellowish-orange. She held her hand over the first pan to make sure it was hot, then laid out four strips of bacon, which sizzled and sputtered almost instantly. She used the spatula to slice off a pat of butter and tossed it into the second pan, waiting until it had liquefied and was bubbling before pouring the egg mixture into the pan.

The toaster popped, and Ryan plucked the first two slices of English muffin from it and put them on one of the chipped plates. He closed his eyes and sniffed the air. "Mm. Heavenly!"

Cara laughed. Without his brother to overshadow him, Ryan blossomed. He was still sensitive and caring, but he also had a quick sense of humor that normally remained hidden behind his serious demeanor.

Cara plated the eggs and bacon, then drizzled honey on her English muffin. She carried the plate into the dining room and grimaced when she saw the stacks of papers covering the table. Turning to Ryan, she asked, "Can you be really careful?"

He nodded and followed her into the living room, where they sat on the couch and balanced their plates on their laps on the sofa by the large picture window.

A scratching sound made Cara jump, sending her plate – eggs, bacon and all – flying to the floor. She wheeled around, hand on her throat, in time to see the woodpecker's tail as he flew past the window to his usual perch in the large oak tree.

"Damn bird!" she spat, leaning down to clean up her mess.

She glanced up at Ryan, who was calmly nibbling on a piece of bacon, trying to suppress a smile.

Cara raised an eyebrow. "Didn't that scare you?"

He shook his head. "Nope."

"Did you see it?"

Ryan nodded.

"Thanks for telling me it was there."

He shrugged. "It doesn't bother me, Mom," he said. "In fact, I think I want to name him."

Cara sat back on her feet and said, "Oh, no. We're going to figure out some way to exorcise that bird. He's driving me..."

"Up a tree?" Ryan offered, giggling.

"Ha-ha," she said. "I'm going to have to call somebody, I guess."

"Didn't Stephan say he'd go away on his own, once you figured things out?"

She flung a piece of bacon onto the plate and considered her son's question. "Yes, he did. But I thought I had already done that."

Ryan shook his head and popped the last bite of bacon into his mouth. "Nope," he said. "It doesn't look like it."

"How'd you get so smart?"

He shrugged again and glanced up at her, mischief in his eye.

"What?" she asked.

"That's another five cents," he said.

She scowled at him carried her plate into the kitchen, returning a moment later with a damp towel to mop up the spilled honey from the carpet.

Ryan chewed his bacon slowly as he watched Cara, and his face grew serious. As she surveyed her work, Ryan swallowed and said, "Do you ever have dreams, Mom?"

She frowned. "Well, sure I do. Everybody has dreams." She hoisted herself from the floor and padded into the kitchen to rinse the towel in the sink. After some clattering of dishes and slamming of cabinets, she sunk onto the sofa with a bowl of cereal.

"But not everybody pays attention to them," Ryan said.

Confused, she looked at him. "What?"

"Their dreams," he said.

She thought about that for a moment and guided another spoonful of cereal into her mouth before answering. "You're saying that I have to pay attention to my dreams before the bird will go away?" she asked him.

"I don't know. But it makes sense, doesn't it?" he said. "That's what happened to me."

"You had a bird?" she asked.

He shook his head. "No. A spider."

"Hm," she said, lowering her spoon into the bowl and stirring it around until she had collected a healthy combination of flakes and raisins. "You have dreams, Ry?" she asked.

He nodded. "All the time."

"What do you dream about?"

He shrugged. "Lots of things. I told you about the one time, when my father came to talk to me."

Cara was quiet for a few minutes, absorbing what her son had said as she chewed another mouthful of her dinner. "I've been meaning to ask you about that," she said. "I didn't know what you meant before, but I think I'm beginning to understand now. You're talking about your *spirit* father, right?"

Ryan exhaled and smiled. "Yes." He sat up taller in his seat, the plate shifting precariously across his lap.

Cara watched until he straightened the plate and took a bite of English muffin. "Who is he? Do you know?" she asked, and lifted another spoonful of cereal to her mouth.

He nodded his head from side to side as he chewed. After he swallowed, he held his hand level and shifted it as he said, "Kind of. He is really big, and people respect him."

So much different from his *physical* father, she thought.

"He's *big* big?" she asked.

He shook his head, frustrated. "I don't know how..." Screwing up his face in thought, he grew quiet for a moment. When he spoke again, his voice was solemn. "There isn't *big* big, there. There's just *a lot*."

Cara sighed and twisted her mouth. "I don't understand, honey."

Ryan's shoulders slumped and he looked down at the floor. After a moment, he looked his mother in the eye. "You know how you are trying to wake up?"

"You mean, trying to remember?" she asked.

Ryan nodded.

"Yes."

"Well, he's big because he never went to sleep," Ryan said.

She took a moment to think about that as she leaned forward to put her cereal bowl on the coffee table. She glanced at the floor, frowned and bent down to pick a few tiny pieces of egg out of the carpet, which she deposited into the empty bowl. "I didn't think there was anyone like that," she said.

"Not someone who has skin and stuff, like us," he said again.

"You're saying that he isn't a person?"

"No. I mean, yes. He's a person, but he doesn't come back and start over, like we do. Not anymore, anyway," Ryan explained. "He stayed behind when we had to come back."

"Hm. Sounds like he's got it made while we're living *Groundhog Day*," she said. She stood up and carried her bowl and Ryan's plate into the kitchen. She peeked around the corner, then plucked a piece of bacon from her plate next to the sink, picked a piece of carpet lint from it and popped it into her mouth.

She returned to the living room carrying a roll of paper towels and a spray bottle of stain remover, and proceeded to blot the grease stains in the carpet. She sprayed the spot, then sat next to Ryan on the sofa, curling a leg underneath her. "Do you mean that, when your job is finished, you don't have to come back as a human anymore?"

"As anything," he said.

Cara's skin prickled. "Anything."

Ryan nodded. "We're not the only people, you know."

She looked out the window and wished she had curtains that covered the entire thing. She suddenly felt very exposed. "You mean that there's aliens and stuff?" she asked.

He made a face. "Mom! That's silly!"

Her eyes grew wide and she held her hands out. "Well, I don't know! If they don't live here, what else would you call them?"

"Not aliens," Ryan said. "That's what they do in the movies, just to scare people."

"So, there aren't aliens. But they aren't people. And they live on other planets?" She raised her eyebrows and looked at him, not sure what type of answer to expect from an eight-year-old boy.

Ryan made a face and thought for a moment. "Sort of," he said. "But not really." He sighed heavily. "I think we need to bring in the big guns for this discussion."

Cara laughed out loud. "The big guns, huh? And who might that be? Your father?"

"Don't be silly, Mom!" he said, shaking his head. "You can only talk to him if he visits you."

The smile faded quickly from her face and her skin erupted in goose flesh, down her arms, across the back of her neck, and across her breasts. She shivered. "Would he visit me?"

"I don't know," Ryan said, and picked up a book from the coffee table, frowning as he read the cover. "What's this?" he asked, holding it up in front of her.

She laughed when she read the title: "Animal Speak: The Spiritual Powers of Creatures Great and Small." On the cover was a picture of a man – obviously Native American – wearing a bald eagle on his head and carrying a deer antler.

Ryan looked up at her, still holding the book in front of her. "Well?"

She propped her elbow on the back of the sofa and turned to face him. "I was trying to figure out what I could do to get rid of the woodpecker," she said. "And I was curious to see if he was responsible for bringing the chipmunk around, and if maybe the chipmunk was planning to move into the attic, once the woodpecker had bored enough holes."

Ryan laughed and lowered the book to his lap. "Chipmunks don't live in attics, Mom. Squirrels do."

"Oh, great! You haven't seen any squirrels hanging around talking to the woodpecker, have you?"

He shook his head, still smiling. "No, Mom." He handed her the book. "I don't think the woodpecker is going to go away until you're ready."

"You keep telling me that. And Stephan has told me the same thing." She frowned. "And Marlene, too, for that matter." Cara sighed. "Can you call in the big guns for me? The people like your father?"

He shook his head. "Not my call," he said.

"Not your call, eh?" she repeated, amused by the adult tone of his comment. "What do I have to do to be ready? Do you know?"

"Sleep," he said. "Maybe the people who talk to me when I'm sleeping will talk to you, too."

"I have to be asleep to be awake? Hm," she said. "Do you think that could happen?"

Ryan nodded. "They talk about you. They try to talk to you, but you haven't been listening. I think they've been waiting for you to hear them."

"Well, maybe if their little woodpecker friend would let me sleep, it would be easier, don't you think?" she asked, glancing at the window to make sure the bird wasn't there.

Ryan took the book from her and put the book back on the table, then jumped off the sofa.

"Where are you going?" Cara asked.

"To brush my teeth," he told her. He stopped at the end of the hallway. "Since Dylan isn't here, could I sleep with you tonight?"

She shrugged. "I don't see why not."

He smiled and bounded down the hallway to the bathroom. She smiled and stood up, carrying the book under her arm. She checked the locks on the doors and turned off lights before padding down the hall into her own bathroom to wash off her make-up and brush her teeth. She unfolded her pajamas from the shelf next to the shower and hung them on the hook while she stepped out of her jeans and pulled her blouse over her head, then she slid into the soft flannel bed clothes and stretched a moment before turning off the light and crossing the room to her bed.

Ryan was already there; he had tossed the decorative pillows to the floor and had the large square pillow propped behind his head. He had brought a school book with him and it was perched open on his lap.

"That was fast," Cara said.

Ryan looked up at her. "I was mostly ready."

"Did you do a good job brushing your teeth?"

He nodded.

"Show me," she said, baring her own teeth at him.

He laughed. "You look funny. Like a chimpanzee."

"Thanks," she said flatly.

He opened his mouth and she examined his teeth. "Not bad," she said. He closed his mouth and licked his lips, then returned to his book.

"What are you reading?" she asked.

He held it up: "The Miraculous Story of Edward Tulane."

"Is it any good?" she asked him.

He shrugged. "Sort of. It's about a rabbit."

"A rabbit?" Cara rolled her eyes. "As long as he doesn't join the menagerie in the backyard, I guess that's okay."

Ryan laughed. "He's not a real rabbit. He's a glass rabbit. He has to learn a lesson the hard way." He stole a glance at his mother, turning away quickly when he realized she had seen him.

"What? Are you saying I have to learn my lesson the hard way?" she asked, feigning hurt feelings.

He smiled, tilted his head to one side, then returned to his reading.

"That wasn't an answer," she muttered, butting him lightly with her elbow until he giggled.

Cara smiled and leaned over to pick up her book from the night stand, feeling a little foolish for having chosen something like that, but she flipped it open to the section on woodpeckers and began reading anyway. "Hm," she said. She hadn't realized she said it aloud until she noticed Ryan staring at her.

"Did you find something interesting?" he asked.

She nodded. "Yup. Apparently, you're right about our little

visitor. He's not going anywhere anytime soon. I'm being stubborn, and I have to listen to him knocking until..." she frowned. "Umph!"

"What's the matter?" Ryan asked.

"It says I have to accept the truth that the woodpecker is trying to reveal," she said.

"So?"

She closed the book and looked at Ryan. "What if all that he's trying to reveal is that I bought a house with bad siding?"

He laughed again and shook his head. "Oh, Mom. You just don't get it, do you?"

She rumpled his hair with her hand before he could pull away, then she pulled him close to her and kissed the top of his head. He smelled like watermelon shampoo, and his hair was still a little damp. "I love you, Ry," she said. "And I do get it. But I'm a lot older than you, and I have to, I don't know, *open* my mind up to being able to believe these things, you know? I've spent a lot of years listening to people tell me that religion is this or that, and that I can't believe in certain things, or that I have to believe in other things. It's really hard, Ryan."

He smiled. "I know. But you already know what you need to know. You have to stop putting it behind the door."

"Behind the door?" she asked.

He nodded. "Yup," he said. Then he put his book on the night stand and stretched his hands over his head, his mouth opening in a huge yawn.

"Tired?" she asked.

He nodded again. "Yes," he said, and tossed the square pillow to the floor with the others. "Good night, Mom."

"Good night, sweetie," she said, and watched as he lay on his side, pulled his knees toward his chest and closed his eyes. In his fetal position, she hardly noticed the additional body in her bed.

She laid a hand on his head and stroked his hair absently while continuing to flip through pages in her book. Out of curiosity, she looked up "rabbit," and was surprised to find that it was associated with teaching and guidance, but also about being open to intuition.

"Listen," Cara whispered, nodding to herself. She glanced at her son and smiled. He was trying to teach her; she had to get past his being her eight-year-old son and realize that he knew things that she needed to learn.

Maybe Ryan was the rabbit, she thought, then nodded as the idea took root in her conscious mind. Interesting, and totally possible.

She turned to the passage about chipmunks and rolled her eyes as she began reading the text. "Oh, yeah. This is me," she said, laughing out loud. She glanced at Ryan, but he was sound asleep, snoring softly. "'The chipmunk does things on his own time, and doesn't like to be told what to do.' Geez, Louise, if that's not my M.O.," she said, and chuckled to herself. "Great. Now I'm identifying with a rodent."

Cara sighed and closed the book and placed it on her night stand, then reached over and turned out the light. She took a couple of deep, cleansing breaths, then lay still and quiet, absorbing the darkness and stillness of her bedroom, and listening to the rhythmic breathing of her child sleeping beside her. She felt herself tense as something made a noise against the side of the house, but she realized it was too big – and too close to the ground – to be the woodpecker, and she tried to force herself to relax.

Remembering the breathing exercises she learned in the single yoga class that Marlene had managed to wrangle her to, Cara placed her hand on her abdomen and focused on expanding her center with each breath. She closed her eyes and imagined the world that Ryan had told her about, where voices from the spirit realm spoke with such authority that it was impossible to tune them out.

She found herself taking long, deep breaths through her nose, holding it for a count of five, then exhaling forcefully, also through her nose. "That can't be right," she said. "I think the yoga instructor said I'm supposed to breathe out through my mouth." She tried that a few times, but it was uncomfortable, unnatural, so she went back to exhaling through her nose.

It didn't take long for the rhythmic breathing to relax her body, allowing her to fall into the edge of sleep. She was still aware of the night noises outside her window, the ticking of the clock on her night stand, and the high-pitched chirp emitted by the alarm system every few minutes. She must remember to replace that battery...

She shook her head to clear her thoughts and forced herself to concentrate on relaxing, beginning with her toes, and moving up her body each time she exhaled. By the time she got to her shoulders, her limbs felt heavy and she was warm and comfortable. "Talk to me," she thought, and smiled as she sensed a warm glow radiating in what would be her peripheral vision, if she had her eyes open.

Cara felt her eyes moving behind their lids, trying to figure out the source of the light, but the glow remained just beyond her line of sight, as if her eyes were the globe and the glow was just below the horizon. Oddly, she did not feel compelled to chase it. Her limbs felt heavy, not her own, although she felt as if she was light enough to be carried away on the first breeze.

She concentrated on the rhythmic rising and falling of her chest, the comfortable filling of her lungs, which was also odd, since she had not used her inhaler before climbing into bed.

Clouds formed above her, swirling like a tornado, but curiously calming. She watched the rotation and realized that it wasn't clouds at all, but a tunnel of sorts whose walls were closing in on her. She remained motionless and relaxed and allowed the rotation to squeeze her, which she felt as a physical sensation, almost like the pulsing of a massage chair, or the throbbing of her leg when she had massaged it earlier. The walls of the tube moved her gently upward, where the glow became more and more pronounced.

When she reached the top – or what she thought must be the top – the glow was no longer white, but golden, like the corona surrounding the sun but not painful to look at. She felt warmth radiating from the inside that seemed to reach out toward the glow, and she felt herself smile.

Beyond the horizon, as she emerged from the tunnel, she found that the glow was not emanating from any one thing, but was a part of her entire surroundings. The entire landscape – not land, exactly, but that was what she would compare it to – was the color of amber, if someone were to shine a light through it.

Someone was walking toward her, although it was more of a presence than a physical body. She felt confused, as if she had *seen* someone, but the image was now gone, replaced by the physical *feeling* of someone beside her.

She heard – or felt – laughter, which she thought she recognized as Ryan, and she wanted to move her arm to see if he was laughing beside her in the bed. She found that she could not actually control the limbs of her physical body, but the realization did not make her panic as she thought it might; rather, she thought, "Oh. Of course. This is how it is supposed to be."

The youthful presence answered her. "You found it! I knew you would." His voice was jubilant, but somehow older at the same time.

"You were right," she told him. "I just needed to relax and let myself be led."

She felt the energy gently laugh once more. "You weren't led. You knew how to get here all along. Actually, you come here all the time, but this time you made yourself remember."

"Oh. Of course," she said, and she felt the glow of herself smiling once more.

"What is this place?" she asked him.

The glow of her surroundings seemed to burn brighter for a moment as the other being moved aside, allowing her to take it all in. "It's here," he said, and she felt – rather than saw – his energy arms spread wide to encompass the entire space.

Although he hadn't entirely answered her question, she felt that she understood, and she stood basking in the amber glow of her surroundings.

"Is there anyone else here with us?" she asked him.

"Of course. Everyone is here," he said. "Some of them are awake, but most of them are not. This is where you go when your body needs to rest."

"Hm," she said, taking a moment to absorb what he said. "Can I see them – everyone else, I mean?"

The presence laughed again. "Can you see me?" he asked.

Cara felt herself looking for the source of the energies she felt before she answered him. "Ha-ha," she said, a little nervously. "No, of course not. I can't see anything except... this." She felt her energy spread wide and she turned around to try to measure the size of her surroundings, but the amber glow seemed to stretch out indefinitely. She returned her attention to Ryan's space - what she thought of as Ryan. "Do they know that I am here?" she asked.

"They have been waiting for you," he told her.

"Ahriel," someone said. The voice was familiar – although it wasn't something she *heard*, exactly. Rather, it resonated with her, and she swelled with pleasure as she recognized the name as her own. She felt entirely comfortable, not at all afraid, as if she had opened a door in her own home to a favorite room that had been forgotten and unused. She felt herself take in a deep breath and exhale, although it was not in the physical sense – the familiar feeling of breathing simply caused her to expand from the core of her awareness.

"I am so glad you decided to join us, finally," someone else said. She recognized the presence as as familiar, a friend, and she felt overcome with a warm glow of joy.

"I'm not dead, am I?" she asked, although she realized she would not have been upset if they told her yes.

"No. You are walking," the voice said. "Some call it *traveling.* Some call it *projection.*" The masculine presence projected humor. "Call it whatever you want. It's just *here.*"

She felt a spark inside herself, where her heart would be if she was inhabiting her body. She glowed again and felt laughter bubble up inside her.

"What do you remember?" he asked her.

"You are Liris, but you remind me of someone I know," she told him, unsure from what part of her that knowledge arose. It just felt right, like the name fit him somehow.

His energy increased, and Cara – Ahriel – recognized it as pleasure at her response. "You do know me. I knew you would remember," he said.

"Keke is here as well," Ahriel said, feeling her own presence expand as she searched for the other energy she recognized.

She felt Keke's presence laugh. "She was more than ready to be aware of her walking," Keke said.

"C'teus brought me here," Ahriel said, proud that she was able to recall the name of the youthful presence. Not Ryan – *C'teus.* With the realization came the feeling of butterflies in the region where her abdomen would be in her physical body. Panic gripped her. Thoughts - memories - were racing too fast, and she felt the tunnel opening beneath her to deliver her energy back to the sleeping body in the bed at home.

She was aware that C'teus moved closer to her, which calmed her. "She must go," he told the others. "Now that she knows the way, she will be able to walk again. But for now, she must rest."

The glow of her other two companions faded just a bit and she felt herself stirring in her sleep. Cara – the physical manifestation of the energy Ahriel - opened her eyes and lay still as they adjusted to the darkness of the room. Ryan still lay motionless beside her.

She turned back the blanket and padded to the bathroom, filling a glass of water from the tap. She felt thirsty, and she drained the entire glass while leaning on one hand against the marble counter top of the sink.

Flipping the switch on the wall inside the tiny commode room, she squinted as her eyes adjusted to the light, then relieved herself, resting her face in her hands. When she rose, she washed her hands and took a moment to examine her face in the mirror. With the light shining from behind her, she thought she looked like her mother, and she leaned closer to try to find evidence of the vibrant being she was just moments before. She thought she detected a faint glow around her head, neck and shoulders through her peripheral vision, but it disappeared when she attempted to look at it directly.

Was she losing her mind? she wondered, trying to remember if "seeing halos" was one of the symptoms of a migraine, although her subconscious reminded her that her head did not hurt.

Fighting a rising sense of panic, she paused to look at her own eyes, which sparkled with a similar amber glow as that which had effused her surroundings at the top of the tunnel. She realized then that it had not been a dream, and she wasn't going crazy. She had *walked.*

Elated, she turned off the light and returned to her bed.

"Good night, Mom," Ryan mumbled.

"I thought you were asleep," she said as she leaned over, patted him and kissed him lightly on the top of his head.

Ryan turned his head toward her. "Mm-mm," he said. "Happy." He yawned and turned his head back and was instantly snoring softly.

She turned away from him to lie on her side and forced her eyes shut. Her physical body was exhausted, but her mind was racing, and she felt disoriented.

For the rest of the night, Cara tried to go back to the place she had been – to walk or simply to experience what she had earlier, but she could not. Sleep eluded her as well, as she knew she had not been asleep when she had walked; rather, she had been in some sort of meditative state. In her excitement over the experience, she was unable to attain it again.

After several hours of watching the clock and listening to night sounds – including what sounded like the blasted woodpecker scratching outside her bedroom window – she curled up facing Ryan, pulled the blankets to her chin and dozed fitfully until the first light of dawn began to filter through the window.

She turned onto to her back and closed her eyes, feeling the morning sun on her cheek and basking in the glow of soft golden light that permeated her eyelids, making her feel as if she were back in the amber place.

As Ryan began to stir, she forced herself to remain still, not wanting to awaken him while it was still so early.

Finally, when she could not lie still any longer, she slowly folded back the covers and slipped from the bed to the floor, padding once more to the bathroom. She relieved herself, brushed her hair into a ponytail and tiptoed from the bedroom and down the hall to the kitchen.

Despite her relatively sleepless night, she felt exhilarated and eager to begin her day. She measured four heaping scoops of coffee beans into the machine, poured in the appropriate amount of water and turned the machine on, cringing at the loud whirring sound it made as it spun the beans around and ground them into powder. She didn't realize she had been holding her breath until the gurgling sound of water dripping through the filter began, and she peeked down the hall to see if the noise had disturbed her son's sleep.

When the timer beeped and Ryan had not emerged from her bedroom, she sighed and poured herself a large, steaming mug. She carried it to the living room and opened the blinds that covered the back door, letting the sun bathe the room in soft morning light.

With both hands wrapped around the mug, she took a sip, then looked around the room. She gasped as she realized the morning sun made her living room the same amber color as *there*, and she put her coffee mug on the top of the television so she could pull one of the small armchairs in front of the door.

Shivering, she reached for the "crazy quilt" - an afghan her mother had knitted when she was learning the craft, when Cara was about nine or ten years old. She dragged it to the chair, retrieved her mug of coffee and sat down, pulling her feet up under her until she was a ball curled up under the quilt.

The chipmunk peeked out from under the tree root, its tail twitching as it surveyed the morning. Satisfied that no carnivorous beast was going to swoop or pounce down upon it, the creature emerged fully from its hole and scampered tentatively across the yard – five feet, stop and sniff, five feet, stop and sniff – until it reached the porch. It hopped up on the rail and inched inquisitively toward the pile of seeds that Cara had laid out for it the night before, then it sat up on its haunches and began stuffing the cache into its cheeks, pausing between each piece and twitching its nose in Cara's direction.

There were a only a few crumbs of seeds remaining on the rail when the chipmunk suddenly sat up and stiffened, then sniffed the air nervously before hopping down from the rail and making a mad dash for its hiding spot under the tree.

Cara moved closer to the window and peered around, wondering if perhaps the neighbor's cat had come into the yard. She would have to talk to Mrs. Woodward about that; she didn't want anything to eat her new little friend, and she particularly wanted him to stay comfortable under the tree root. If he felt threatened on the ground, he might look to the safety of a high-rise and decide that her attic would be a comfortable home after all, despite Ryan's certainty that chipmunks did not make their homes high above ground.

Seeing nothing out of the ordinary, she sat back in her chair, adjusted the crazy quilt and closed her eyes as she inhaled the mug's contents then took a long sip of her coffee.

She felt Ryan's presence before she heard or saw him – *C'teus*, she thought. Turning toward the hallway, she saw him standing in his pajamas, his hair sticking out in all directions, squinting in the sunlight and wearing a sleepy smile.

"How'd you sleep, buddy?" she asked.

"Great," he said, his voice still rusty, and his face contorted. He sported a crease from the pillow on his right cheek.

"Do you want breakfast? I can make some oatmeal," she said.

He rubbed his eyes with the back of his hand and nodded. "That would be great," he said. "Can I eat it in here with you?"

She looked around and shrugged. "As long as you promise not to spill – and not to tell your brother!"

He grinned, still squinting, and nodded. "Deal," said the little man of few words.

Cara tossed the crazy quilt over the back of her chair and rose carefully, carrying her coffee mug with her to the kitchen to fix breakfast for her son.

"Are you going to have some?" he asked.

She shrugged. "May as well," she said, and measured out three cups of water instead of two. "Would you grab the box of oats from the pantry?"

Ryan yawned, stretched and turned toward the pantry to retrieve the box of cereal. He handed it to his mother and asked, "can we put berries in it?"

Cara nodded. "Sure."

"And maple syrup?"

She raised an eyebrow and looked at him as she dumped the first cup of dry oats into the pot. "Uh-huh."

Ryan grinned. "How about chocolate chips?"

She laughed. "Good try, buddy. Not today." She re-sealed the round box of oats and handed it to her son to return to the pantry shelf. "There's orange juice in the fridge," she told him.

He nodded and opened the door to retrieve the carton of juice. "Ooh. It's heavy!" he said.

"Yup. It's new," she told him.

She stirred the oats with a wooden spoon, then opened the spice cabinet to the right of the stove. Moving a couple of bottles around, she said, "Ooh, Ry. How about we have cinnamon in it instead?"

"Yeah!"

He went back to the pantry and rummaged through the plastic bin on the bottom shelf, returning with the bag of dried cranberries, which he handed to his mother. She dumped several into the pot of bubbling goo, then looked into the bag and dumped the rest of the berries in, much to Ryan's delight.

She poured herself another cup of coffee, then filled two bowls with the oatmeal, the smell of cinnamon wafting under her nose and making her senses tingle with pleasure. "One of the good things about a chilly morning, eh, Ry?" she said, raising her bowl to him with one hand and placing a second bowl in front of him.

Ryan nodded and stabbed his spoon into the bowl to shovel a large helping into his mouth, then opened his mouth and waved his hands frantically in front of his face. "Hot!" he garbled as his eyes began to water.

"It did just come off the stove," she reminded him, smiling.

He shrugged and began to blow on the contents of his bowl as he followed Cara into the living room.

She dragged a second chair in front of the glass-paneled door and Ryan scooted down the hall to his bedroom to retrieve the goose-down throw from the end of his bed. He snuggled up under it and reached up as Cara handed him his bowl, and he resumed blowing on his cereal.

Cara chuckled and set her coffee and oatmeal on the floor beside her chair as she snuggled into the chair underneath the crazy quilt.

The two of them sat quietly, eating their breakfast and watching the sunrise, and Cara was amazed by the feeling of peace, to which she was unaccustomed of late. She also felt a presence nearby, similar to the one she had felt when she was walking the night before. *C'teus*, she thought again.

Ryan finished his cereal and reached over the back of the chair to put his bowl on the television shelf, then he licked his lips and snuggled deeper under his down blanket. He watched Cara until she had finished her cereal and rested her bowl on the floor beside her chair, then he shivered and made a tiny noise that caught her attention.

"Are you cold?" she asked.

He shivered and nodded.

"Well, the oatmeal will warm you," she said. Inclining her head toward him, she added, "that blanket will, too. It's the warmest one in the house."

"You did it, Mom," he said suddenly.

Cara smiled and scrunched her shoulders up toward her ears. She took a tiny sip of her coffee, froze for a moment, then nodded. "Yeah. I did." She felt a shiver of excitement mingled with self-conscious embarrassment, speaking about it with her son.

"They're glad, you know," Ryan said, staring out the window at the sunrise.

"Who?" she asked.

He didn't have time to answer her before the phone rang, and Cara glanced at the clock and frowned. Eight-forty-five. *This can't be good*, she thought.

She picked up the handset and smiled when she looked at the Caller ID. "It's Stephan," she said to Ryan, then pushed the "TALK" button. "What are you doing up so early?"

"Good morning to you, too, sunshine!" he said. "Didn't you sleep well?" There was a teasing tone in his voice, which confused her. Stephan was definitely not a "morning person."

"Well, no, if you want to know the truth. I slept like crap!" she told him.

"Mom!" Ryan scolded, twisting around in his seat to frown at her over the back of his chair.

"Sorry," she mouthed to him, and smiled as he held out his hand, palm-side up. "*Crap* is not a cuss word," she said.

"Excuse me?" Stephan asked.

"Oh. Not you!" she said, and laughed. "Ryan is trying to break me of a terrible habit."

"Good for him!" Stephan said. "Everyone needs a useless hobby. Mine is golf."

"Ha-ha."

"Well, that and smudging," he said. "So, do you want to get together?" he asked, before she had time to process his comment.

"What? Now?" She glanced down at her flannel pajamas and touched her free hand to her pony-tailed head.

"Not this very minute. But not too late. I was thinking coffee," Stephan said. "Do you have the little men all day?"

"Yes," she said. "No. I mean, it's just me and Ryan."

"That's great! Bring him," Stephan said. "We can get him a hot chocolate or something."

"He'd like that," she replied. "But I'm not even dressed yet."

"Let me guess. You've been watching the sunrise," Stephan said.

"Is that a crime?" she asked, feeling a bit defensive.

"Hardly," he said. "It's just so unlike you to just sit peacefully and relax, particularly when you've been working as much as you have lately."

"Hazard of a Type A personality," she said.

"Slow down and things won't be so difficult," he told her.

"What do you mean, 'Slow Down'?" she asked. "I have hobbies. I'm not always going ninety-to-nothing."

"Only most of the time," he scolded. "Okay, then. Finish watching the sunrise, then get dressed and meet me at the coffee shop. It's almost nine now – want to meet me at ten?"

"Says the man who tells me I don't take enough time to relax," she said, laughing.

"This is different," he told her. "I think we should talk."

"About..."

She could almost hear his grin through the telephone. "I think you know," he said, the teasing tone creeping back into his voice.

"Maybe you could let me in on what it is you think I know?"

"Good try," he told her. "Go get dressed. I'll meet you there in an hour."

"Okay," she said, and clicked the phone off and returned it to the base. "Want to go get some hot chocolate, Ry?" she asked as she reached to pick up the crazy quilt, which she folded and draped over the arm of her chair.

He nodded enthusiastically and leaped from his seat, carrying the two empty oatmeal bowls to the sink and filling them with water and a squirt of dish soap. Then he raced down the hallway and closed the door to his bedroom. Cara laughed when she heard the drawers of his dresser sliding open and slamming shut as Ryan hurried to get dressed. She wrapped both hands around her coffee mug, absorbing its heat, then went into her own bedroom to get ready to meet Stephan.

Of the two of her boys, Ryan liked Stephan the best, perhaps because his own father was so dismissive of him. Dylan was the more athletic of the two, the more like his father, and found Stephan to be too conversational for his taste. Generally, when Stephan was visiting, Dylan would slink off to his room to listen to his i-pod or play his hand-held video games. Ryan would linger at the table and eavesdrop until his mother tired of watching her language and told him to find something to do.

Occasionally, Stephan would bring his acoustic guitar to the house. Ryan would jump up and down with excitement and hold the front door open when he saw Stephan lift the black guitar case out of the back seat of his Prius. He would sit and listen for as long as Stephan would play, and was on top of the world when the man took a few minutes to teach him some chords. It was not an interest that Dylan shared, and the older twin would slink off to his bedroom, earbuds streaming music from his iPod in his attempt to ignore his mother's lifelong friend and the attention he paid to his shy, nonathletic brother.

Because Dylan was not with them and they were meeting Stephan at a coffee shop, Ryan was on top of the world and hummed happily in the car during the entire ride.

Cara glanced at him in the rear-view mirror. "You're excited about going to see Stephan?" she asked.

He nodded, continuing to hum and tap his hands on his knees.

"You like Stephan, don't you?"

"Yup. He's pretty cool," Ryan replied without turning his gaze from the window.

"There's nothing between us. We're just friends, you know," Cara said, wondering why she felt the need to explain herself to her son.

Ryan shrugged. "I'm good with that."

Cara nodded and turned her attention back to the road. At the stop light, she asked, "What is it that you like so much about him?"

Ryan frowned and poked out his lip in thought, temporarily distracted from his humming and tapping. He looked up at the mirror and said, "well, he pays attention to me, and he teaches me music."

Cara smiled and he added, "and he's like us." Then he nodded and said, "are you going to go?"

Her pulse quickened with her son's offhand comment, and she turned her eyes back to the front of the car and noticed the green light. She did a quick check to the left and right to ensure that the intersection was clear, then stepped on the gas. Moments later, her heartbeat back under control, she pulled the car into a parking space behind Jitter Beans Coffee Shop and turned off the engine, laughing as Ryan unfastened his seat belt and practically flew out of the car.

Stephan was already there and had commandeered a table for the three of them. His coffee mug sat steaming on the table next to a white plate with a half-eaten cranberry-orange scone. He smiled when he saw them. "Hey, buddy! I was so glad when your mom said you were coming with her," Stephan said. He didn't speak in the little-kid voice that Brandon used when he addressed Ryan, which Cara added to her tally of reasons Ryan preferred spending time with Stephan.

"Yup. It was just me and Mom last night. Dylan stayed at Dad and Claudia's." His face brightened and he leaned in close to Stephan and whispered, "I got to sleep in Mom's bed last night."

"You did?" Stephan asked.

Ryan nodded, covering his mouth with one hand.

Stephan leaned over close to the boy and whispered, "Why is it a secret?"

Ryan shrugged and said, "I think it helped her." He glanced at his mother out of the corner of his eye, but quickly turned away to avoid making eye contact.

"Oh?" Stephan asked and looked up at Cara with his eyebrows raised. "Was it this young man who chilled you out enough? Or was he the tour guide on your path to enlightenment?" He was smiling, like the cat who had swallowed the canary.

Cara was startled and felt the blood drain from her face. "What? I didn't tell you anything," she said, holding a hand to her throat. "How did you know?"

"I was there. Don't you remember? We had a conversation as clear as you and I are having right now," Stephan said, still smiling.

She stared at him for a moment and shivered as the hairs raised along her forearms.

"Forgive me," he said. "I haven't even given you two a chance to sit down or get a cup of coffee!" Stephan pulled out a chair for Cara and patted the bench seat next to him for Ryan to sit. "Do you want some hot chocolate or something, Ry?"

Ryan nodded. "That sounds awesome!"

"How about breakfast? Did you guys eat?" Stephan asked.

Ryan looked at Cara as he replied, "Mom made some really delicious oatmeal with cinnamon *and cranberries!*"

"She did? That sounds awesome. I'm sorry I missed that," Stephan said, glancing at Cara, who was still staring at him a little nervously. "Well, do you want something else?" Stephan asked the boy. "I mean, it is after ten. And eight-year-old boys are known to be bottomless pits."

Ryan laughed. "Okay!" he said. "What do they have today?"

"Come with me and pick something out," he said. He glanced at Cara. "What about you? Would you care for something to eat?"

Cara held up a hand. "I'm good, but I will take a cup of hot tea, if you don't mind." She rummaged in her purse for her wallet, but Stephan laid a hand on her arm. "No, no. I've got this one. Consider it a celebration of sorts."

"Really? What for?"

Stephan smiled. "Let's just call it your birthday," he said.

She put her purse back down beside her chair and sat back in the cushy seat, laying her head against the top and closing her eyes in a brief moment of serenity.

Ryan accompanied Stephan to the counter and came back carrying a large, steaming paper cup of hot chocolate with a cardboard wrapper around the middle to keep him from burning his hands. He placed the cup on the yellow wood coffee table and bounced happily onto the leather sofa in front of the purple-blue wall that was covered end-to-end by black-and-white photographs and art by local talent.

Cara heard Ryan land on the sofa but said nothing in the way of a reprimand. He was so rarely this exuberant that Cara wanted to let the moment stretch out a little longer. Perhaps she would have to give some thought to splitting the boys up once in awhile. She felt herself nod, and made a mental note to talk to Brandon about that.

Stephan returned to their seats carrying Cara's tea in a cup similarly adorned in the brown cardboard wrapper, but sporting the string and yellow-and-black tag of a Twinings Earl Gray tea bag. She accepted the cup and held it to her nose, inhaling the heady scent of Earl Gray through the plastic lid.

"Did you want sugar or anything?" Stephan asked.

If they had been at the other shop, she'd have asked Karen for some honey. She shook her head. "Nope. Straight is good." She smiled and wrapped both hands around the cup, taking one more deep whiff before setting it down on the table in front of her to steep. "Thanks for this, by the way."

Stephan nodded to her as he sat down and placed a white plate with a steaming blueberry muffin on it in front of Ryan. "Wait a minute on that, buddy. You don't want to burn yourself. They just popped it into the microwave for a minute, but it will blister your fingers – not to mention your tongue – if you eat it just yet."

Ryan nodded and leaned forward, sniffing the steam as it rose from the muffin.

Stephan looked between the two of them and laughed. "What the hell have the two of you been doing this morning?" he asked. "You're like a couple of scent-starved animals!"

Cara smiled and shrugged. "We've just enjoyed a very calm, quiet morning," she told him. "We moved a couple of chairs in front of the porch window and ate our breakfast there while we watched the sunrise."

"The chipmunk was back, too," Ryan said. "Mom left some food out for him last night and he came up to the porch and had breakfast with us. He must have been really hungry, too, because there was hardly anything left, and the pile of seeds was pretty big."

Stephan raised an eyebrow. "Really?" he said to Cara. "You, who wants the little woodland creatures gone from her life, left food out for the rodent?"

"What can I say," she told him. "I had some stuff in the pantry and I thought the little guy looked skinny, especially going into winter."

"You want me to believe you keep seeds in your pantry?" Stephan said, laughing. "Come on, Cinderella, admit it. You bought that stuff specifically for the chipmunk!"

Cara felt herself blush as she shrugged and took a sip of her tea.

"Well, I'll be..." Stephan said. He smiled, picked up his ceramic mug of coffee, which he had refilled at the counter, and sat back in his chair to take a long, slow sip. When he set the coffee on his thigh, he looked at it for a moment as though gathering his thoughts, then he looked up at Cara with a quizzical smile. He cleared his throat and said, "So... do you feel ready to share?"

She cocked an eyebrow at him and grinned back. "What *ever* do you mean?"

Stephan looked at Ryan. "She knows that I know, right?"

Ryan shrugged and took another sip of his cocoa. Somehow, even with the plastic sip-cap, he had managed to smear a thin line of chocolate across his upper lip, giving him what looked to be a pencil mustache.

Cara leaned forward and handed him a napkin. "He knows what, Ry?" she asked.

Ryan shrugged and took the napkin from her, wiping his face, then licking his lips again and creating another line.

"Well?" she asked, looking from Stephan to Ryan and back again. She cocked her head to one side and stared at her friend.

Stephan sighed and shook his head. "Okay, then, I'll start," he said. "I thought you understood when I told you I was there. You walked last night. What did you think?"

"Wow. To the point, aren't you?" she asked.

"Someone has to be."

"And you tell me *I'm* rushing!" she said.

"This isn't rushing. Consider it a *de-briefing* of sorts," he said.

She lowered her chin. "A de-briefing."

He nodded.

"Okay. So... what did *you* see?" she asked.

Stephan nodded. "Very good." He moved his cup to the table and folded his hands in his lap in a decent imitation of a therapist. "Well, you know who you are now... your name, at least. That's a start."

"And what might that be?" she asked.

Ryan was picking blueberries out of the muffin and popping them into his mouth. Without looking up, he said, "Ahriel."

Her eyes flew open and she stared at her son. "So it was real!" she whispered.

"Of course it was," Stephan said. "What did you think? You don't dream stuff like that – not that vivid."

"I've always thought dreams were the journey, like, in a restorative way," she said. "That's what all the psychological studies say, anyway."

Stephan nodded. "Sure. True dreams do have a purpose. But you weren't dreaming. You were *walking*," Stephan said. "There's a difference."

Cara frowned, processing what he said before she would reply. She took a deep breath and, concentrating on a spot just to his left, she said, "so, you're saying that the little glow-place where I was last night is something I visited on a *walk*. But it wasn't a dream. It was... what *was* it, exactly?"

Stephan looked at Ryan, who was smiling without looking up from the muffin. Neither of them said anything, allowing Cara to cycle through her thoughts at her own pace.

And cycle she did – she sat back, fingers twitching in her lap as she frowned, glanced up at Stephan, opened her mouth to ask a question, then changed her mind. Stephan and Ryan sat back in their seats, amused.

Finally, Cara leaned forward and whispered to Stephan, "Was it some sort of out-of-body experience? I've read about those..."

"Yes – and no," Stephan said, unsuccessfully fighting to control a grin. "You were still very much in your body last night, which is one of the reasons you came back so quickly."

Cara sat back, feeling deflated. "There's more to it, then?" she asked.

"Oh, yeah," Stephan told her. "Lots more. Right, Ryan?"

Ryan nodded and peeked at his mother without raising his head. His smile widened and he picked off a huge chunk of the muffin and stuffed it into his mouth.

She slumped in her chair, staring at her son for a few minutes, her mind racing. "Is that where you met your father?" Cara asked, her cracking voice evidence of her struggle to accept that it was anything but a fantasy concocted by Stephan and Ryan.

He shook his head, still chewing. When he swallowed, he said, "it was kind of the same, but it looked different. My father is from the green place."

"The green place?" she asked. "I don't understand. What I saw was a glow, kind of like looking at everything through amber."

Stephan nodded. "That's healing," he said, "or protection, or both." He paused for a moment and stared over her shoulder as if he were listening to someone, then added, "I'm thinking that, since it was your first time, it was probably protection."

"What? Something could hurt me there?" Cara asked. Skeptical or not, she didn't want to do anything that might hurt her in some way.

He laughed a little nervously. "No. Of course not. Well, unless you face a truth about yourself that you're not quite ready for."

"And that could hurt me?" she asked.

"Not physically, no," he said, without looking her in the eye. "But there are a lot of things you just aren't ready for yet. You need to relax and enjoy it, and take it slow. We have forever. We're not going anywhere."

She frowned. "But you were so impatient for me to get there," she said.

Stephan shook his head. "Not really. You've been aware of your ability to do this for a long time, but it was subconscious. It's part of the reason you were so conflicted - you had a hard time letting go of the guilt that everyone piled on you about it."

"Guilt?" she asked. "I don't understand. I didn't do anything wrong, so what do I have to feel guilty about?"

Stephan shrugged. "You don't. You're just following your instincts – or your energy is. But you know there are those so-called 'mainstream people' who are so caught up in their own lives that they think everyone who believes differently is going to hell," Stephan said. "It's the reason we can drink beer at a bar we have to drive to on Sunday, but we can't buy a six-pack and drink it in the safety and comfort of our own home. Those same people who want to uphold 'religious freedoms' only do so for certain ways of thinking. Heaven forbid you want to embrace the truth, you'll be pursued by an angry mob."

She nodded. "There sure are a lot of those."

"You're surrounded by that, so you fought what you knew was there because of, I don't know, fear, maybe? Denial? Probably a little of both," Stephan said.

"So, you're telling me that the crazy notion I've had for a long time is real?"

"Yeah. Probably," he said, smiling as Ryan chuckled beside him. Stephan picked up his coffee mug and took another sip. "Do you want to tell me about it?"

She laughed. "You sound like a shrink!"

He shrugged. "Maybe I am," he said. "A spiritual shrink. Hm. That sounds pretty cool. Maybe I'll hang out a shingle."

"Yeah, hey, good luck with that," Cara said.

"Stranger things have happened," he said.

She laughed again. "I can see it now: 'Brother Stephan – Spirit Shrink,' on a hand-painted sign with a hand with one of those eyes staring out from the middle of it."

"Not all of them are off-base," he said. "Some of those people are dead-on. But the quacks who bastardize the practice give everyone else a bad name."

"One bad apple?" she asked.

"Exactly," he said. "Just like those goof-balls that the national news people always find to interview after a tornado. They're always the toothless whack-jobs who speak with an exaggerated accent and whose aluminum trailer is now in the bottom of a duck pond. Unfortunately, those are the rest of the world's idea of people in Georgia and Alabama, when we're just like people in New York or Washington State."

"Do they have toothless whack-jobs in those places, do you think?" she asked.

He nodded. "Absolutely," he said. "Have you ever been to Upstate New York?"

She shook her head. "Nope. Well, I've passed through. I grew up in New England, though. We had plenty of people in little bungalows who reminded me of the witch in 'Hansel and Gretel'."

"Well, there are more than a few of those who give our religion a bad name," he said.

"Religion?"

"For lack of a better word, yes," he said. "Although I don't like the stigma attached to that word, either."

"Bible-thumpers used to burn people at the stake for offering differing views of religion," she said.

"They still do, although not quite literally. They lock people up in asylums or put them on medications to keep them from walking or other things. Funny thing is, they do it, too - or they could if they'd get their energetic heads out of their religious assholes." Stephan covered his mouth as he heard Ryan laugh beside him. "Oops! Sorry," he said before he continued. "You still have to be really careful what you say, and to whom."

"Is there, like, a community of people who believe in... ah..."

"Tell me what it is that you believe, Cara," he said, touching his thumbs and forefingers together in a diamond shape under his chin. The symbol made Cara shiver.

She sat back and felt a lump rise in her throat. Ever since she was little, she had *known* things, but when she mentioned them to anyone, they had told her that what she was hearing was the devil tempting her, and she was thrust into youth programs and religious studies at her parents' church. "I've never thought that a billion people in Asia are going to hell because they don't believe that Jesus is their savior," she said thickly.

"Of course not," he said. "But that's what they tell you. That's, unfortunately, what a lot of people believe."

"Do you think they are not aware that they are being coerced?" she asked. "These followers, I mean. People like me who didn't have the courage – or the encouragement – to accept that there might be a different truth?"

He shook his head. "I think that a lot of people are just too scared to admit that they have had a vision or heard a message or had an experience. Society tells them that it's crazy. For centuries, there have been people who were go-betweens, telling their followers what was 'the truth' and what would damn their immortal souls. There were generations of common people who were not allowed to learn how to read and write, so they relied on these religious leaders to tell them what to believe."

She frowned. "The Bible?"

"Oh, there's a lot of truth in there," he said. "I mean, through the entire Old Testament, there are stories of people who listened to the voice of God speaking to them directly, and most of them weren't condemned or thought of as crazy. Moses transcribed his conversation with The Creator onto a couple of stone tablets, and the Ten Commandments still are followed all over the place today. And look at old Noah. If it hadn't been for his conversation with The Creator, we'd be lacking an entire history of religious belief that existed up until that time."

"Not to mention zebras and giraffes and elephants," Ryan chimed in, smiling.

"Yeah. That, too," Stephan said with a laugh.

"Do you really think that happened?" Cara asked. "Noah and the ark?"

Stephan nodded. "I don't *think* so," he said. "I *know* it did."

"You were *there*?" she asked, her eyes wide.

He smiled, raised his hands palms-upward and shrugged. "All I know is, back in the days when the Old Testament guys were talking to God directly, nobody questioned them. Everybody talked to God back then. It was normal, accepted."

"Everybody?" Cara asked. "Surely, not."

Stephan laughed. "Okay. Not everybody *did*. But everybody had the ability, just like they do today. They just didn't do it. The guys we know as the prophets realized that they had something, and they were just the first ones to the patent office with their transcripts."

"Hmpf," she said, furrowing her brow as she reached for her cup of tea. She cradled it in both hands before taking a sip, then lifted off the cover and removed the tea bag, placing it on the edge of Stephan's empty plate.

"What's the matter? Am I throwing too much information at you?" he asked.

She looked at him for a moment, her elbows resting on her knees as she leaned forward, then she shook her head. "No. I don't think that entire generations of people could be left to believe something that is so unbelievable if there weren't some ring of truth to it. I just always thought it was more of a fable."

"Which story? Noah and the Ark? Moses?" Stephan asked.

"All of it," she said. "But, for the sake of argument, let's stick with Noah."

He grinned and his eyes sparkled with mischief. "And what was the moral of the story, Cara?"

She thought about that for a moment, then smiled, shook her head and said, "Have faith."

Chapter 6

Cara finished sorting through the mountain of paperwork that her latest client had dropped off in a collection of plastic shoe boxes and began to enter the items in the appropriate places on the ledger sheet on her computer. The muscle in her jaw had been clenched for so long that she now had a the equivalent of a wall of rock all the way around her neck to the base of her skull, and she found herself more and more often putting the pen down, leaning her head forward and massaging her neck to try and loosen the knot of tension there.

The boys were away with Brandon and Claudia for the weekend. They had decided last-minute to take a trip to Blue Ridge to ride the train that Claudia had seen advertised in the newspaper the previous Sunday. Brandon had rented a cabin for the weekend, which Cara balked at initially, but finally relented. It was, she supposed, no worse than the boys spending time with their father at Claudia's house, where Brandon now lived.

Cara made a mental note to call her attorney about Brandon's living arrangement, but just the thought drained her energy. She didn't want to fight with Brandon anymore. She just wanted things to get back to normal, whatever normal was after an affair and divorce. Perhaps normal included a mind-numbing tension headache every time she saw the woman. She was sure that the pressure in her neck had more to do with seeing Claudia than it did with Mr. Fowler's or Miss Larue's plastic bins of business receipts. At the very least, the woman's presence in her driveway earlier had not done anything to relieve the latest bout of "receipt neck."

Claudia had stayed in the car while Brandon came to the door for the boys' things. Standing at the front door, giving kisses, Cara had noticed that Claudia was layering on another coat of thick black mascara with the aid of the visor mirror. Why the woman thought she needed multiple coats of eyelash make-up in the mountains, Cara could only guess, and she struggled to maintain the plastic smile on her face until Brandon took the boys' rolling duffel bags to the back of the SUV.

When they had left, Cara dove into the paperwork, finishing the ledger sheets for two of her least organized clients before starting in on Miss LaRue's. As one of Cara's oldest clients – in both literal senses – Cara put up with more from her than from other clients, but the multiple plastic shoe boxes were beginning to take their toll.

"Miss LaRue, what happened to the filing system I gave you last year?" Cara had asked.

The older woman had simply laughed politely and waved her hand in front of her face. "Oh, can't teach an old dog new tricks, dear!" she had said, and foisted the three boxes into Cara's arms. "I did organize them based on the types of receipts, though."

"You did?" Cara had asked, dubiously eyeing the boxes, which appeared to have confetti in them, as opposed to actual, legible receipts.

Miss LaRue had nodded proudly. "Of course! I labeled them for you, too. The top box is – ah, let's see – grocery store receipts, the middle one is gas and credit cards and the bottom one is charitable donations."

"Donations?" Cara had asked, raising a hand to her lips to quell the wave of nausea that arose just thinking about the task.

Miss LaRue had smiled, nodded and tapped the box, which Cara noticed was stuffed with the tags pulled from dozens of garments. "You donated new things?" she asked.

"Don't be silly, dear," Miss LaRue had said. "I save the tags to all of my clothes. That way, I know what they're worth when I give them away."

Cara had a sinking feeling in the pit of her stomach and said, "but I've never seen them with your things before."

"No, no. I realized just this year that I've had them stacking up," Miss LaRue had said sweetly. "There were several on a single hanger, and I realized that I had forgotten to give them to you for the past few years."

"So, you brought me just the ones from this year, right?" She had felt her head beginning to spin and her cheeks ached from forcing the smile.

"Oh, no, no. I just tossed them all in there. You can go back, can't you?" Miss LaRue had asked, cocking her head to one side like a little bird. "Oh dear," she added, noticing Cara's pale expression. "I hope it won't be too much trouble."

Cara had taken a deep breath, took the boxes from Miss LaRue and said as sweetly as she could manage, "I'll see what I can do."

Miss LaRue had turned and waved as she stepped daintily from the porch. "Thank you. I knew I could count on you, dear!" the old woman had said. "Just call me when you're done, dear. See you!" And she had sped off in her shiny new red VW Beetle. Certainly not the car for an "old dog," Cara thought.

With the boys gone and the receipts finally sorted, Cara sat bleary-eyed at the table rubbing her temples with her fingers. "There's got to be a way to get through to that woman," she said. "Maybe I'll let her know that organizing bills will incur an additional fee." Then she laughed – if only to keep from crying. "Who am I kidding? According to her receipts, she paid seven hundred dollars for a single pair of shoes!"

It was dark by the time she entered the last of the items onto the ledger sheet, filling in the maximum amount allowable for "Charitable Donations."

"Well, that will just have to do," she said, and she slipped the ledger sheets into the file marked "LaRue."

Pushing her chair back from the table, she stood and pressed the heels of her hands into the small of her back, luxuriating in the popping and stretching that would surely launch her chiropractor, Dr.

Elizabeth, into a full-blown lecture. Her muscles were tight all the way down to her buttocks, which were numb from sitting in one position for so long in the hard wooden chair. During a second, deeper stretch she felt a single, loud pop that released the tension along her spine, and she breathed a deep sigh.

She turned to leave the dining room and gasped at the appearance of a shadow on her front porch. The door bell rang and the blood pounded in her ears. Panicked, she picked up the first thing she could find and walked to the door. She turned on the porch light and peered through the peep hole, then let out the breath she hadn't realized she was holding.

"Damn, Steph! Why didn't you call and tell me you were coming over?" she asked as she slid the chain from the door and turned the handle.

"Well, hello to you, too!" he said. "You did say today was Miss LaRue's day, didn't you? I figured you were hip-deep in plastic boxes full of receipts and could use a break. Need some dinner?"

She eyed the bag he held in front of him. "Mm. Sushi?"

He nodded and looked down, then burst into laughter. "Please tell me that you weren't thinking of protecting yourself with that!" he said.

Cara blushed as she realized she was holding one of the empty plastic filtered water bottles that were next to the front door awaiting the delivery man. She quickly dropped it back with the others and rolled her eyes.

Stephan shook his head. "I can see the headlines now: 'Musician disfigured by plastic bottle. Story at eleven!'"

Still blushing profusely, she moved aside to let him in and locked the door behind him.

"So, are you hungry?" he asked. He glanced at the neat stacks that were lined up on the dining room table and raised an eyebrow. "Impressive! If those neat stacks are the receipts that belong to Miss LaRue, I would say the answer must be yes."

"Why didn't you call?" she asked again. "You just about scared me to death!"

He shrugged and placed the bag on the kitchen counter. "It has never upset you before," he said. "If you recall, I usually bring dinner when you tell me you're working on Miss LaRue's final quarter paperwork." He pulled two cardboard boxes out of the plastic bag with the yellow smiling face and turned to look at her. "From the looks of you, maybe I should have brought some adult beverages as well!"

She closed her eyes and nodded. "That probably would have been good," she said. "But I think I may have a couple of beers left in the fridge. Do you want one?"

"Beers left in the fridge? That's not something you hear every day," Stephan said. "Left over from when?"

"Halloween, I think. Remember, we sat out in the driveway around the little fire pit and drank beer?"

"That was, like, three weeks ago," he said.

She nodded. "Yeah. So?"

He shook his head and snorted. "You are *so* not a guy!"

"Thank God for that!" she said. She peered around him at the boxes. "So, which one's mine?"

"Get those beers and I'll bring your food to the table," he said. "It's a surprise."

"Ooh!" She brightened and opened the refrigerator, from which she produced two Coronas from the produce drawer. "Tah-dah!"

He sighed. "Girlie beer," he said, then smiled. "Oh, well! Beggars can't be choosers, right?"

"You got it, mister. The alternative is a juice box," she said.

"Mm. Sushi and juice box," he said. "Careful. We might start a new trend!"

She rolled her eyes and removed the caps from both bottles, stuffed the roll of paper towels under her arm and followed Stephan to the dining room table, where they set up their meal at the opposite end from the mountains of paper. She collapsed into a chair from which she could avoid seeing the piles of work, as long as she kept from turning her head to the right. She picked up a stone coaster from the box in the center of the table and placed Stephan's beer on it, then took a long, grateful sip of her own before placing it on a second coaster.

Stephan laughed at Cara's blissful expression, then handed her a paper sleeve containing a pair of chopsticks and waited for her to open the package and break them apart before unveiling her dinner. "Voila!" he said as he released the folded paper lid.

"Eel?" she asked, grinning.

He nodded, pleased with himself.

"Mm! My favorite!" she squealed, then scooted her chair closer to the table and began clicking her chopsticks together.

"You must be part mermaid, as much as you like raw fish," Stephan said, laughing.

Cara laughed, but felt chill bumps rise on her forearms. She shivered before removing the green blob of wasabi and pouring some soy sauce over the top.

"Are you cold?" Stephan asked.

She looked up at him. "Hm? Oh. No. Just a goose walking on my grave," she said. "Happens a lot these days."

He sat back and regarded her as she mixed the soy sauce and wasabi with her chopsticks. When she realized he was watching her, she stopped and looked up at him. "What?"

He shook his head, frowning amusedly. "Goose on your grave, eh?"

She shrugged. "It's something my grandmother always said."

He nodded. "Yeah. That's not quite it."

She dipped a piece of eel roll into the soy sauce and popped it into her mouth. She closed her eyes and chewed slowly, savoring the taste and texture of the fish, all the while aware of Stephan staring at her over his untouched box. She pointed at his box with her chopsticks. "Aren't you going to eat that?"

He sat forward and picked up his paper sleeve, emptied the contents into his left hand and broke the chopsticks apart. "Yes, of course," he said, scooping a glob of wasabi into a small plastic cup.

"Why are you acting weird all of a sudden?" she asked.

He shook his head as he poured the contents of one packet of soy sauce into the cup and stirred the wasabi into it. "No reason."

"Bull," she said. "If you know something, then tell me."

He picked up a bite of yellowfin, swirled it in the soy-wasabi and popped it into his mouth, chewing for a moment as he contemplated his response. When he swallowed, he gestured with his chopsticks. "When was the last time you walked?" he asked her.

"Changing the subject?" she said.

He shook his head. "No. It's relevant, I promise."

She frowned. "Just... well..." She frowned, then looked at him blankly. "It's been awhile."

He grinned at her and shook his head. "No, it hasn't."

"How do you know?" she asked.

"Because I've seen you. We've talked," he told her.

She felt the blood drain from her face. "How often?"

He shrugged and picked up another section of roll, gesturing with it as he spoke. "Let's just say *often*," he said, and popped the roll into his mouth. He reached over his box and picked up a stray piece of rice to avoid looking directly at her, which he knew infuriated her.

Cara frowned. "How come I don't remember?" she asked.

Stephan finished chewing and took a sip of his beer. He regarded the bottle and said, "That's actually pretty good," then took another sip and placed the beer back on the table before frowning in thought. "What time have you been going to bed at night?" he asked.

She shook her head and hiked a thumb toward the opposite end of the table. "I'm trying to get all of these clients caught up before the holidays, so I've been burning the midnight oil," she said.

He smiled. "There's your answer," he told her.

"I'm too tired? You mean, I'm actually *sleep walking?*" She laughed out loud, thinking the idea was hilarious. "That's just crazy! How can I be too tired to dream?"

He shook his head again. "I've told you before. It's not dreaming. It's a different state of consciousness. You must be getting pretty good at it, though, because we've moved on from the place where you were stuck."

"The amber desert?" she asked.

He laughed. "Is that what you call it? Well, I guess that's pretty accurate. It seems kind of barren."

"Barren? Really?"

He shrugged. "Yeah, sure, in comparison to other places."

"Other places?" she asked. "You mean I'm going somewhere that actually has scenery and stuff and I'm missing it?"

He laughed. "Once you quit burning all that midnight oil you'll be able to appreciate all the energy work you're doing when you aren't aware of it. In the meantime, you can be content in your little barren amber desert all by yourself."

"Except for all of the little voice-people who talk to me," she said.

"Voice-people?" he asked.

Cara nodded. "Yeah. And they have those weird names, too. I have a hard time remembering all of them. I'm Ahriel, remember? I know that because that's how all the voice-people address me and I answer. I don't know how I knew it was me – it's not like I can *see* anyone addressing me."

He laughed and she continued. "Then there's Keke, who I think is, like, my best friend or something. Can we have those there? Best friends? Anyway, she – I think she's a she – is always there to greet me when I get off the elevator..."

"The elevator?" he asked, nearly choking on a sip of beer as he laughed.

"What else would you call it? It's the swirly thing that picks me up and brings me to the amber desert. Kind of like an elevator." She frowned and waved her hand. "Never mind that. There's also Liris, who seems to think I know way more than I do. He – he reminds me of you, actually – isn't impatient, but I get the idea he wants me to remember faster. You're kind of infuriating in that way. I mean, he is."

She paused, glaring at Stephan, who was laughing silently and shaking his head. He hid his grin behind his hand and she took a sip of her beer, then nodded.

"Oh, yeah. And there's C'teus. I can't tell if that one is male or female. I get the feeling C'teus can be either one, or both. He was there the first time. I think he's like Ryan, actually. When Ryan is in the room, even when I don't see him, it feels the same."

Stephan, still grinning, shook his head as if he was overwhelmed. "Miss Popularity! Is that all?"

"That's all the names I can remember. At least, those are the only names I'm aware of. There seemed to be a lot more people – or whatever they are..." she said, feeling her face grow hot. "What's so funny?"

"You take an elevator to the amber desert?" he repeated.

She shrugged self-consciously. "I told you – I don't know quite what to call it," she said.

He smiled and popped another piece of sushi into his mouth, nodding as he chewed. After he swallowed, he took a sip of his beer and grinned. "And you talk to voice-people?"

She nodded and leaned toward him. "What? I know it sounds crazy."

"Certifiable, actually," he said.

"Great," she huffed, and stabbed at her box with her chopsticks.

"Don't get mad," he said, still grinning.

She glared at him. "You are definitely like Liris, actually. You're almost as infuriating!"

He paled a bit and cleared his throat, taking another sip of his beer. "Right. Um... how's the woodpecker problem?" he asked.

She was busy chewing a bit of eel roll and poking at the pickled ginger with her chopsticks, but she paused and frowned. When she finally swallowed, she looked up at Stephan with an odd sort of grin. "Huh," she said.

"Is he gone?" Stephan asked.

"No. Not gone. But he isn't on my house anymore," she said. "He seems to have taken up residence in the big tree in the back yard. You know, the one where the chipmunk hides under the roots?" She smiled and sat up a little straighter. "Huh. Maybe that little rodent is needing to pay some closer attention to something, like storing more of the food I'm putting out there for him!"

Stephan laughed. "Wonderful," he said, shaking his head. "You take elevators to amber rooms and wish for rodent enlightenment."

147

"Hey, we're all one energy, right?" she asked.

"Now you're starting to sound like a Disney movie," Stephan said.

"That would make me Cinderella, and I am perfectly okay with that," she told him, raising her chin a little higher. "Well, as long as I don't have my little rodent friends working in a sweatshop in the basement to make some sort of goofy garment for me."

"No sweatshop rodents. Check."

Still smiling, she shook her head and captured a piece of pickled ginger with her chopsticks, turned it over once or twice to examine it, then put it in her mouth, savoring the slightly spicy flavor and unique texture. "I love this stuff," she said. "But it's so cool. You can't eat a whole lot of it, or you'll get sick." She gestured at her box with her chopsticks. "The Japanese have got the right idea. Natural portion control. I love it."

Stephan laid his chopstick diagonally across his now-empty box, dabbed his lips with his napkin and smiled at Cara.

"What?" she asked.

"You seem so much more at ease now," he said.

"More at ease, as compared to... " she shrugged. "Are you saying I was uptight before? If you think it's easy to sleep at night when your ex is running around on you with the bimbo who broke up your marriage, and one of your kids thinks that guy hung the moon, and when you can get to sleep you have a stupid bird drilling holes in your house right outside your bedroom window... well, then, I had a reason to be uptight."

As he watched her he fought back a smile, and she halted her rant. Her face felt hot and she sighed, feeling sheepish. "Sorry," she said. "You were saying?"

"Yeah, about that. Maybe 'at ease' isn't quite the phrase I was looking for," he said.

"Probably not." Cara took a sip of her beer, then picked up the last piece of pickled ginger with her fingers and popped it into her mouth. She thought for a moment, then her brows knitted together. "What were you saying about my being stuck?"

He shook his head. "No. You aren't. That's just it," he told her.

"But the problem is that you keep thinking you're dreaming, so you're losing some of the experience."

"The experience," she repeated.

He nodded. "Yeah. You know – when you go to sleep and you feel really relaxed and you have very vivid dreams?"

She leaned toward him. "Uh-huh."

Stephan shrugged. "I'm just saying that maybe you ought to keep a notebook by your bed, that's all. Some of the stuff is probably not dreams."

"You said the amber desert isn't the only place I go walking," she said. "Do you really think I can remember the other places?"

He shook his head. "Absolutely. If the only thing you could remember was the amber desert, I don't know too many people who would want to return night after night. Do you?"

Cara laughed. "I guess not. All of that barren wasteland would get a little boring after a while."

"Not barren," he told her. "It's what you needed at the time. If you hadn't experienced the amber desert first, you wouldn't know how to get started walking."

"But I still don't," she said. "Because I'm not making myself go there. I guess I just sort of wind up someplace and that's that. I don't control it at all."

"Cara, are you listening to yourself?" Stephan asked.

She frowned. "Yeah. If I were any good at this, I would have it down by now. Hell, Steph, I've been talking to God since I was, like, ten. I'm thirty-six now. I should have the hang of it after all this time."

He laughed and shook his head, looking down at the table. When he recovered, he looked at her, mirth still evident on his face. "Cara, you need to relax. It isn't about control. It's about being open to what you can learn. You can't learn if you don't listen."

"But I told you, Steph, I heard the voice-people talking to me. They told me what my name is. And somehow they made me aware of what I should call them – well, the names I should use when I refer to them, anyway. That's listening, isn't it? I mean, some of those names are a little tough to pronounce."

"You're missing the point, Cara. This isn't a mission with a due-date, like your accounting projects. This is something that is ongoing. You don't have a specific mission, per se. Nobody is assigning you a task that you have to complete. You have to just... well, *be.*"

"Are you kidding?" she asked. "What's the point of all of this," she held out her arms and looked around, "if there isn't something we're supposed to do? If you haven't noticed, Stephan, the world is kind of a shit-hole right now. People hate each other just because of what they believe. We're killing our planet because we're too stupid or lazy to look for alternative resources. Everything is so... *messed up* right now. I can't believe that we're supposed to just sit on the sidelines and let everything around us go to pot!"

Stephan inhaled audibly, then exhaled in almost a whistle. "Oh, Cara. Some lessons are so hard to learn."

"What lessons?" she asked.

He looked tired all of a sudden as he searched her eyes for some sign that his lecture was getting through to her. "You have to stop thinking that you have to control everything. You can't act alone, Cara."

"What's the point of figuring out this stuff and walking and all of that if we aren't going to do anything with it to improve the world?"

Stephan laughed. "Now you just sound like Doctor Evil."

She laughed in spite of herself. "Doctor Evil? Really?"

He smiled. "You know what I mean. You're acting like this is some sort of grand-plan project and you're trying to fit all the pieces in place so you can do some big job. You don't have to control it, Cara. Do you want to be so busy there that you recreate the tension you feel here?"

"No, of course I don't!" she said. "I'm not trying to rule the world; I'm just trying to help other people see what they're doing."

"They have to find out for themselves," he said. "This..." he paused and searched for the right word, but sighed frustratedly and waved a hand between them. "This *gift* we have: it's not just for us, you know. It's something everybody has the potential for. They just are too busy to listen."

"Is that what I am?" she asked him.

"Too busy?" he asked. "Sort of. Yes."

"Really?"

"You always want to take charge, Cara. Sometimes you just have to take time to pause and be grateful."

"Be grateful," she repeated.

"I feel like I'm talking to a parrot," he said.

"You know, I tried doing one of those gratitude meditations one time," she told him.

"And how did that work out for you?"

"About as well as the time I took a yoga class."

"You took a yoga class?" He raised his eyebrows. "Do tell."

"I don't think I quite have the patience for yoga or meditation," she said. "I'm more of a get-in-there-and-sweat kind of girl."

"Hard core."

She nodded and smiled. "Exactly!"

"Figure it out and get it done," he said.

She nodded again and raised her beer bottle to him in a mock-toast.

"Which is what gets you in trouble, Cara."

Her smile faltered. "I'm in trouble?"

"No. Not trouble, really. But you need to watch yourself or you'll become one of *them*," Stephan warned.

"That sounds scary. Who are *they*?"

"Not scary," he said. "Well..." He paused and took another sip of beer. "I guess they can be scary. Remember when we were talking about the politicians and the old religious leaders and all of that when we were at the coffee shop?"

She nodded. "History," she said. "The people who kind of knew what was going on but wanted to make sure nobody else did. But I thought that was ego, just in one lifetime. They don't get to do it over and over again."

"Right – sort of. See, the thing is, we don't get to figure out that we've made these mistakes before," Stephan said. "We have to trust that, at some point, our spirit is going to know what feels right and what feels wrong. It's just the nature of the spirit to enjoy the sensation of power – of ego – when it's acting alone. What we need to remember is that there's way more power in working together, in harmony with other people, even with the environment, than there is in acting alone."

"Uh-huh."

"I don't know if it's energetic memory or what, but sometimes those egomaniacs make the same mistakes over and over, incarnation after incarnation, trying to rule things, trying to bend others to their will," he said. "I'm just speculating, of course. No one can every *really* know what they've done before from one life to the next – not without really trying, anyway. But I don't think that acting alone to complete a task is what we're supposed to be doing."

"But I am not trying to act alone, Steph," she said. "I'm want to teach people what I know so they can change for the better."

"You can lead people with the best of intentions, but they're still *your* intentions, Cara," he said.

She frowned. "I don't understand."

"Taxation without representation," he said. "Sound familiar?"

"History lesson?" she asked. "Don't tell me I was a British monarch or something."

He laughed. "Hardly. I'm just using a documented example," he said. "In the Revolutionary War, the people in England thought the poor, naïve little colonists had no idea what was best for them, so they taxed them out the wazzoo and ruled them from afar. Heck, the ruling class had never even set foot on American soil. They didn't know where the colonists were coming from."

"Right," she said, leaning forward to encourage him to continue.

"Right. The British thought they were doing what was best by leading people in the only way they had ever known." He shrugged and gestured with an upturned palm. "You don't know the experiences or the needs of other people. They may be doing bad things to themselves and to each other, but this – peace, love and understanding - is not something that you can just force down their throats."

"They have to figure it out for themselves?" she asked.

"Basically," he said. "And so do you."

Cara frowned and fidgeted with the lid to her sushi box. When she looked up, her eyes were filled with concern. "But what if they find out too late?"

Stephan sighed and shook his head patiently. When he looked up at her he was smiling sympathetically.

"What?"

"There isn't a *too late*, Cara," he told her. "What is, is. Don't you see?"

She shook her head. "No. I guess I don't," she told him. "Now that I know there's something out there, some sort of underlying *reason* for everything, a connectedness, I don't think I can just sit idly by and watch people ruin themselves and everyone – hell, *everything* – around them. Around us. Is it fair? I mean, really, Stephan, you would think that there is some reason we've been given the ability to see what is going on."

He narrowed his lips and frowned, then simply said, "No."

She waited for a moment, watching him. He didn't look up at her, but took a sip of his beer and set it back down on the table. As the silence between them grew, he picked the bottle up by the neck and swirled the last of the amber liquid around the bottom, watching it intently.

Finally, he put the bottle back on the table, folded his hands and looked at her without saying a word.

"What?" she asked, frustrated. "Aren't you going to say anything?"

He shook his head.

She let out a long, angry breath, and crossed her arms like a petulant child. She frowned at him, but held her pose, until she realized she couldn't drink her beer with her arms folded across her chest.

Trying to maintain some sense of dignity, Cara reached across the table for her beer, keeping her eye on Stephan. She overshot her target and knocked the bottle with her fingers, sending it spinning, nearly tipping over onto the table.

Stephan reached out for it at the same time Cara did, and the two of them bumped foreheads over the table with a sickening crunch.

"Ow!" Cara said, smacking her palm to her forehead. "Oh, God, that's going to hurt!"

Stephan was blinking, his eyes glistening with the sudden pain, but he triumphantly held up the beer bottle and forced a smile. He handed her the bottle and sat back down, rubbing his head.

Cara snatched the bottle with her free hand, took a swig, then held it to her forehead. "Damn. It's not even cold anymore."

She got up from the table and pulled a bottle of raspberry preserves out of the refrigerator, then returned to her seat and proceeded to sip the rest of her drink with the jar of preserves pressed to her head. "So," she said. "You know it isn't in my nature to just sit back and watch things happen. Hell, Stephan, I've slammed on my brakes when a squirrel runs out in the street in front of my car! If I'm not going to let a squirrel turn into road kill, I'm certainly not going to let an entire generation of human beings destroy themselves and the planet we live on if I can figure out some way to stop it!"

Stephan fixed her with a level gaze, then inhaled deeply through his nose. When he spoke, his voice was very quiet. "Cara, listen to yourself. What I am trying to tell you is that, regardless of your intentions being good or bad, you can't go rushing out into the world with sword in hand and expect to change everybody's minds or actions or anything else. That's your ego talking. And you can't let your ego rule your actions."

Cara shifted the jar of preserves so that another cool spot pressed on her bruise, and she shook her head. "You're saying my ego will get me into trouble?" she asked.

He answered her with a half-smile, and sat back in his chair.

She nodded and stood up. "I see," she said. "So what is this all for, Stephan?"

Without waiting for him to answer, she picked up both of the empty bottles and the empty sushi boxes and walked into the kitchen. She rinsed the inside of the boxes and turned them upside-down in the drain board, then did the same with the bottles. She picked up the jar

154

of jam, looked at it, touched her head gently with her fingertips, winced and opened the refrigerator to switch to a cold bottle of sugar-free orange marmalade.

Cara returned to the dining room, crossed one arm across her middle and looked at Stephan from beneath her bottle. "Would you like to sit in the living room? I, for one, have spent way too much time in here today and my butt is going numb."

He laughed and stood up. "Sure," he said, and he followed her out of the dining room, pausing to flip the light switch off before he left the room.

Cara plunked herself sideways in her favorite armchair, her legs hanging over the arm on one side, her head leaning against the overstuffed cushion that served as the back on the opposite side.

"Do you want water or something?" he asked before he sat down.

Cara shook her head and pointed to the side table. "I still have mine from earlier," she said. Then she frowned, realized she hadn't spent any time at all in the living room all day, and picked up the cup to inspect its contents. She made a face, then turned and handed the cup to him. "On the other hand, I don't need the protein that's doing a backstroke in here," she said, "maybe a fresh cup with ice would be nice. Thanks."

He inclined his head toward her. "As you wish," he said, bowing slightly as he quoted the line from her favorite movie, *The Princess Bride.* She sighed and tossed a pillow at his retreating back.

Chapter 7

Cara had a feeling that Thanksgiving was going to be a nightmare. Since Brandon would have the boys for the holiday, he had originally suggested that Cara join them for dinner at Claudia's – until, of course, he mentioned it to Claudia. The woman threw a raging fit and somehow decided that Cara had invited herself – of which Cara had been unaware until she ran into an old friend at the grocery store .

Rather, the friend had run into Cara, after doing such a poor job of avoiding making eye contact that she panicked in an effort to escape the conversation Cara had started near the dairy case.

"Mindy?" Cara asked, feigning surprise while knowing full well, of course, that it was indeed who she thought it was making a mad dash down the pet food aisle, despite her strict no-animals policy. Feeling devilish, Cara made her way quickly down the beer and wine aisle and intercepted Mindy near the cat toys. She felt like a fox pursuing a chicken, and it gave her quite an adrenaline rush!

Mindy was intent on looking over her shoulder, wondering if Cara would follow her. It was a combination of Mindy's panic and Cara's wanting to see the woman squirm that made her bump into Cara with her grocery cart.

"Oh, sorry!" Mindy said, the blood draining from her face when she realized it was Cara she had run into.

"Hey! Mindy? I thought that was you! What's up? You look like you've seen a ghost!" Cara said, smiling. She gave her friend a playful punch in the arm. "I haven't seen you in – well, *forever*. It must have been at least before Brandon left with that bimbo!" She bit her lip, wondering if she was taking it too far. "What have you been up to?"

Mindy stammered as she struggled to gather the coupons that had fallen out of her hand and were now mingling with the items in her grocery cart. "Oh, you know, just – ah – getting ready for the holiday," she said. "You?"

Cara enjoyed watching the other woman squirm when she realized the direction in which the conversation would surely lead, having now mentioned the holiday. Cara smiled broadly and said, "oh, you know, Brandon and the boys are going to be spending the day together. I was thinking maybe I'd rent a bunch of movies and make myself a turkey-and-cranberry-sauce sandwich and just not even get dressed all day. It has been *years* since I was able to spend the day in my jammies. Heck, I might not even shower!"

The other woman's face was pale, and Cara, enjoying the game, shifted her shopping basket from one arm to the other. "Whew!" she said, glancing at Mindy's already-overflowing full-size shopping cart. "I'm glad I'm just cooking for one. The thought of spending all that time in the kitchen cooking for a bunch of ingrates shoveling food down so they can get back to their football game is *so* not appealing!"

Mindy frowned as Cara's words sunk in. "That's odd," she said. "I got together with Claudia the other day and she said you were planning to have dinner with them. Of course, I thought *that* was odd, and would be uncomfortable for everyone involved, but..." She looked up at Cara and her eyes widened.

"Oh! I mean..."

Cara waved a hand, giving Mindy an opportunity for a graceful escape, which, of course, she didn't take.

"God! That sounded awful, I know!" Mindy said as her hand flew over her mouth. She forced a smile and cocked her head to one side. "I guess that's not the case, then, hm?"

"Which part? It being uncomfortable for everyone? No – I think that part's right on the money," Cara said, struggling to control the level of ice in her voice. "I wasn't planning on having dinner with them, either. In fact, the thought of spending the day with them would rather spoil my appetite, I should think."

"Gosh, Cara, I'm so sorry!" Mindy said, her hand again flying to her mouth to stifle a gasp. "That was so insensitive of me!"

Cara shrugged. She would doubt the sincerity of the statement from anyone else, but she happened to know that Mindy had a completely underutilized batch of gray matter under that perfect coiffure.

"So, you weren't planning on it? Spending the day with them, I mean?" Mindy bit her lip and frowned. "The way Claudia talked about it, you had sort of invited yourself, since the boys were going to be there..."

Cara sighed and rolled her eyes. Because she never connected her brain and her mouth, Mindy was truly the most tactless person Cara had ever met. She was almost glad that Brandon got her in the divorce! She forced a smile and replied, "No. Brandon invited me, which I thought was very nice of him, but of course I declined. I thought the same thing, you know, about it being uncomfortable for me to be eating Thanksgiving dinner in the house with my two sons and my ex-husband and the woman he slept around with before our divorce." She put her hand over her mouth and smiled demurely. "Oops! Did I say that out loud?"

Mindy's eyes opened so wide they might have popped out of her skull, and Cara thought the woman would certainly keel over of embarrassment right there in the middle of Kroger. Cara struggled to keep from laughing out loud as Mindy dropped her coupons again and cussed under her breath, bending down to scoop up the brightly colored slips of paper that had scattered beside the grocery shelf. As it was, a snort did escape, and Cara did her best to disguise it as a coughing fit.

When Mindy straightened again, her cheeks wore twin burning spots of red and Cara decided she had had enough fun for one day – almost. She picked up the one last coupon that had fallen under the woman's shopping cart – for his-and-hers lubricant - and handed it to Mindy with a bright smile. "Here you go! Hey, if they have you over for dessert, don't eat the pumpkin pie." She looked around conspiratorially, then whispered, "I heard that one was meant for me!" She straightened and managed to keep a straight face as Mindy's eyes grew wide and her mouth dropped open into a perfect "O."

"I hope I see you again soon," she added, in her best ladies' social club accent. "It's just been way too long! Say hi to Bob and the kids for me, will you?"

Then she turned around and walked purposefully to the yogurt section without looking back once, trying hard to contain her laughter.

When she heard Mindy's cart squeaking in the opposite direction, she allowed herself a quick "ha!" then covered her mouth as she tried unsuccessfully to control a hiccup. "Serves me right for messing with that woman's mind – what there is of it," Cara muttered to herself, and proceeded to pluck the thirty-nine-cent yogurts from the shelf and put them into her basket, then headed to the check-out lanes feeling a little guilty for so thoroughly enjoying her encounter with Mindy.

* * * * *

Brandon picked up the boys around two o'clock on Wednesday afternoon, after Cara had overseen their packing and made sure that they brushed their teeth and stood on the back porch to brush the mud from their tennis shoes. "Have a good time, but make sure you mind your manners," Cara reminded them, as Brandon's car pulled up slowly in the driveway. She knew what both of her sons were capable of when they were forced into doing something they didn't want to do.

"I don't want to go," Ryan said, confirming her fears.

Dylan frowned at him. "I don't want to, either, but it's Dad's holiday. Remember?" He gulped and Cara's heart broke. What a horrible thing to do to a child – create a calendar by which days belonged to Dad and which belonged to Mom. She rubbed his shoulder in what she hoped was reassurance.

Ryan nodded sadly, his eyes lowered and his lower lip poking out. "But what's Mom going to do all day by herself?"

Cara squatted down and straightened Ryan's collar – he practically lived in logo T-shirts, and Cara had bought him a single rugby shirt for special occasions. Although she had purchased it during the back-to-school shopping expedition, Cara had to remove the tags that very morning. "Now, Ry," she said, rubbing his cheek with the backs of her fingers, "you know you'll have a good time. I think Dad bought a new puzzle for you guys to do together this weekend. It has, like, five thousand pieces!" she told him, hoping to lighten his mood with the mention of one of his favorite Thanksgiving traditions.

He shook his head and she saw tears well up in his eyes. "But what are you going to do without us?" he asked again and she felt her heart swell with pride and compassion for her little protector.

She smiled at him reassuringly and said, "Oh, don't worry about me, Ry. You know I'm a resourceful old gal. I'll be just fine. I might even dig out one of the old puzzles and do it myself, and think of you guys while I'm putting it together." She made a mental note to dig out a puzzle and work on it some. The boys would not forget what she told them, and would surely check when they came home on Sunday to make sure she hadn't been bored or lonely.

"See?" Dylan asked, elbowing his brother in the arm, earning him *the look* from his mother.

She straightened and leaned over to give both boys a hug and kiss. "I'm going to miss you both, but I want you to have a good time," she said. "And let's swap stories when you get home on Sunday, so we can see who had the best time, okay?"

Ryan smiled and wiped his nose on his sleeve, his head bobbing up and down excitedly. Dylan elbowed his brother and rolled his eyes.

"Ow!" Ryan said, rubbing his arm. "What did you do that for?"

"Idiot," Dylan said under his breath. "She's just saying that so we go to Dad's without a fuss. She's going to sit at home and do nothing. She'll make up something to tell us when we get home so we don't worry about her. You know that, right?"

Ryan's eyebrows shot up in a concerned point. "Really?"

Cara lowered her chin at Dylan, then raised a finger to her lips and shook her head.

He looked down, then turned to his brother and smiled

unconvincingly. "Nah. Sorry I said that."

Ryan sighed, visibly relieved. He turned back to his mother and beamed. "You tell such great stories, Mom," he said. "Try to have fun, okay? So you can tell us all about it when we get home."

She returned his smile and rubbed is head. "I will. I love you guys."

"Us too, Mom," Dylan said, and pulled Ryan by the sleeve out the front door.

She stood on the porch and waved as Brandon backed down the driveway. He stopped about mid-way and was obviously saying something to one of the boys. Cara watched him turn around and face the porch, move his arm, then shake his head, then the car started moving backwards once more. She watched until the tail lights disappeared over the hill, then she rubbed her arms with her hands and went back inside the house, wondering what she could do that would sound exciting to the boys when they returned home.

Cara stood in the doorway and stared into her empty house, a momentary panic rising within her. "Silly," she told herself. "You enjoyed living by yourself before you had kids. You can handle it for a long weekend." She forced a laugh and looked around, grateful that no one was there to hear her talking to herself.

Despite her usual preference for energy conservation, she walked around the house and turned on a few lights – the reading light in the living room and the table lamps in each of the boys' rooms. Although it was warm for November, she also gave a moment's thought to turning on the heat, but opted for a cup of hot tea instead. She went into the kitchen and filled the kettle with enough water for a single cup, then rummaged through the drawer for a flavor that would chase away the loneliness that was closing in.

Something with chamomile, she thought, and she rummaged through the cabinet until she found the box of chamomile and mint. She panicked when she picked it up, thinking it was empty, but a quick shake offered relief at the sound of a single tea bag inside. She tore open the paper and held it under her nose, inhaling the calming scent of chamomile under the stronger mint smell before dropping the bag into her favorite chipped ceramic mug, shivering involuntarily at the white chip standing out so starkly against the deep amber color of the mug.

She stood over the stove and waited for the water to boil, turning off the burner just before the kettle began to whistle. She filled her cup with the water, then stood warming her hands over the rising steam as the tea bag steeped.

The telephone rang, startling her so that she nearly spilled the tea. She picked up the cordless receiver from the kitchen counter and checked the Caller ID, which only read a number. "Hello?"

"Cara?" It was Marlene's voice. "You sound like shit, sweetie? What's going on?"

Cara coughed, followed by a short laugh – almost a squawk. "Mar? You are, honestly, the most blunt person I have ever known."

"Ah, but sweetie, you love me for it," Marlene said. "You wouldn't have me any other way. But don't change the subject. What's eating you, honey?"

"I swear, Marlene, you are worse than my own mother," Cara said.

"Mm-hmm."

"But better in some ways, too," she added.

Silence.

"And I appreciate it. Really. I do. You have no idea how much..."

"You are such a kiss-ass," Marlene said. "But flattery will get you absolutely nowhere. Are you drinking?"

"What?" Cara spluttered.

"Wine? Beer? Oh, hell, honey – have you started on the hard liquor?" Marlene asked.

"I'm drinking chamomile tea, thank you for asking," Cara said indignantly. "And I haven't had a chance to put anything else in it yet, as I had just finished pouring it when the phone rang. But I'm thinking a drizzle of that honey you gave me would be just the right finishing touch."

Marlene laughed. "That's my girl."

"Huh?"

162

"I've been worried about you all day, Cara," Marlene said. "You've been on my mind."

"I have?"

"Of course," Marlene told her. "You're stressed. I can hear it in your voice. Talk to me."

"Marlene," Cara said. "We haven't spoken for at least two weeks. I am the single mother of twin eight-year-old boys. I am an accountant to some people who are so disorganized that I'm not sure how they have made it to the ages they have. My ex-husband is living with a life-sized Barbie doll – actually, I think the doll has accomplished more than Claudia has..."

"There it is," Marlene said, her grin audible through the receiver.

"There *what* is?" Cara asked her.

"The source. I felt it when you mentioned Claudia."

"The source?"

"The source of your stress, sweetie. Honestly! Are you not paying attention?" Marlene huffed. "I'm trying to help you, here, but you have to give me something to work with."

"I didn't realize I needed help..."

"Tut, tut! Of course you did, even if you didn't use your words," Marlene said.

Cara put her hand to her forehead, squinted her eyes and exhaled. "I am very confused," she said. "Why did you call?"

Marlene laughed. "Cara, honey, you called me." She paused. "Last week. Don't you remember?"

"Um." She racked her brain but truly could not remember calling Marlene. She'd been very busy. "Maybe I butt-dialed you?"

"I don't think so. We spoke," Marlene insisted, then her voice was more sing-song. "No matter," she said. "The fact is, Cara, that you asked me for help and I've been trying to answer you, but you don't respond. I don't think you even heard me."

Cara frowned. "When did you call?"

"Every day," Marlene said. "Like clockwork, when the sun came up. Actually, there were a few days when I called you both in the morning and at night..."

"Really?" Cara asked, picking up her cell phone and scrolling through the missed calls. "Did you call me on my home phone or on my cell?" she asked. "Did you leave a message? Because I honestly have no record..."

Marlene laughed. "Really? You didn't hear me?"

"Come again?"

"Cara, I called you on the phone today because you haven't responded to my other methods, even though that's how you contacted me," Marlene told her.

"Are you saying that I talked to you..."

"Some people call it telepathy. I prefer to say you dialed direct," Marlene said, laughing at her own joke.

"Hm."

"You're not ready for that?" Marlene asked.

"I'm not sure," Cara said.

"That's pretty funny, coming from somebody who talks to woodland animals," Marlene said. Cara could hear a hint of humor in the older woman's voice.

"Woodland animals..." Cara repeated.

"You've been feeding the chipmunks and making deals with woodpeckers, from what I hear," Marlene said.

"You've been talking to Ryan," Cara said. It wasn't a question.

"Oh, honey, Ryan and I talk all the time," Marlene said. "He's so unpretentious. It's very refreshing!"

"Of course he is, Mar. He's eight!" Cara said.

"Well, when we talk, we're more like peers, really," Marlene told her. "He's quite insightful." Her voice was playful, and Cara felt a little queasy when she thought of what Brandon might say if he caught Ryan on the phone with Marlene. She also felt a twinge of jealousy, thinking about how her son and one of her oldest friends spoke regularly and she had not a clue.

"He is normally so shy about talking on the phone," Cara said, swallowing her misgivings. "I'm glad you were able to get him to talk." She frowned. "Wait a minute... When did you talk to him? He's been spending a lot of time at Brandon's – well, Claudia's. Brandon hardly

164

lets him call *me* . And, no offense, Mar, but Brandon doesn't exactly approve of you. I doubt he'd appreciate you calling Ryan when he's over there."

"Oh, no offense taken, Cara. Actually, I probably think much less of Brandon than he does of me. But I have not been talking to Ryan on the phone." Marlene chuckled. "Actually, your son is very comfortable using dial direct."

"Dial direct? I don't understand."

Marlene exhaled with a sound like a racehorse. "Really, honey. Just when I thought you were making progress," she said. "I meant mind-to-mind. No ten cents a minute that way, you know."

"You're kidding, right?" Cara asked.

"Not at all," Marlene said. "That son of yours has a gift, and the best thing is that he's aware of it. He uses it, and he isn't afraid." She paused for a moment, then added, "you're doing a great job with him. He's very mature for his age. And you could learn a lot from him, if you take your time and relax a little bit."

"He's my son, Mar..." Cara said, her voice a bit higher pitched than usual.

"He's a natural talent, Cara," Marlene countered. "He told me you've been visiting. Well, he confirmed what I already knew. But he's very excited about it. He's proud of you, you know."

"He... wait a... *what?*"

"He said he was there the first time you succeeded. He thought I was, too, so he called to me to confirm that I was there. We've been talking ever since," Marlene said.

Cara felt chills, but excited at the same time. "Wow. I had no idea..."

Marlene laughed. "You did, but you had a hard time getting it past your rather annoyingly logical nature."

"He *called* you?" Cara asked.

Marlene laughed again. "Oh, stop it, Cara. You're killing me. He didn't call me on the *phone*, honey. I said he called *to* me. We've been talking while we're walking." She hooted at her own joke. "Oh, honey, I crack myself up."

"Wait a minute..." Cara said.

Marlene was silent, waiting for Cara to connect the dots.

"C'teus?" Cara asked quietly.

"Now you're catching on," Marlene said as she caught her breath. A few final chuckles escaped. "I thought you already knew."

"Well, I had a feeling, since Ryan was so excited for me, even before I said anything," she said.

"Uh-huh. Go on," Marlene said, ever the patient therapist.

"And you were there when I... what did you call it? 'Went visiting'?" Cara asked.

"Yes. Exactly," Marlene said. "About damn time, too."

"What's that supposed to mean?"

Marlene blew out her breath. "Forget it," she said. "You've been making the rounds for a while now, but it's just now starting to hit your conscious mind."

"Hmm," Cara said, trying to wrap her brain around the idea of being in two places at once. "Okay. If Ryan is C'teus..."

"Sort of," Marlene said. "Energy is a little different than flesh and blood and bone. But for all intents and purposes, yes, Ryan is the energy called C'teus."

"Right. And that's why he recognized me. His energy, I mean."

"Sure. Although it doesn't always happen that way," Marlene said. "Sometimes you run with a very different crowd in another dimension than you do here as a physical being."

"Is that so?" Cara asked.

"It is," Marlene chuckled.

"And you are..."

"Excuse me?" Marlene asked.

"You said you saw me, so I must have met you, right? *There*, I mean," Cara said.

"Oh, sure," Marlene said. "We've been running around together for a long time, so it was nice that you finally recognized me on both sides of the curtain."

"So who are you? *There*. What's your name?" Cara asked.

"Uh-uh. You know, and you just don't want to admit that you

know." Marlene's voice was smug.

"Stubborn," Cara muttered.

"Well, if that ain't the pot calling the kettle black!" Marlene said.

"I told... I thought... *Keke?*"

"Now we're talking."

"Okay. So, you've visited me for how long?" Cara asked, as she sighed and looked out the window. The whole idea of walking and visiting when she assumed she was sleeping was suddenly making her very tired.

"A very long time," she said. "You actually knew it, but you just didn't remember when you were awake," Marlene said. "That's what I meant when I said that it took you awhile. We really have been running around together for a very long time. But it's nice to have a chance to be awake in this realm before you for a change."

Cara held the phone away from her and stared at it, goose bumps rising on both of her arms. "What did you say?"

"It's nice to be awake before you for once," Marlene repeated. "Why? Is that a problem?"

"No. I mean, I guess not. But it's the same thing Stephan told me," Cara said.

"Is it, now?" Marlene asked.

"Yes."

"Interesting."

"Is it?" Cara asked.

"I think so," Marlene said. "I don't remember it happening before."

"Is that a bad thing?"

"What's good and what's bad, in the grand scheme of it all, Cara?"

"How am I supposed to know?" Cara asked. She bit her lip and frowned. "Is there a grand scheme?"

Marlene was silent, thinking.

"Just what is the purpose of all of this, Mar?" Cara asked.

"Are you kidding me?"

"No, I'm not. Isn't there some sort of grand plan or something?" Cara asked. "I mean, you're the one who brought it up."

Marlene sighed. "Oh, Cara. You really must learn to just relax."

"That's what Stephan says," Cara said as she sunk down into her arm chair. She turned her head as she saw something move on the back porch. The chipmunk skittered past the window to the little dish of seeds that Cara had left out for it on the porch rail. She breathed a light laughter into the telephone.

"Cara?"

"I'm relaxing, Mar," she said in monotone.

"Oh, now, don't get all huffy," she said. "Is something wrong?"

"No," she said. "It's my little rodent. He's come back."

"Your little what?" Marlene asked.

"I have a chipmunk, remember?" Cara told her.

"The chipmunk? Really?" Marlene asked. Her voice rose with excitement.

Cara frowned. "Yes. Why?"

"How long have you been feeding him?" Marlene asked.

"Oh. I don't know... since September or so? Labor Day, maybe?" Cara told her. "But I haven't put anything out there for a few days, at least. I thought maybe he was hibernating or something..." she said, but Marlene wasn't listening.

"About the time you and I met at the coffee shop?" Marlene asked. She could scarcely contain the excitement in her voice.

"What?"

"Is that when you started feeding him? Around the time that you and I met at the coffee shop?" Marlene asked.

"Yes. About then, I guess. Why?"

"Interesting timing, that's all," Marlene told her.

"I take it that's a good thing?" Cara asked.

"Of course! But you have to pay attention," Marlene told her.

"And what does the chipmunk mean, other than that he was a little behind on gathering his food for the winter?" Cara asked her.

"It is not a coincidence that he caught your attention when he did," Marlene said.

"What? Labor Day?"

"Well, of course, that, too. But tonight, I mean. During our conversation," Marlene said. "You were asking the meaning of everything."

"And you tell me that there is meaning in my seeing a *chipmunk*," Cara said, trying to recall what she had read in the book about animal spirits.

"Yes."

"But, what is the meaning of everything else? Of you and Ryan and Stephan having different names and talking to me while I'm sleeping..."

"Not sleeping. When you, Ahriel, are *awake*, but when you – *Cara* – are asleep," Marlene said.

Cara frowned and pinched the bridge of her nose with her fingers. "You're confusing me, Mar," she said.

"It's not all that difficult to grasp if you stop trying to make it so complicated," Marlene said.

"Are you going to tell me?" Cara asked. "Or is this another one of those things that you're going to tell me I already know?"

"Listen to your chipmunk, Cinderella," Marlene said.

"What's he saying again?" Cara could feel the beginning of a headache, although thankfully she did not hear any humming noises that might accompany a dizzy spell – or worse.

Marlene sighed. "Chipmunks do things when they want. You can't direct them. You can't tell them what to do. They are very, *very* independent little creatures, despite their size," Marlene said.

"Is he talking to *me*?" she asked.

"Of course!" Marlene said. "There's also the little side note about gathering nuts for the winter."

"I have you and Steph, don't I?" Cara said, rubbing her temples while balancing the phone.

"Very funny, Cara," Marlene said. "Seriously. You've always been very good about this, but it probably isn't a bad idea to make sure to not neglect your money situation."

"I'm doing okay," Cara said.

"But as things change, that could, too," Marlene told her. "It's part of the chipmunk's message. I thought it best not to leave that out."

"I said I'm fine, Mar," Cara snapped.

"Don't sound so pissed off, young lady," Marlene said.

"Great. Now you really do sound like my mother."

"I don't hear you complaining about it at other times," Marlene said. She could have been perturbed, but there was humor in her voice. Cara wished she could see the older woman's face. As if she knew what Cara was thinking, she added, "did Brandon come and take the boys already?"

Cara frowned. "Yes, he did. Just before you called."

"I knew there was something wrong," Marlene said. "It just didn't feel right."

"Great. Are you, like, Yoda or something? You felt a disturbance in the Force?" Cara chuckled.

"Don't laugh," Marlene said, sounding suddenly serious.

"Oh, God. You think you're Yoda?" Cara sat up and placed her free hand at the base of her neck, massaging the beginning of a knot there. "And I'm supposed to be taking financial advice from rodents. This is beginning to sound like a bad movie."

"Cara. You've known me long enough to know that I'm not some bumbling nut-job. Give me a little credit, won't you?" Marlene said.

"I would if I knew what the hell you were talking about," Cara said, frustrated. She inhaled deeply and stretched, her hand at the small of her back, then asked, "Have you had dinner, Mar? Do you want to get together and chat for a little while? I'm getting a crick in my neck from holding this phone."

"Oh, my poor little sweetie," Marlene said. "Can't have that. And dinner sounds like a lovely idea. What do you feel like eating?"

Cara sighed. "Honestly, I don't have much of an appetite," she admitted.

"What's the matter, honey? You invited me, remember?" Marlene said.

"I'm trying to understand," Cara said, squinting her eyes tightly. "You are one of my closest friends, Marlene. But you are driving me a little crazy, if you want to know the truth."

"I'm so sorry that you feel that way," Marlene said, although she didn't sound the slightest bit contrite.

Cara sighed. "So, if we have dinner, will you tell me what the hell I need to know?"

"I'll think about it," Marlene said.

"Hmm."

"Tell you what, Cara," Marlene said, "you don't feel like eating, but you need to or you're going to get sick. And you can't do that, because those boys need their mama feeling well when they come home from Brandon's. You know that. So, why don't I bring over some chicken soup?"

Cara chuckled. "Chicken soup? Are you serious?"

"Of course."

"Canned or from the dinner counter at Whole Foods?" Cara asked.

"Neither. I should think you know me better than that!" Marlene said, her chicken-soup-wielding feathers sounding more than a little ruffled. "As it so happens, I was making a pot today, so I have some fresh that I'm willing to share with my friend."

"You've been cooking today? Really? A pot of chicken soup the day before Thanksgiving." Cara laughed. "You really are my Jewish Mother, aren't you?"

"Hey, don't knock it," Marlene said. "Everyone should have one. I'm here when you need me."

"That's true. I can't even remember how long we've been friends," Cara said, hoping Marlene would take the bait.

"It's not important," Marlene said. "But that was a good try."

Cara sighed again. "You're not going to share anything, are you?"

"Mm-mm. Not until I see you," Marlene told her.

"Fine. Chicken soup it is," Cara said. "I have some wine. Would that be acceptable?"

"Wine is always acceptable," Marlene said, chuckling. "I'll see you in an hour."

The phone clicked and Cara smiled, staring at the receiver in her hand and shaking her head. She walked into the kitchen and replaced the phone in the cradle, then uncorked the bottle of red wine to let it breathe. She opened the glass-front cabinet and removed two of her special bowl-shaped wine glasses without stems and inspected them for dust and spots. Satisfied that they weren't filled with spiderwebs from lack of use, she placed them on the counter next to the bottle and went to her bedroom to freshen up.

She used the bathroom, then splashed cold water on her face. When she caught a glimpse of her reflection in the mirror, she paused to take a good, long look at herself. "God, I *do* look like shit!" she said, poking and prodding her cheeks and her eyes and feeling every bit like Scarlett O'Hara as she pinched her waxy cheeks to give them color.

Even with the two little pinch spots, her face was pale and she had dark, bluish circles under her eyes. She picked up a hairbrush and pulled it through her hair, wincing as it snagged the tangled parts. She frowned as she picked several long strands out of the brush, stared at them for a moment then lowered them into the trash can beside the sink.

"Stress," she said. She looked at her reflection once more in the mirror. "I don't want to be alone for Thanksgiving, or Christmas or New Year's..." She snatched the brush through her hair with a bit too much force, leaving her scalp feeling as if it had been raked. She stopped when she noticed tears in her eyes and realized she had inflicted pain without even realizing she'd done it.

Cara lowered her head, grasping the brush firmly with both hands, and allowed herself a moment to wallow in self-pity. The feeling welled up inside her chest and constricted her breathing, and she let her thoughts grow angry as she considered the circumstances that had brought her to her current status of divorced woman, single mother, struggling to make ends meet by handling other people's messed-up accounts.

She closed her eyes and looked at herself once more in the mirror, then steeled herself, stood up straight and nodded to herself. "I hate it when I do this," she said out loud, her voice sounding strange to her own ears as it echoed in the empty bathroom.

She replaced the brush on the counter top and turned off the light as she left the bathroom. She put on a pair of thick, mismatched socks and padded down the hall, startled by the sight of headlights in the driveway. She frowned. "That can't be Marlene already. She just called."

Cara went to the door and squinted against the brightness of headlights directly in front of her. Whoever it was had pulled into the driveway with their brights on. When the lights went out, she blinked to clear the purple and blue orbs that dotted her vision, waiting to see who was exiting the car and coming up the driveway to her door.

Against her better judgment, she opened the door and leaned out. "Mar?" she shouted.

"Not quite," said a male voice, muffled as its owner leaned into the hatch back to retrieve something. She heard a grunt as he lifted whatever it was, then the clunk of metal against metal as he slammed the trunk with his elbow. "Sorry I didn't call. You're not going to hit me with an empty water bottle, are you?"

She heard Stephan chuckle as he stepped onto the porch carrying a cardboard carton of Coronas and a small plastic bag of limes. He held them up to her and smiled. "This is the way you like them, right?"

She nodded and hugged her arms, smiling softly. "That's great, Steph. Thanks."

He shrugged. "It's the least I could do, considering I downed your vintage bottles the other day." He smiled and raised an eyebrow as he looked around. "You alone?"

She nodded again and looked over her shoulder at the uncharacteristically quiet house. "Yeah. Brandon came by and got the boys about an hour ago."

"Oh, that sucks," Stephan said, and frowned. "I really should have called first. I'm sorry. Do you want to be alone?"

She shook her head. "No. But..." She cocked her head to one side and smiled, shrugging her shoulders. "No, it's fine."

He raised his eyebrows and a slight smile crossed his lips. "Cara Porter – are you seeing someone?"

She rolled her eyes and snorted. "Hell, no. Are you kidding me? Been there, done that. Thanks, but I'm not planning to make that mistake again."

"Oh, Cara. You can't write off every man just because your marriage to Brandon was all messed up," Stephan said.

"I'm not. But it's kind of recent, you know? And I have two little boys who need the full-time attention of their mother," Cara told him. She raised an eyebrow back at him. "You aren't applying for the job, are you?"

He choked as a blush rose from his collar. "Uh, no! Not to disappoint you or anything, but if I were to date you and things got serious, it would be like sleeping with my sister. I hope that's not upsetting to you."

She laughed. "No. It's a relief, actually. I don't ever want there to be anything weird between us."

Stephan stopped and raised his eyebrow again. "Really?"

"Okay. Maybe I meant I didn't want it to be any *more* weird," Cara corrected, removing a lime from the bag and rinsing it under the faucet.

He laughed. "So, do you want me to stay? Or would that be weird?"

"Well, I don't know," she said. "A friend is coming over to bring me dinner. She was worried about me not eating..."

She paused and looked over Stephan's shoulder as headlights topped the hill and slowed in front of her house. The car turned into the driveway and Cara shoved her hands into her pockets and shrugged. "Well..." she said, glancing at the clock over the wall oven. "That was fast!"

Stephan deposited the box of beer on the tile counter, paused as he took in the bottle of wine left to breathe, and hiked a thumb over his shoulder. "I should go, then," he said, clapping his hands together as he backed away.

"No, no," Cara said, touching his arm. "Since she's here, I'll introduce you. I can't believe that, as long as I've known both of you, you've never met each other."

He laughed nervously. "You know, you run in different circles, depending on where you are at the moment," he said.

She jerked her head around to look at him. "What did you say?"

He shook his head. "Just saying."

Cara eyed him warily, then laid the knife down on the cutting board and went to the front door.

The car pulled up alongside Stephan's car and the engine cut off; the lights went off and Cara listened for the tell-tale squeak of Marlene's driver-side door. She smiled when she heard the noise, followed by the shadow of Marlene's head popping over the door. "Hello, hello!" she said. "Looks like I'm not the only one who thought you needed a little bit of company." Her voice was perky, very Marlene-like, and Cara sighed in relief.

Cara looked over at Stephan and smiled. "Well, it looks like Marlene doesn't think three is a crowd.

"How do you feel about chicken soup?"

His brows furrowed. "Are you kidding me?"

"Nope," she whispered, and inclined her head toward the car.

"What?"

"Hello there, handsome," Marlene said, her smile moving from his face to his biceps, one of which she reached out to squeeze. "You look like you work out regularly. How do you feel about helping me out by carrying this pot of soup into the house?" She walked around to the passenger side of the car, approached the two of them and craned her neck to look up at Stephan. "Besides, if you do it without spilling any, I'll let you have some!" she added brightly.

Stephan laughed. "Wow! What a deal!"

Marlene smiled at Cara, then grabbed Stephan by the sleeve and dragged him to the car. "Here you go. Careful – the pot is a little hot. Here. Use these," she said, and handed him a pair of pot holders.

He looked back at Cara with an amused grin on his face. She shrugged and watched him lean into the car to remove the pot of soup. "Smells delicious!" he said.

"Thanks," Marlene said. "It's my specialty. I always make a pot the week before Thanksgiving. Keeps me from gearing up for the big meal, you know? This way I don't overeat."

"I don't know. I bet I'd gorge myself on this stuff!" Stephan said.

Marlene opened the back door to the car and removed a reusable grocery bag with a baguette sticking out of the top. She shut the door with a squeak and a slam, and smiled at Cara. "I would have been here a little bit sooner, but I stopped at the store to get a bread." She smiled at Stephan's retreating back as he carried the hot pot toward the house.

"Are you kidding? You're here way earlier than I thought you would be," Cara said.

"Anything for my babushka," she said, reaching up to pinch Cara's chin.

Cara laughed. "You act like you're eighty sometimes, Mar," she said.

Stephan grunted and raised his chin toward the door. "Hey, gorgeous. Want to grab that for me? I've kind of got my hands full."

Both women's heads spun toward him, and they laughed. "Here, I'll get that," Cara said.

"I think he was talking to me, but by all means..." Marlene muttered, loud enough for Stephan to hear.

Cara shook her head, laughing as she opened the door and held it for both him and Marlene. As Stephan continued walking toward the kitchen, Marlene leaned over and whispered, "My, my, honey. Wasting no time, are you?"

Cara rolled her eyes. "It's not like that, Mar," she said. "I've known Stephan since we were teenagers. He's one of my best friends."

Stephan came back to the door and leaned on the frame. "And I just got finished telling Cara that it would be like kissing my sister if we were more than friends," he said. He stuck out his hand. "I'm Stephan Rust," he said. "And you must be Cara's Jewish mother?"

Marlene threw her head back and laughed. Cara loved the way her friend never held back – the older woman's laughter, sadness, anger – each emotion was fully embraced. It was her laughter that Cara loved best.

"You've heard about me, I see! Yes, I'm Marlene Luzell. Nice to meet you, finally," Marlene said, hitching the bag over her shoulder and shaking Stephan's hand. "Oh, hell!" she said, and pulled him into a hug. "I've heard so much about you, I feel like we already know one another!"

A strange look passed between them, followed by a glint of mischief in Marlene's eye. "Now let's get inside and eat. The temperature is dropping out here and that soup is much better when it's piping hot!"

Cara stepped back and let her friends enter the house, then followed them, flicked the porch light off, closed the door and locked it. She hesitated, then slipped the chain into its channel as well before she joined them. They were already in the kitchen and Marlene was rummaging through the cabinet to retrieve the soup bowls. She had emptied her bag, which included a stack of cloth napkins Marlene had brought from home – she didn't approve of paper napkins, which were what Cara usually used.

Stephan was rubbing his hands together, and he turned to the two women with a crooked smile. "What the hell is in that pot, bricks?"

Marlene chuckled. "It's not canned soup, sweetie," she said. "It's made from scratch. There's some good stuff in that pot – cures whatever ails you!"

"That, I can believe," Stephan said. "I'm sure it sticks to your ribs, too, as heavy as it is!"

Marlene reached over and squeezed his muscle again. "I thought you were stronger than that," she said, smiling as he frowned at her. "Your arms aren't so big as they are solid, though."

He yanked his arm from her grasp and rubbed it as if he had been burned.

"Spoons?" Marlene asked, as they were not in the drawer she had opened that held the rest of the silverware.

"Oh. Sorry. We don't use soup spoons very often," Cara said, retrieving three large spoons from a drawer near the stove, and a ladle from the canister on the counter top. "The boys' mouths aren't very big. They eat with cereal spoons when I make soup."

Marlene raised her eyebrows in surprise. "You make soup?"

Cara laughed and pulled a can opener out of the drawer, holding it up for Marlene and Stephan to see.

177

"Figures," Marlene said, grunting. She shook her head and grumbled to Stephan, "I really think that kids would do better in school if mothers relied more on soup bones and big pots and less on just-add-water and microwaves."

"I... uh..." Stephan stuttered. "She doesn't pull punches for anybody, does she?" he asked, and looked helplessly at Cara, who just laughed.

"Welcome to my world," she said to Stephan.

Cara put the spoons on the counter next to the stack of bowls and reached up to squeeze Stephan's bicep. "Not bad," she whispered, teasing him. "I wouldn't let her get to you."

"Huh? I didn't think I did!" he said. "You've never complained when I've come to your rescue, so I guess I'm not that much of a wimp!" He glared at Marlene, then began ladling soup into their bowls, making sure to drag the ladle along to bottom of the pot to dredge all of the meat and vegetables.

"Tsk!" Marlene clucked, with her hands on her hips and facing Cara, feigning insult. "And here I thought I was being a shoulder to cry on, your rock, your refuge from the storm..."

"Oh, gag!" Cara said, hugging her friend. "I'm sorry. I love you for coming over to my rescue. Both of you!" She looked around. "Wine, anyone? Or beer?"

"Mmm, yes!" Marlene said, holding out one of the glasses toward Cara. "That would be absolutely heavenly. Red, I assume?"

"Of course," Cara said.

Marlene shot a motherly glance in Stephan's direction. "Since you've known each other for *so long*, I assume you know that white wine..."

"Gives her horrible headaches," Stephan finished. "Yup. In fact, I'm the one who told her husband..."

"*Ex*-husband, thank you very much," Cara said, halting in mid-pour and giving Stephan the Evil Eye.

"Right, right. Ex-husband. Took long enough to convince you," he said, popping the top off a bottle of Corona and chucking it into the trash can. He slid a small knife from the block beside the stove and sliced into one of the limes, creating a perfect wedge, which he squeezed into the mouth of the bottle. He put his thumb over the opening and turned the bottle upside-down, forcing the lime to rise through the beer.

"Neat trick," Marlene said, watching him.

He grinned at her when he was sure she was being sincere. "Thanks," he said. "If you don't do that, it keeps getting stuck in the mouth of the bottle and it's a real pain in the ass."

"Stephan was a bartender," Cara said.

"Bartender *extraordinaire*," he corrected, smiling.

"Why do they do that?" Marlene asked, ignoring their exchange. "Put limes in the beer, I mean. Is that a Mexican thing?"

Stephan took a good, long slug and shook his head, smiling. "Nope. Although that's a nifty urban legend."

Cara grinned. Stephan loved telling this story.

He set the bottle down and propped himself against the counter, then cleared his throat and assumed his "story-telling voice." "There's a lot of speculation about the origin of this practice," he began. "Some people say it started to take the aluminum taste out of beers that were stored in cans. Others insist that the acidic properties of the lime somehow disinfected the rim of the bottle, making it safer for us *gringos* to drink it when we're South of the Border." He waved his finger in front of them as his eyes grew wide. "But neither these, nor a multitude of similar stories, are true."

Marlene sighed and crossed her arms, raising an eyebrow. "Okay, so what is the origin? What's the big mystery?"

Stephan smiled and picked up his beer, taking another sip and watching the lime sink back to the bottom of the bottle before sharing his secret. "It was a dare," he said, his voice barely breaking a whisper. He looked around conspiratorially and opened his eyes wide.

"A *what*?" Marlene asked.

He shrugged, reassuming his nonchalance. "Yeah. Basically, some bartenders in Texas started this thing. They were serving beer and this one guy told his co-worker that he could start a trend, putting a lime in a Mexican beer." Stephan held up his bottle and grinned. "Guess he won!"

Marlene shook her head. "That's just silly," she said.

"Why is it silly?" Stephan asked. "There are a lot of other traditions that have origins just as off-the-wall, don't you think?"

She turned her head and regarded him through the slits of her eyelids. "I guess you're right," he said.

"Stuff that's passed down from generation to generation, starting with those who *know what really happened*, then spreading among those who merely want to feel like they're a part of something..." Stephan said.

Marlene narrowed her eyes at him and crossed her arms. He raised one eyebrow, lifted his beer bottle in her direction, then raised it to his lips and took a healthy sip.

Cara glanced at them nervously and laughed. "He's pretty good at protecting the mystique when he's not among friends," she said. "You're privy to a little-known-secret that only the most elite bartenders are aware of."

Marlene shook her head, not taking her eyes off Stephan.

"You're saying I was one of the elite?" Stephan asked, rubbing his knuckles on his t-shirt collar. "I feel so honored!"

"Of course you are," Marlene said, so focused on him that he jumped back as if he had been shocked. She turned to Cara and rubbed her hands together, grinning broadly. "You always have had a knack for collecting people who are the best at what they do!"

"I'm not sure..." Cara began.

"She has, hasn't she?" Stephan interrupted. He was holding his beer in one hand, rubbing his knuckles with the other.

Marlene nodded, her smile broadening. Apparently, she had accepted Stephan into her fold; he had passed her little test.

Cara looked back and forth between the two of them, staring at each other and grinning like idiots. "Um, excuse me. Am I missing something?" she asked them.

They didn't take their eyes off one another, just stood there with odd smiles on their faces, searching each other's features as if they were trying to place them.

"You two haven't met before, have you?" Cara asked. "I mean, I've known both of you for a million years... Maybe at a Christmas party or something?"

Marlene shook her head. "Nope. I don't do Christmas parties."

"You don't?" Stephan asked. "Why not?"

Marlene shrugged. "Nope. Christmas is too commercial. I stay at home and celebrate quietly," she told him.

He nodded. "Sounds good to me," he said. "It would sure save a lot of people a lot of grief if they remembered the real reason for the holiday."

"And what is that, exactly?" Marlene asked.

He frowned. "Putting others first," he said as he lifted the lid from the soup pot and began ladling some more of the stuff into his bowl. "It pisses me off how all of these holier-than-thou types make a big deal about trimming the tree and buying gifts and showing up in church in their new clothes and making sure everyone knows how much they spent..." He shook his head and replaced the lid on the pot, and took a few mouthfuls of the burning liquid, closing his eyes to fully appreciate the heady combination of tastes and scents.

"And you disagree with all of that..." Marlene said.

He opened his eyes. "Of course," Stephan said. He put his bowl down on the counter and reached around to find a napkin.

"So you don't buy gifts and all that?" she asked.

"I didn't say that," he told her, grinning. "But I keep it in perspective..."

"Steph's the one who inspired me to do the three-gift thing with my boys," Cara said.

He smiled. "Not that Brandon agreed with that one."

"Brandon didn't agree with anyone on anything," Cara sneered. "It's one of the many reasons he's not here."

"Hmpf," Marlene said as she took a sip of her wine. She lowered the glass and squinted. "Tell me about the three gifts?"

"Jesus only got three gifts, so we keep the boys' gifts to three each," Cara said. "I thought I told you this." She frowned. Marlene shook her head, so Cara continued. "It helps us keep things in perspective, and the boys aren't disappointed when they don't get the entire stock of Toys R Us under the Christmas tree."

Marlene nodded. "I like it," she said. "Where are we eating, young lady? Surely we aren't going to spend the evening standing around the kitchen balancing soup bowls and wine glasses!"

Cara laughed and looked at Stephan. "She does this to me all the time. She's only a couple of years older than me, but she acts like she's ancient. I tell her she'd better watch out – if you're only as old as you feel, then she's going to be making a premature move to the nursing home."

"Bah!" Marlene said, mock-frowning. "You'll never catch me in one of those places!"

"Good," Cara said. "Let's eat in the living room. It's cozier, and there isn't a pile of paperwork mocking me in there."

"Poor baby," Stephan said. "Still being haunted by the terminally disorganized, are you?"

"And how," Cara said. She topped off her glass of Sangiovese and followed her friends into the living room, where she set her soup bowl on the side table and made herself comfortable in the arm chair she had been sitting in when Marlene had called nearly two hours earlier.

"*Salud!*" Marlene said, raising her glass when they were all seated.

"Cheers!" Stephan said, raising his beer, the lime bobbing gently in the bottom of the bottle.

Cara raised her glass and simply smiled. "I'm so thankful to have friends like you two," she said. "To friendship!"

"Hear, hear!" Marlene said, then took a sip of her wine. "Oh, goodness!" She put the glass and the bowl of soup on the coffee table and jumped up to the kitchen.

"What's the matter?" Cara asked.

"No, nothing. Nothing. I'll be right back!" Marlene said as she rustled around the kitchen.

Cara heard crunching and rustling and the clatter of the silverware drawer, then saw the light from the refrigerator illuminate the wall in the hallway. Marlene returned moments later carrying a basket lined with paper towels, filled with slices of the baguette and the butter dish, a small spreader stuck in the top of the stick. "Almost forgot this, and it was hot when I bought it. It's going to be scrumptious with the soup!"

Marlene passed the basket around and each took a few slices of bread.

Stephan was quiet, except for the occasional tinkle of the spoon hitting the side of his bowl. Cara curled up in her chair, spooning the soup into her mouth with appreciative comments from time to time. Marlene ate her meal more slowly, taking time to enjoy both the food and the enthusiasm with which the other two ate.

Stephan excused himself and went into the kitchen, returning with another full bowl of soup. He paused for a moment before sitting down. "Does anyone else want more, while I'm up?" he asked.

Cara waved her hand toward him and uncurled herself from the chair. "Sit, sit. I'll get it." She stood up and turned to Marlene. "Mar?" she asked, raising both her bowl and her eyebrows.

Marlene smiled and shook her head. "I had a bunch of tastes this afternoon," she said. "I'm good. But thanks." She picked up her glass and drained it. "Why don't you bring the wine in, though," she shouted as Cara rounded the wall to the kitchen.

The younger woman popped her head around the wall and grinned. "Good idea! Steph? Another beer?"

He looked up from his soup long enough to bob his head, causing both the women to laugh. "Okay," Cara said, laughing. "I'll take that as a yes!"

She returned with the beverages, then went back to retrieve her soup and curl up once again in her chair. She fished a down throw from inside the leather foot rest and draped it across her legs, then spread her cloth napkin over the top of the blanket on her lap. "Anyone?" she asked, offering blankets to her friends, who shook their heads, and Cara closed the lid again and propped one foot against it.

When she finished her second bowl of soup, Cara set the bowl on the side table, leaned her head back and held her stomach, groaning. "Oh! Who knew you could get so full eating just chicken soup?"

Stephan nodded in agreement. "You're right about this being way more filling than the instant stuff," he told Marlene, patting his stomach. "I don't usually eat so much of anything at one sitting. What do you put in that to make it so addictive?"

"It's an old family recipe," the older woman said as she smirked. "And one that I plan to take to the grave!"

"A lot of good that will do," Stephan said. "I don't know too many spirits who can appreciate a bowl of home made soup."

Marlene looked at him sharply and caught a glint of mischief in his eye.

"Nobody makes soup at home anymore," Cara said, still rubbing her stomach and missing the interplay between her two guests. "I love it when Marlene brings it over. She's kept me and my boys healthy for years."

"Really?" Stephan asked, still looking at the woman curiously. She seemed so familiar, and yet...

Marlene nodded, then set her wine glass on the table before her and folded her hands in her lap. She glanced at each of her companions, then took a deep breath. "Stephan, the reason I came over this evening is that Cara is having some – ah – *issues* about accepting her new experiences."

Cara blushed and coughed. Marlene was certainly not one for subtlety, but she didn't even *know* Stephan; they had only met for the first time an hour or so before.

Stephan didn't seem at all surprised by Marlene's blunt announcement. He casually crossed one leg over the other and frowned thoughtfully. "Really? How so?" he said.

"I'm assuming you are the other person who has been helping her, acting as a guide, perhaps?" Marlene asked, cocking her head to one side.

Cara watched her, then frowned and looked at Stephan, who did seem surprised by the older woman's question.

"Oh, no. Not a guide," he said, shaking his head. "Cara and I go back a very long way – as I believe the two of you do as well – although not *a million years,* as she suggested in the kitchen." He grinned and glanced at Cara before turning his attention back to Marlene. "I'm sorry I haven't quite placed you yet. You do seem familiar - unless *you* are a guide? In which case I have made a very wrong assumption."

"No, no. Not me," she said, laughing. "I didn't mean *guide* in the literal sense, my boy. I simply meant that you are helping her as Cara remember herself as the one we all know and love."

"All?" Stephan asked. His eyebrows shot up and Cara felt the little hairs rise at the back of her neck.

"Oh, we all love her," Marlene said, her face stretching into a wide smile. "Some of us more than others. Although it is very clear that there are more than a few – ah - *folks* out there who would rather she remain oblivious to her past for a little while longer."

Stephan laughed and nodded. "So true. I've hesitated myself, although I regret doing so," he said. "It's not good for her to avoid her calling. We need her to know almost as much as she does."

Cara felt as if she were watching a tennis match, and while she knew that what they were saying made sense to each other, she had absolutely no idea what their words meant.

"Uh, hello? I'm sitting right here," Cara said, annoyed. She frowned at Marlene, then looked at Stephan. "Before you came by tonight, I had been talking with Marlene about my chipmunk," she told him, then blushed, realizing that the statement sounded more than a little absurd.

Stephan laughed at her red face and looked past her toward the deck, but it was too dark outside to see anything. "So the little guy is still hanging around, is he?" he asked. "That's good, right?"

She glanced over her shoulder, and flipped on the porch light, but there were no woodland creatures peering over her shoulder, so she turned it off again and turned her attention back to her guests.

"Well?" Stephan asked.

"She's feeding him," Marlene said disapprovingly.

"You're still feeding him? Well, that's not all bad," Stephan said. "She has always been very good with animals, after all."

"Oh, I have?" Cara asked. "Good to know."

"All kinds," Stephan said, the devilish glint dancing once more in his eyes as he raised a brow. "Even some that we don't see much anymore."

Marlene cackled and took a sip of her wine, raising her glass in a toast to Stephan. "I like you, Stephan. You have a wicked sense of humor," she said.

"That's one way of putting it," Cara said. She frowned and picked up her wine glass, swirling the red liquid around the bottom of the glass without sipping. "I thought you two were getting together to fill me in on things, let me know my mission – if I choose to accept it – and all that jazz," she said. She frowned and glanced at Marlene accusingly. "Actually, I thought you were coming over to feed me, not to gang up on me."

Marlene looked at Stephan and sighed. Stephan shook his head slightly and shrugged. Cara watched the exchange with interest.

"Oh, honey, we're not ganging up on you," Marlene said. "It's just an interesting situation we find ourselves in, that's all. Ganging up? No. Reveling in the moment? Absolutely."

Stephan cleared his throat, bracing himself for the coming storm.

"Are you sure you two have never met?" Cara asked, her face darkening as she fixed each of them with a hard gaze. "Did you plan this little meeting?"

Stephan lowered his head and raised the beer bottle to his lips in an attempt to hide a smile. Marlene smiled openly. "I've never known him as Stephan Rust," she said. "But I've called him lots of other names."

Cara chuckled, her dark mood lifting slightly. "Funny. I have, too."

Stephan eyed her and she added, "Dumb-ass, Sir Chucklehead..."

"And those are the clean ones," Cara said, raising her wine glass in a toast to herself.

Marlene laughed. "She's full of herself, isn't she?"

"That's for sure," Stephan said. "And, to think, I came over with beer to help her not feel in a funk with the boys gone."

"It did the trick, apparently," Cara said brightly. "But I'm still in the dark. So, at the risk of sounding like an impatient kid at Christmas, would you two please tell me what the hell is going on? I feel like you both know something that you're hiding from me, and it's really pissing me off!"

"Well, we do," Stephan said, without looking at Marlene. "You do, too. You always have."

"That's what Marlene said on the phone," Cara told him. "If I know it already..." She made a "zip the lip" gesture and sat back in her chair with her arms crossed, ready to listen to Stephan.

Marlene inhaled deeply and took a sip of her wine, then she smiled at Cara. "How long have you known things, honey?" she asked.

"Um. What?" Cara asked.

Stephan leaned forward. "You know, the kinds of dreams that give you deja vu? The little chills up your spine that warn you about things? The stuff you call coincidence, even when you know in your heart that it isn't?"

Cara frowned. "All the time," she said, shrugging. "Doesn't everybody?"

Marlene smiled. "Of course," she said. "But not everybody is as aware of its significance as you."

"And you think I'm aware of the significance of strange dreams and prickly skin?" Cara asked.

"You know you are," Marlene told her.

"What did you tell me about your church when you were growing up?" Stephan prodded.

She sighed heavily. "I couldn't understand why all the people around me kept saying they were 'saved' and then they thought it made them part of some sort of elite group. The feelings they described were feelings I had had since I was about four or five years old – the feeling of ease and calm, like someone was always with me, making sure I didn't get hurt." She let out a little laugh. "It really ticked off Caroline Hightower when I had my born-again moment. Up until then, she had been the queen bee of Sheldon First Baptist. I got a bad reputation, which I thought would end once I was a true, saved member of the church. Boy, was I wrong!"

"What happened, Cara?" Marlene asked. She turned to Stephan. "I've never heard this story before."

Cara thought for a moment, then picked up her glass and took a sip of wine. She put the glass back on the table and watched the pattern the swirls made on the wall before continuing. "Everyone got mad at me when I described my experience," she said, staring at a space above Stephan's left shoulder on the wall across the room. "God actually spoke to me. Not the standing on a hill, write down these commandments on a stone tablet kind of talking. No, he actually spoke. In plain speech. Like the three of us are talking right now."

"And what did he say?" Marlene asked.

"That things weren't working out the way they were supposed to. The more we got better, the worse things became." She frowned and shook her head, focusing her vision once more on the two other people in the room. "I'm afraid I'm not explaining this very well."

"It's okay. Take your time," Marlene said.

Cara took a deep breath and closed her eyes. When she exhaled, she squeezed her eyes shut tighter for a moment, then opened them and looked at her friends. "Just remember... you asked."

Stephan smiled and Marlene nodded in encouragement.

"Okay. So, I had a dream that I was walking around with Jesus, like around the time he was supposed to be killed. The soldiers were already looking for him. The disciples were all on edge, you know? Like kids can be, sniping at one another, acting like each one was Jesus' best friend, but none of them wanted to stand up next to him when the time came. It made him really sad," Cara said.

Marlene was staring at her friend in rapt attention. Stephan uncrossed his legs, then crossed them the other way and sat back as quietly as possible in his chair. He winced as the chair made a tiny creaking noise, but Cara didn't seem to notice.

"Well, I thought I was just watching him in my dream, but he stopped by a tree and sat down on a rock and looked right at me, then he invited me to sit down next to him," Cara said. Her eyes were fixed once more on the point over Stephan's shoulder across the room, but both he and Marlene knew that she wasn't seeing the wall behind him. She was sitting on a rock somewhere in an ancient Biblical desert.

"He called me Anna. He wasn't speaking English, but I

understood him. It was weird." She shook her head and closed her eyes before continuing, her forehead creased. "He said that things were going to change a lot, and that he had done the best he could, but that people weren't going to use the message the way it was intended. He said that's what made him most sad, knowing that his time on Earth was finished. He said that people were going to take his words and his lessons and twist them around to divide people, when his intention was to bring people together so they could work together and just help each other."

"He taught the message of love. Ultimate love, a father giving his son," Marlene said in a whisper. "The Bible got that right."

"But that's not what he was here to tell us," Cara said as she shook her head. "He was one of us. He was human, but he was spirit, too, just like all of us. He knew early on that the spirit is what binds us all together. That's what he was talking about. Not that God is some white man with a beard and a white robe sitting in a chair in the clouds and passing judgment on everyone. God isn't some impartial third-party who sticks his finger into a situation and makes people die or get better, or get richer or get poorer. And God couldn't care less which church thinks it's the most holy."

"That's what he said to you?" Marlene asked.

Cara continued, as if she hadn't heard Marlene's voice questioning her. "God is not going to send a billion people in China to hell for all eternity because they go to a temple and worship Buddha or whoever, instead of a church that worships Jesus Christ. But that's what people did. They used the teachings of Jesus to divide the world, instead of bringing it together, when that's all he wanted to accomplish."

"Bringing people together?" Stephan asked.

She nodded, closing her eyes. "That's all. And so many souls have tried since then, but they can't claim to be one with God, because you see where that got Jesus."

"That's blasphemy, in the context of the church, Cara," Marlene said, lowering her voice as if someone outside the three of them might hear and take offense. "You realize that people have been burned at the stake for saying things like you're saying."

"I know," Cara said, her eyes flying open and blazing with the passion and truth of her words. "All throughout the ages, there have been people who wanted nothing more than to enlighten spirits or souls or whatever you want to call them, and bring them together. The fewer souls who realize what they are, the more out-of-sync the world becomes."

Marlene looked over at Stephan with a smile on her face, which she hid slightly when she turned to look at Cara. "You know this? You've seen it?"

"Of course!" Cara said. "There are so many things that people do to shut each other out, when all we need to do is recognize each other as connected beings, as kindred spirits, if that's what you want to call it. We all come from the same place. And the reason we're here with all of this negative energy and the world dying around us is because there are people out there who worship their own egos instead of the Source."

"The Source?" Stephan asked.

"Yeah. You know. The *Source,*" she said, moving her hands as if trying to conjure the right words that would explain what she knew was true.

She took a deep breath, glanced at the ceiling to gather her thoughts, then balled her hands in her lap and looked at Stephan. "The humming we heard at the beach? It made me sick because it was so strong," Cara said. "The ocean, the clouds, people, animals, we're all connected – although we all have different energies.

"But once in a while we recognize someone we've been with before. Oh, our bodies change." She made a gesture to her body with her hands and continued talking. "But our energy is the same. We all come from the same Source. We're born wide-awake, with all this knowledge packed inside our heads, but we can't speak." She laughed as a thought occurred to her. "Maybe that's why babies have such large heads in relation to their bodies."

"Some babies look so old and wise right from the start," Stephan said. "My daughter, your son."

"Right. They know things, but they can't communicate them to us, who have spent so much time in this world already," Cara said. Her cheeks were red and her eyes were blazing. She was on a roll. "And these little babies spend so much of their energy on trying to master their new bodies, trying to absorb the physical world around them." She shook her head, a sad expression on her face. "Then they start to walk and talk and manipulate things, and they have such wonderful expression and joy, because they still remember where they came from, who and what they really are."

"And that is..." Stephan asked.

"The Source!" Cara said, slapping her knees with the palms of her hands. "They're energy! They're light! They're full of information and knowing! Every last one of us is born with all of this *knowing!*"

"But why is it that some people know this and others don't?" Marlene asked. She looked at Stephan, who was frowning and staring at Cara. "That's the part that has always confused me," Marlene added.

Cara nodded. "Of course. Well, go back to my conversation with Jesus. How people misuse the message," she said. "There are some energies that, while they are aware of what they are, they get drunk on the power of being able to control others, to keep them asleep, in a way – I'm only saying that because *asleep* is the opposite of *awake.*"

She looked at Marlene and Stephan to make sure they were following, then nodded and continued. "Anyway, those energies, the *ego-driven* energies, made rules that allowed for those who acknowledged the Source to be burned at the stake or silenced in some other horrid ways. It's a shame, really. That leaves lots of... of... *people* – energies - who stay asleep for their entire lifetimes, or are awake but never allowed to say what they know to be true."

"For risk of being crucified," Marlene said solemnly.

"Exactly," Cara whispered. "The poor little children. The old souls in their tiny bodies." She closed her eyes and inhaled deeply. "They grow up in these families where they are told what to do and what to believe and what not to believe, and sometimes they're punished for speaking a certain way or acting a certain way." She shrugged. "Eventually, they grow up and it's just easier to let their true selves, their energies, lie dormant, rather than fight. It takes a lot of energy to fight, you know."

Marlene nodded. She had grown up in just such a family. "It's part of the reason I have such a hard time celebrating certain holidays," she said.

"But it isn't just that," Cara said. "It's everything. It's people who think the only way to win is to fight."

"It isn't?" Stephan asked.

Cara shook her head. "Of course not," she said. "It's actually easier to influence people – and I'm talking about large numbers of people – with simple, quiet messages of love and light and peace," she told him. "If we can do that, rather than fight all the time, more people will wake up. But they have to be ready. They have to understand the message. And they have to be willing to accept it for what it is."

"And what do you think it is?" Marlene asked.

"It's the truth," Cara said.

Marlene nodded.

"So what is happening now?" Stephan asked. "You are awake, but you have been for a long time, by your own admission, and you're just now accepting who you are."

Cara nodded. "My mother is Baptist. My father is Baptist. We're not Southern Baptist, but the preachers aren't that much different up north. I'm from a little town, where everybody knows everybody. Jimmy Montague was practically hung from a tree when he admitted he was gay. It was unnatural, they said. It was a slap in the face of the Lord." Twin spots of red darkened her cheeks and she clenched her fists and took a deep breath before looking up at Stephan. "Could you imagine what would have happened if I had started spouting off that I'd sat on a rock and had a heart-to-heart with Jesus Christ?"

"They'd have called you a witch," Stephan said.

"They already did," Marlene added.

Cara's eyes widened and the color drained from her face – not just the splotches on her cheeks. She turned to Marlene and frowned. "What do you mean?" Her body tingled, as if little electric shocks were feeding through her fingertips and traveling lightning-fast through her spine and her back, making the hair stand up on the back of her neck. She shivered.

Marlene raised an eyebrow. "I don't think I need to explain, love," she said.

Stephan laughed. "Marlene, she's as white as a sheet."

Marlene looked over at Stephan, a slight smile on her lips. "You remember? Was it like that for you, too?"

"Remembering? Oh, yeah," he said. "I felt like the little guys with the white suits and the butterfly nets were going to pop in at any moment and hand me a one-way ticket to La-La Land!"

Marlene laughed. "That's one way to put it."

"What are you two talking about?" Cara asked. Her hands were on her hips and she felt as if she were watching a tennis match as the two of them spoke rapid-fire.

Marlene and Stephan turned to face her. "Well, in the really old days they threw stones at you or tried various methods of torture to exorcise your demons," Stephan began.

"And more recently, you were yanked from your home and doused in a river then burned at the stake," Marlene added.

"Nowadays, they are much more civilized," Stephan said, his tone sarcastic.

Marlene snorted. "Sure. They make you think you're crazy and toss you in a padded cell and feed you drugs to calm the voices in your head."

"But there are people who really do hear voices and need that sort of thing, aren't there?" Cara asked.

Stephan shrugged. "Oh, sure. There are some who can't control their bodies here somehow, and they malfunction..."

"Like a bad spark plug in a car," Marlene suggested.

"Or just a total lemon," Stephan added. He shrugged again and turned toward the window. "I mean no disrespect. It happens sometimes," he said quietly.

Cara swallowed hard, remembering Stephan telling her about his brother who had overdosed on some drug when they were in high school. "Suicides?" she whispered.

"Sometimes," Marlene said. "Who knows why it happens. Maybe sometimes there are issues beyond our control..."

Stephan turned around quickly, startling both women. "It's to teach us to be careful," he said, the emotion making his voice crack. He cleared his throat and looked at his hands. "I don't think anything is an accident," he said, more quietly. "Not really. I mean, we all get to make our choices and all that..."

"That's what it says in the Bible," Cara said.

Marlene nodded. "Exactly."

"So you believe that the Bible is true?" Cara asked.

"Mostly, yes," Marlene said.

"Mostly?"

Stephan sighed. "You've heard about Constantine?"

"Sure," Cara said.

"It is widely believed that he picked and chose which stories to include in the modern version of the Bible," Stephan said.

"So he was one of those egomaniacs you were talking about?"

Marlene nodded. "There have been plenty of them," she said.

"There's that," he said, "but you also have to remember that the Old Testament guys who heard God talking to them didn't write the stuff down – well, except for Moses!" he laughed at his own joke, then cleared his throat as the two women continued to stare at him, waiting for him to finish. "Anyway, the stories were passed down by story-tellers, so who knows how much was changed as it was passed from speaker to speaker, then eventually written down."

"So you *don't* think it's true," Cara said.

"I think they got the basic ideas right," Stephan said. "But you know how hard it is to get a message right in a room full of people playing 'telephone.' Five or six people in a circle change the message as it goes around the circle. Some do it by mistake, but others do it intentionally."

"Okay, so..." Cara said.

"So, all I'm saying is that a few thousand years of playing telephone, and the original guys who heard the voice of God already well past the ability to correct the errors, leaves a lot of opportunity for inconsistencies from the original message," Stephan said.

"I see your point," Cara said.

"Of course, a lot of the egomaniacs took the original texts and had them destroyed," Marlene said. "There were a lot of those nut-jobs back then who believed burning the word or busting stone tablets would bend the world to their way of thinking."

"They had an advantage back then in that most regular citizens couldn't read. It was a lot easier for them to control what people heard and thought," Stephan said. "Of course, there still are a lot of those people today, although most of them are the everyday Joes and Janes you won't necessarily read about in the history books."

Cara's eyes opened wide. "You're kidding! Like who?"

"Next-door neighbors who are those judgmental religious zealots," he said. "You know, the folks who stick the fish on their cars like it's some sort of license, and give big donations to the churches to see their names on bricks and pews, then go to brunch at a restaurant on Sunday..."

"Even though they don't believe in working on Sunday," Marlene interjected.

Stephan smiled and nodded. "Right. And they wind up abusing the poor waitress and leaving her a tip that's pitiful – or none at all - because they feel all pious for having tithed at church an hour before."

"Meanwhile, they leave a mess in the restaurant, complain about everything and snub everyone around them, while wedging their over-sized bodies into little booths or chairs..." Cara said, feeling her face grow hot.

"Even though gluttony is a sin," Marlene said.

Stephan smiled. "You get it, too, don't you?" he asked Marlene.

She nodded. "Of course. It's one of the reasons I started having my own conversations with God. It's quieter there, when it's just me and God in the car without the radio on, or me and God in the garden with the birds chirping in the background..."

"Or the chipmunk snatching seeds off the porch rail," Cara added, smiling, her legs crossed under the throw on her lap.

Marlene and Stephan smiled. "Exactly!" they said in unison.

"I think I get it," Cara said. "But it's a little off-putting, don't you think?"

"At first it is," Stephan said. "Some people figure out what's going on, then they become possessive of their abilities, like they're some sort of chosen people." He snorted.

"When actually it's that they've chosen to accept what they know, but not the responsibility that goes along with it," Marlene said.

"Responsibility?" Cara asked.

Marlene nodded. "Living in the higher vibrations, protecting against the lower vibrations..."

Stephan cleared his throat and made a face, shaking his head as he took a sip of his beer and cast a nasty glance at Marlene.

"What? It's true, isn't it?" she asked him.

He shrugged.

"Lower vibrations?" Cara asked. "You mean, like, evil energy or something?"

Stephan laughed without humor. "That's what we're here for, darling," he said, but his voice was strange.

"Steph?"

He waved a hand in her direction and pinched the bridge of his nose. "Time enough for that," he said. "You need to be ready."

"Yes, she does," Marlene said. "Thank goodness she's been practicing."

"The traveling?" Cara asked, frowning. "I'm not really *practicing* that. It's kind of hard to do, and it's frustrating when I can't."

"Oh, it's great fun, once you get used to it," Marlene said.

"Isn't it exhausting?" Cara asked. "I mean, when do you sleep?"

Stephan took a deep breath and considered her closely. "You've traveled already, haven't you? I mean, it sounds like you have. I *think* you have, from what we've talked about."

She opened her mouth to speak, frowned, then closed it again and shrugged. "I guess," she said at last. "I'm not really sure. It always just feels like I'm dreaming."

"Keke?" Marlene asked.

Cara wheeled around to face her. "What did you say?"

Marlene smiled like the cat who had swallowed the canary.

"Guess that answers my question," Stephan said. "Remember the de-briefing at the coffee shop?"

"I thought you were kidding!" Cara said, her face white.

He shook his head. "How could I? I mean, even your son knew I was being completely truthful with you."

"I thought you two had talked..." she said quietly, gulping as she saw Stephen giving her *the look*. "Yeah. I guess you didn't have time for that, did you?"

Marlene laughed and took a sip of her wine. "Honey, you've been at this long enough to know that everything Steve's telling you is the truth."

Stephan smiled. "You're funny."

Marlene shrugged and lowered the wine glass. "Sorry. *Stephan.* Or would you prefer *Li?*"

"Only sometimes."

She laughed.

Cara looked from one to the other and frowned. "You two have only just met," she said. "How is it that you have inside jokes that I have no idea about? Have you been keeping secrets from me, too?"

"Not secrets, sweetie," Marlene said. "I've known for a long time that I would meet Stephan when the time was right. I just didn't know his name – not Stephan, anyway."

"I don't get it," Cara said.

"Yes, you do. You're just trying not to." Marlene put her wine glass on the table in front of her, unfolded her legs and leaned forward, pressing the corners of her lips upward into what Cara referred to as her *lecture* expression. "I have known you as Ahriel since you were born. Not born in this lifetime, but a thousand lifetimes ago. I came looking for you because I knew that this time would be really hard for you."

"Hard? How so?" Cara sat up straight and blinked, looking from Marlene to Stephan. "I don't understand."

"Well, to tell the truth, Cara, you're a bit bossy in your spiritual side," Stephan said. He raised one eyebrow and cast a crooked smile her way, adding, " A bit hard to believe, I know."

"Ha ha," she said, feeling more perturbed than amused. "Why don't I remember anything? I mean, you two seem to remember a lot."

Marlene shook her head. "Each incarnation is pretty much a clean slate." She paused, frowned and shook her head. "No. That's not right. You're born into the baby's body, full of spiritual knowledge, but with no context in which to put it. You may have been here, or you may have been... *somewhere else*... in your previous life."

"Or lives," Stephan corrected.

"Right," Marlene said.

"But..." Cara began, but stopped, closing her mouth and frowning slightly. Just watching the two of them, trying to keep the conversation straight, was making her feel dizzy. She closed her eyes and rubbed her temples, then turned her attention to Stephan, who was waiting patiently, nursing his beer, while she regained her balance.

He raised his eyebrows at her and she nodded. "Something like ninety percent of our brains are untapped," Stephan added. "Or so modern science will have us believe."

"That's because modern science is equipped to measure those things that it understands," Marlene said.

"They don't get things like spiritual maturity and past lives and faith," Stephen said.

"So that's what is in that ninety percent?" Cara asked.

Both Marlene and Stephen nodded, wearing nearly identical smiles. Cara could almost feel the air in the room intensify, as if their pleasure with her learning was having a physical reaction. She shuddered.

"It is, isn't it?" Marlene asked, lifting her wine glass once more for another sip.

"What? I didn't say anything," Cara said.

"I know," Marlene winked. "But you feel it. The room is changing."

"I just felt a chill, that's all," Cara said.

Marlene shook her head. "It's not getting colder. It's the

vibration. You felt yours shift, elevate, ever so slightly. You learned something, or rather *remembered* something, and your spirit recognized it."

"It works like that?" Cara asked.

Stephan nodded. "Not exactly, but sort of," he said. He frowned and thought for a minute. "Think of it like a physical science lesson," he began, and Marlene frowned at him, crossing her arms. "I'm going to put it into terms you can understand from a modern science point-of-view," he said, turning his head to ignore Marlene's disapproving stare. "If you pick up a single wire and hook it up to a battery then touch it to your finger, you're not going to get any sort of reaction, right?"

"Right," Cara said, leaning forward, her spine tingling as he spoke.

"But if you put another wire on the other register and touch the two of them together, you get a little bit of a spark or shock, yes?"

Cara nodded, a frown creasing her brow as she processed the lesson with her brain. From the energy pulsing through her, she felt certain that her energy understood perfectly.

Stephan and Marlene stayed quiet, glancing at one another, then turned their focus back to Cara.

"The three of us here..." Cara began, then stopped again and sighed, making a face. "It's really kind of hard to believe, you know?"

"It is, but so are a lot of things," Stephan said. "I mean, you take it for granted that there are twelve hundred fifty calories in a fast food cheeseburger because some report came out on it, right?"

She nodded.

"Did you actually conduct the data?" he asked.

"What? About the cheeseburger? No. Of course not," she said. "That was done by some, I don't know, *cheeseburger expert* in a *cheeseburger lab* somewhere."

"So how do you know that what they're telling you is true?" Stephan asked, resting his elbows on his knees and folding his hands, making an arch with his thumbs as he waited for her reply.

"It's a scientific study..." she began. "They have to give us that information."

"How do you know it's accurate?" Marlene asked.

Cara shrugged. "I don't know. I just assume..."

"Faith in the system," Marlene suggested. "You trust what someone tells you as fact because they have the credentials to back their findings and they tell you they conducted the research."

"Right, but..."

"When one of your kids has a fever, what do you do?" Marlene asked.

"I take his temperature," she said. "And if it's over one hundred, I give him something to relieve the symptoms, and I plop him on the couch with juice and chicken soup and blankets so he's comfortable until the fever goes away."

"Who told you to do that?" Stephan asked.

Cara shrugged. "Nobody, really. Parts of it are things my mom did with me. Others are just..."

"Instinct?" Stephan asked.

She nodded. "Yeah. I guess that's right."

"So you know instinctively that juice and chicken soup and some sort of baby aspirin thing is going to make your child feel better until the symptoms go away and he's back to normal?" Marlene asked.

She nodded again. "Well, not baby aspirin. They've said that's bad..."

"Who said?" Marlene demanded.

"You know, doctors... researchers," Cara told her.

"People in a *baby aspirin lab*?" she sneered.

Cara nodded. "Well, yes. I suppose..."

"Hmpf!" Marlene pursed her lips and shook her head. "Take away all that the body recognizes as good and natural healing and replace it with some synthetic trash that pollutes the body and makes it less resistant to the next bout of -"

Cara cleared her throat and looked at Stephan. "Do you believe that? That the body can heal itself if you feed it things that are natural?"

"Sure," Stephan said. "Like your chicken soup."

She nodded. "Of course."

They were quiet for a moment, Marlene and Cara each taking sips of their wine, Stephan quietly contemplating the lime floating in the bottom of his beer bottle among the bit of foam that remained there. Finally, he took a deep breath and looked up at Cara. "What about the beach?" he asked.

"What about it?" Cara's head snapped up to look at him, startled.

"You smelled something at the beach that day, and you were frustrated with me when I told you all I smelled was fish and salt water," Stephan told her. He was wearing another crooked smile.

"I told you I smelled..."

"Electricity. Energy," Stephan said. "You *felt* the energy."

"Was that those stupid surfers?" she asked. "Did I feel the fear that they felt?"

"Maybe," Marlene said. "But more than likely you felt the storm."

"The storm isn't human," she said.

"It doesn't have to be," Stephan told her.

"I heard it, too," Cara said. "It's what made me black out. The noise was – well, it wasn't *loud*, exactly, although it was deafening. It drowned everything else out. Kind of swirled around inside my head, you know?"

Stephan nodded. "We're all a part of this energy. That's probably what you heard," he told her.

Marlene shot him a look and he raised his hand ever so slightly and closed his eyes, gathering his thoughts for a moment before he continued. "The earth is polarized, with magnetic forces keeping it on its axis and on its path around the sun, which also has magnetic forces that keep everything spinning around it and keep it centered in its place in the universe..."

A look of realization came over Cara's features and she considered both Marlene and Stephan before speaking. "So you're saying that we're part of this overall force field..."

"Energy, yes," Stephan said, nodding.

Marlene chuckled.

"What?" Cara asked.

She shook her head and looked at Stephan, who was also smiling. "'Force field' sounds so woo-woo," she said.

Cara frowned and Stephan added, "George Lucas tossed the idea out there, that there's an all-powerful force binding all of us in the universe. Unfortunately, his use of certain terminology is permanently linked to death stars and light sabers."

"Ah," Cara said, nodding. "So you're saying that there are a lot of normal people out there who subscribe to this philosophy, but they just keep it under wraps?"

"Something like that," Marlene said. "If you want to call them *normal.*"

"Blockbuster movies aren't exactly what I'd call *keeping it under wraps,*" Stephan said, laughing. He reached for his beer and took a sip, wiping a bit of foam from his lip with the back of his hand before replacing the bottle on the table. He looked pointedly at Cara before continuing. "I think people like him have this message swirling around inside them and they know that it's their job to put it out there, to make people think, to open up the window for those poor mainstream people who haven't had the same learning opportunities we have."

"By mainstream, you mean *normal* people, right?" Cara asked.

Marlene snorted. "What is normal? If you mean the suit-wearing, conformist, apple-pie kind of person, sure. There are plenty of them, but there are plenty of us, too." She sat up straight and waved a hand in front of herself with a flourish. "I mean, we're a lot more *normal* than you think."

Cara frowned. "Really? I wouldn't think I could walk up to anyone on the street and talk about... what we're talking about, without them making a call to the authorities."

Stephan laughed. "Encountered some bad *juju,* have you?"

Cara rolled her eyes. "I guess you could say that. I was at this little shop a few weeks ago. The woman who owns it is Native American..."

Marlene held up one hand. "Say no more."

"What?"

Marlene shook her head. "I think I know this woman. She's a bit snobbish when it comes to our kind of folks."

"I asked her about energy and earth spirits and she sort of snorted at me and said she doesn't *do New Age*," Cara said. She huffed and added, "I didn't say anything about *New Age*. And I certainly wasn't waltzing around her shop in long skirts and flower wreaths asking for incense and all that."

"That's the thing," Stephan said. "The Native Americans actually got it. Well, them and the Mayans..."

"Who were, in fact, Native Americans," Marlene interjected, raising her chin to make a point.

"If you come right down to it, yes," Stephan conceded. He frowned, then nodded. "Yeah. You know what? You're absolutely right!"

"About..." Cara prodded.

"Look at all of the stuff that's written and passed down about earth energy and early religions," Stephan said. "It's all pretty similar."

"So where does that put people like us?" Cara asked. "I mean, my parents were Baptist, but they were born Catholic, for God's sake!"

"There are a lot of enlightened Catholics," Marlene said. She drained the last of her wine as if emphasizing her point.

"Really?" Cara asked.

"More than you'd think," Stephan said. "I mean, look at them. They use incense and candles and ointments and all that."

"And they understand the power of colors and the human spirit," Marlene added, scooching to the edge of her seat and peering into her glass, hoping some more wine would simply materialize.

Cara reached over to the table next to her and handed the bottle to her friend, who took it and poured the remaining contents into her glass.

"And Jesus actually tried to teach people about everything we believe today. In fact, I believe you confirmed that with your little testimony earlier," Stephan said. He folded his arms and sat back in his seat, nodding for emphasis.

"So why were the Catholics so hell-bent on burning witches at the stake?" Cara asked. "And why are there so few women in the church? Well, except for nuns and stuff."

"Think about it, Cara," Marlene said. She leaned forward and Cara watched the wine as it sloshed around perilously close to the top of the glass. "What is it that men want more than anything?" She turned to look at Stephan, her head leaning to one side, smiling lopsidedly, "No offense, Stephan."

He shook his head and shrugged. "None taken," he said. "The truth is what it is, you know."

Cara frowned and looked down in thought. "I don't know what you mean," she said, shaking her head.

"Power," Stephan suggested. He stood up and walked into the kitchen. The light from the refrigerator shone against the dark wall in the hallway, followed by the clinking of glass and, finally, the pop of a cap being removed from a bottle. He strode back into the living room moments later, thumb over the mouth of the bottle as he held it upside-down, watching a tiny wedge of lime float upwards, then sat down in his chair, the bottle resting between his knees.

"But they would have it, wouldn't they? If they followed the rules?" Cara asked.

Marlene burst out laughing. "Rules? Really? Oh, honey, you have so much to remember!"

"Huh?"

Stephan lifted the bottle to his lips and took a long swallow. "You're like one of your babies, who knows what she knows, but has it locked away somewhere because she was told it was improper." A sharp look from Marlene made him stop abruptly. "I think Marlene is suggesting that you're a bit naïve," he said.

"But don't I have to remember so I'm not thought of as naïve?" Cara asked.

He shook his head. "Sort of," he said. "You do this a lot."

"I do what a lot?" Cara asked, a little testily.

"Selective memory, honey," Marlene said, her eyes lingering on Stephan. She turned to look at Cara and said, "You don't drag stuff from one life to the next. You, I don't know, bury it in some sort of cosmic bunker somewhere instead of dealing with it."

"A cosmic bunker?" Cara laughed. "You've got to be kidding me!"

"It's why you've come back so many times," Stephan added. "At least, that's my theory," he added, catching another of Marlene's warning looks, which had grown sharper as he continued speaking.

"So I didn't have to come back?"

"Who knows," Marlene said, rising from her seat and crossing the room to sit on the foot stool in front of Cara. Stephan reached for his beer and leaned back in his seat, red spots staining his cheeks as he avoided Marlene's gaze. "Want more wine?" she asked Cara.

Cara shook her head. "Thanks, but no. I think what I need is some milk and cookies, after listening to you two. It seems like I have a lot to learn." She caught Stephan's frustrated expression out of the corner of her eye as he shot an angry look in Marlene's direction.

"What is it with you two?" Cara asked. "You're sparring with each other. It's like you're protecting me against something that I should know, but it's almost like you don't want me to know." She looked hard at both of them. "I'm right, aren't I?"

Stephan's face was blank, but she could see the muscle working hard in his jaw. Marlene stood beside him with the wine glasses and Stephan's empty beer bottle in her hand, and her face was pale. Their expressions told Cara all she needed to know. She nodded to herself, then sat back on the sofa. "Okay, then. Talk. I want to know everything."

"But..."

She shook her head. "No. If you've been waiting for me, then there's some reason. If there's some sort of schedule for things to happen, then we're just wasting time dancing around a subject that I know nothing about. And if you wait for me to dig it out of some – what did you call it, Mar? A cosmic bunker? - Haha. Well, we could be waiting around for a long, long time." She sat back in her seat and folded her arms across her chest, fixing the two of them with a steady glare. "The only way to avoid that is for one or both of you to come right out and tell me what I need to know."

Stephan and Marlene looked at each other. Marlene's eyes were wide and she shook her head, muttering something unintelligible in a slightly panicked voice. Stephan, however, raised his eyebrow. "She's right," he told Marlene, whose shoulders slumped in defeat. She turned on her heel and took the glasses and the empty bottle to the kitchen, where Cara could hear her pitch the bottle with unnecessary force into the recycling bin.

"She's pissed," Cara said to Stephan.

"You think?" he asked.

"I have a right to be!" Marlene shouted from the kitchen.

Stephan laughed and shook his head, returning to his seat, his jaw working as he avoided Cara's gaze.

"Is it really that bad?" Cara asked. "I didn't, like, *kill* people or anything, did I? Was I some sort of bad person... before?"

They heard a surprised gasp in the other room, followed by a coughing fit. Marlene re-emerged from the kitchen, red-faced, her jaw open slightly.

"What?" Cara asked. Then she looked at Stephan, who also was silent, but his eyes were dark as he stared at her. "Oh, God. I did, didn't I? Was I the female version of Jack the Ripper?"

"No," Stephan said. "Nothing like that."

"You weren't insane," Marlene said quietly. She crossed the room and handed Cara a full glass of red wine. "You were..."

"People said you were power hungry," Stephan suggested.

Marlene nodded quickly and took her seat. "I don't think it was that, so much as taking a stand," she said. "You've always been powerful, but you were trying to prove a point."

"To whom?" Cara asked. She looked at the glass of wine, sniffed it, then took a tiny sip before placing the glass on the side table.

"Followers," Marlene said. "You had a lot of them."

"Idiots," Stephan said. "Actually, they were worse than idiots. They were wannabes."

"Huh?"

Marlene shook her head. "I really don't think you're ready..."

"She has a right..." Stephan began, but Marlene cleared her throat.

"Some of us don't know exactly what happened, and it's best not to guess," Marlene said to Stephan, without looking directly at him.

She turned to look at Cara and reached across the arm of the chair to pat her hand. "You'll know what you need to know when it's right for you to know."

"Aren't we running out of time?" Cara asked, narrowing her eyes at the woman.

"Time for what?" Marlene asked. "You're acting like this is some sort of planned thing, like we're pawns in some sort of game." She laid a hand on Cara's knee. "We're not, honey. It's been like this for millions of years. We come, we inhabit, we do our thing, we go, we come back." She shrugged.

"We don't have to," Stephan muttered. His mouth snapped shut and he scowled as Marlene shot another warning look in his direction.

"But we change history," Cara said. "Don't we?"

"Sort of. I mean, who's to say it's change?" Marlene told her. "If it isn't predetermined in the first place, the simple act of our breathing can make a change."

"The butterfly effect?" Stephan snorted. "Really, Marlene?"

She frowned. "Well? It's true, isn't it?" Marlene growled. "We're not little chess pieces. There's not some all-knowing being in a director's chair with a script, feeding us lines and giving us place markers. We make our own choices. The Catholics got that part right, anyway – we have free will, to do good or ill as we please."

"So what's the point of remembering?" Cara asked.

Marlene sighed. "To learn from our mistakes," she said quietly. "So we don't keep repeating the same crap over and over again."

"It's the same reason we study history books," Stephan said. "So we can maybe learn from what our predecessors did and not repeat it."

Marlene sighed and a sad laugh escaped her. "The problem with history books is that it's written by those same power-hungry men who want us to remember only the bits and pieces that made a major impact on a lot of people."

"But nobody can burn our memories," Cara said.

"Can't they?" Stephan asked.

"That's enough!" Marlene spat. She closed her eyes and took a deep breath, then forced a smile and turned back to Cara. Her voice was still shaking with emotion as she spoke: "You'll remember what you need to when you do. There isn't any rush, honey."

"It is important, though, that I remember," Cara said. She looked back and forth between her two friends. "Well? Isn't it?"

"Sure," Stephan said. "But there's so much more than that."

"What could be more than remembering?" she asked.

He shrugged. "You want to make sure that your memories are true and accurate, not skewed."

Cara cocked her head to one side. "Like *telephone*?"

"Right," he said. "Remembering your name is pretty easy. Once someone says it, you feel a tremor, a flutter in your chest as you recognize the name as your own."

"I must have watched *The Little Mermaid* a gazillion times," Cara said. "I know that's silly…"

"But her name was *Ariel*," Stephan said. He smiled. "Who knows? Maybe that movie was made for the masses in the hopes that you would remember. She was a mermaid, after all."

"A mermaid?" Cara asked. "Oh, come on, Stephan." She looked at Marlene, then back at Stephan, and her voice changed. "I wasn't a mermaid, was I?"

"Heavens, no!" Marlene said.

"But you do have an affinity for the sea," Stephan added.

"And that's important?" Cara asked.

"It could be," he told her. "They're your memories."

"Was I somebody big and important?" Cara asked. "I think it's funny that everybody always thinks that in a past life they were somebody famous, when there were so many more chances to be somebody not famous."

"But equally important," Stephan said.

"Were they?" she asked.

"Of course they were," Marlene said. "Think of all the people who are into ancestry now. What is their reason for doing that?"

"What? Researching their own family?" Cara asked. She thought for a moment. "They want to know something about their own families."

"But why?" Marlene asked.

Cara shrugged. "Well, the history books don't have the stories about all the thousands of Joe Smiths who came over in steerage on big boats to work on some little farm in Upstate New York or plow fields in some corn field in Iowa or work on the assembly line at some production plant somewhere..."

"Aha! Exactly!" Marlene said, slapping her knee and startling Cara.

"What? That's not important to anyone but the immediate family, or their descendants. And it's just trivia, really."

"Is it?" Marlene asked.

"Well, I thought so."

Marlene looked up at Stephan. "What do you think? Is it just trivia?"

He shook his head. "No," he said, a frown creasing his forehead. "You win. It's the butterfly effect."

Cara frowned, so Marlene smiled triumphantly and continued. "Did you ever see that Christmas movie with Jimmy Stewart?"

"*It's a Wonderful Life*?" Cara asked. "Of course! I watch it a million times every year!"

"Mphm," Marlene grunted. "Anyway. Remember the part when he gets his wish and he sees what happens if he was never alive?"

Cara nodded. "Sure. Everything changes."

"But not just in his little town, right?" Marlene said.

Cara shook her head. "No. His absence had effects on people all over the world." She grew quiet for a moment, considering her reply. "But what I did in the past is done. There's no going back and changing it. It had its effect, and now we're living with the consequences, good or bad."

"Right. But knowing what you're capable of is important, don't you think?" Marlene asked.

"I suppose." Cara bit her lip, deep in thought. "And all of those descendants. They're alive because one person lived long ago. And one of them had to have made some sort of impact. At least one of them."

"And some of them might actually *be* their ancestor," Stephan suggested. "Well, not really. The body has changed, but the energy is the same. They've just inhabited somebody on their family tree."

"Or not," Marlene said.

Stephan shrugged. "Or not."

Cara frowned, trying to process the new information. "But, if they inhabit someone in their family tree, wouldn't it be easier to remember?"

"Not necessarily," Stephan said. "But it does give them a little bit of a head start. They're more likely to hear the stories of their own relatives – in this case, themselves – if they hear it passed down in the family lore. They don't have to go tracking down obscure history somewhere, and not have any physical connection to confirm what they think they know."

Cara massaged her temples. "This is unbelievable. I mean *really* unbelievable. Science fiction, you know?"

"Not really," Stephan said. "And energies, spirits, whatever you want to call them, don't come back every time to the same place. Sometimes they do when they have a job to finish, and they weren't able to do it before."

"So they come back, hoping to finish something..."

He leaned forward in his chair and began gesturing with his hands. "It's like a little kid in school. If they had to learn their ABCs every time they started a new school year, they'd never advance."

Marlene looked up at him and smiled. "Nice analogy!"

He shrugged and smiled smugly before tipping the beer bottle to take a quick sip. "Thanks."

Cara picked up her wine glass and raised it to her lips, then paused as she remembered something and lowered the glass again. "Steph?"

"Hm?"

"I think I get it now."

"Okay..."

"That day you were trying to tell me I was acting on my own intentions, even if there were people following me..." She began to tingle all over and she put the glass on the table, crossed her arms and began rubbing her goosebumps, even though she wasn't chilled. "I was power-hungry, wasn't I?"

"Sort of," he said.

"More like drunk," Marlene said. She stood up and walked around the room, pausing to look at a collection of odds and ends Cara had displayed in frames on the wall, and taking another small sip of wine from her glass.

Cara frowned at her. "So you're loading me up on wine so I remember things?" she shot over her shoulder. "That doesn't sound very productive!"

"Ha-ha," Marlene said. "No. I mean, there were too many people following you. They wanted to be with you…"

"You have always had a certain charisma, Cara," Stephan said. "People admire you. They put you on a pedestal. They want to…"

"Bask in your glow," Marlene suggested, spreading her arms wide. She returned to her seat and perched on the edge of it, leaning toward her companions.

"Yecch!" Cara said. "I don't like crowds."

"Not now, you don't," Stephan said. "That could be something you learned before and brought back with you, to protect you this time."

"I don't think she ever has liked crowds, even then," Marlene told him, then she turned to Cara. "It wasn't her choice to have all of those people around all the time. If I remember correctly – and I think I do – she wanted solitude. She has always been a thinker, and she likes her privacy."

"You're right," Cara said. "That hasn't changed. Although I do like people around me, they have to be people I choose. And only a few at a time." She laughed. "That's why I always thought it was funny that I had twins. The thought of one other person sharing my space, twenty-four, seven was daunting. Sharing with two scared me to death at first."

"And now you wouldn't have it any other way," Stephan said.

"Of course not. They're good for each other. They take care of each other, somehow," she said. She turned her attention back to Marlene. "But you said I had followers? A crowd? What did I do that made people want to follow me? Did I do something then that I wouldn't even dream of now?"

Marlene shrugged and shook her head. "Your preferences don't ever really change. In each life, you'll find that your energy expresses itself in a way that it is familiar with or that makes it comfortable. Maybe someone who was a farmer in another time may live in the city now but has plants in every room. Or someone who was a scholar before may teach at a university now. Even computer programmers had their thing back then. They were astrologers or mathematicians – people looking for ways to solve problems. Times change, situations change, but we continue to seek opportunities that put our souls at ease."

"So, I'm an accountant now, in this life," Cara said flatly. "I don't exactly feel fulfilled in working on other people's books."

"It's because that's not exactly what you're supposed to be doing," Stephan said. "If you followed your true calling, you'd be much more content."

She laughed. "My dream is to live on some farm somewhere in the boondocks and drive a beat-up old pickup truck and make goat cheese and grow vegetables." She shook her head. "How did I get to be a number-cruncher if my dream is so totally opposite?"

Stephan drew his brows together in concentration and raised a finger. "Think about it for a minute," he said. "What drew you to your job?"

Cara shrugged. "I don't know. I get to work at home and be with my kids when they get off the bus. I really hated it that few years I had to drive in traffic and work in a dark, windowless office every day."

He nodded. "Right. Right. You have windows here that look out over your lawn and trees and garden."

"This is hardly a farm, Steph," she said.

"Think about it for a minute," he said. "You were working in the city, or something similar to it, but your energy craved a more flexible schedule so you could be a caregiver to your children. You may not be making goat cheese, but you are growing your own vegetables and herbs."

"In an itty bitty plot in the back yard, and a couple of pots on the porch," she said.

"Sure, but it comes close," he told her. "Growing a few things you can eat yourself while earning your own way is similar to how things would be if you lived on a farm. You'd be self-sufficient, taking care of your own books – and probably other people's too, because you're a nurturer."

"But an *accountant?*" she asked. "That's a stretch, even for you, Stephan. I don't even really *like* numbers!"

"No, but numbers are rows, like you would plant in rows. You like things that are logical and orderly," Marlene said.

"Great. Now I'm Mr. Spock!"

"Another enlightened person, I believe," Stephan said. "He had a great following."

"But he was totally campy," Cara replied, grinning.

He shrugged. "Whatever. When you can get such a large group of people to follow you for generation upon generation, I'd say that's a pretty successful campaign, wouldn't you?"

"Even if a large number of them are just doing it for the cool factor?" Cara asked.

"It gets people thinking," Marlene said. "Do you know many people who can get an audience of millions? I mean, if you get five people thinking and one of them actually *gets* it, I'd argue that you've done a good job."

"Is that what they teach you in sales school?" Stephan asked with a slight snort.

Marlene made a face. "Yes. Return on investment. Absolutely," she said. She sniffed at being called out on her previous line of work. "My argument may be textbook, but think about it: Roddenberry's ideas had a huge impact on people all over the world, even if his delivery methods were a little commercial."

"A *little?*" Stephan asked. "That's an understatement, even from you!"

"Fine. A *lot* commercial," Marlene conceded. "But you have to admit that there would be a lot of people who never would have looked up if they hadn't ever watched an episode of *Star Trek*."

"Looked up?" Cara asked. She felt the shiver of recognition, even though she wasn't sure which part of the conversation she was supposed to recognize. Shaking her head, she said, "I'm confused. We're not talking about alien populations here. We're talking about our planet."

"Same difference," Stephan said.

"Really? Aliens?" Her eyes grew wide.

Marlene nodded. "Sure. We'd be awfully closed-minded to think we're the only intelligent species in the entire universe, wouldn't we?"

"Well, sure, but..."

"The universe is infinite. Energy created the whole blasted thing..."

"Literally," Stephan said, snorting at his own joke.

"Right," Marlene said, shaking her head at his juvenile reaction. "The energy chooses different ways of manifesting as individuals, depending upon the conditions. Just because we don't see creatures we would recognize as sentient beings doesn't mean they don't exist elsewhere," she said.

"Are you saying that there really could be life on Mars?" Cara asked.

Marlene shrugged. "I suppose there could be, but there isn't right now," she said. "People – and by that, I mean the energy that inhabits the body - choose where they're going to manifest," she told Cara. "For one life you might be in some realm far, far away..."

"Like Princess Leia?" Cara laughed.

"Ha ha," Marlene said. "But that's not such a far-fetched idea. As I said, George Lucas also stretched the boundaries of human thinking on the subject when he came out with his first movie."

"How so?"

"*Long ago? Far, far away?*" Marlene said. "I mean, until that time, common thought was that all of the space travel stuff was futuristic with Earth-based technology."

"And it isn't?" Cara asked, tilting her head to one side as if to alter her perspective of the conversation.

Marlene shook her head, and Stephan cleared his throat, a smile on his face. "It's a far-fetched idea, but I think that things like the pyramids and the ley-line markers come from some advanced technology from another place that maybe stopped here – long ago, from far away."

"Inter-breeding with humans?" Cara asked, her eyes wide. "Now you're getting a little hokey, Steph."

He shrugged. "Who knows? It was all way before recorded history. But the fact remains that we have no answers about how those things got here and what they were used for, so why not?"

"You have a point," Cara said. "It's a little creepy to think of aliens, though."

"What if you were one?" Marlene asked.

Cara frowned. "Silly thought," she said. "I know who my parents are. I look just like both of them..."

"On the outside," Marlene interrupted.

"So you're saying there is alien energy?"

"Not so much alien, when you consider that we're all made of the same stuff, when it comes down to it," Stephan said. "So there wasn't interbreeding so much as infusing memories of advances that were brought from a previous existence."

"Wow," Cara whispered. She stood and paced the room, trying to absorb the new ideas. "I never..."

"You have, you just didn't remember," Stephan said.

"We do digress, don't we, Steph?" Marlene asked. "I mean, our Cara has only just realized the possibilities that we've been aware of for some time. And she's having a hard time swallowing everything right now."

"Shrinking aura?" Stephan asked, squinting at Cara.

Marlene nodded, her head tilted to one side. "A bit," she said.

"I feel it, but you see it," Stephan said to Marlene.

Marlene shrugged. "She's just feeling a little overwhelmed, is all."

"My *aura* is shrinking?" Cara asked, pausing in mid-stride to stand and blink at her friends. Her skin went pale as she asked, "Is that bad?"

"I don't think it's anything you should be concerned about, honey," Marlene said. "Your aura glows bigger when your confidence is higher, and it shrinks when you are doubtful or timid or in a situation that makes you uncomfortable."

"A safety measure, of sorts," Stephan suggested.

"Really?"

He and Marlene both nodded.

"Safety measure for what?" she asked.

"Not for you, exactly," Stephan said. "It's a form of communication. Energy doesn't normally have a voice, unless it manifests in a body that affords it one. So energy grows bigger and shrinks smaller so we can recognize and truly communicate with one another. It helps us figure out our jobs or passions, too, and our origins."

"So, what does my aura look like?" she asked Stephan. "What does my aura say about me?"

He shrugged. "Not my area," he said. "I feel energy growing or shrinking. Marlene, though. She's got a knack for it."

"Usually," Marlene said. She hesitated, and Cara noticed her friend blushing a little.

"Are you embarrassed?" Cara asked. "Wow! That's a first!"

"Huh?" Marlene asked. "Oh, well..."

"She's actually really good at what she does," Stephan said. "But she gets a little shy about admitting how powerful she is."

"*Powerful* is not a word I like to use, Stephan," Marlene scolded.

"Right," he said, nodding at her. Turning to Cara, he whispered, "but she is."

Marlene rolled her eyes. "Talented, yes. Gifted, absolutely. Powerful is akin to manipulative, and I certainly don't want to manipulate anyone."

"You're really touchy about that," Cara said. "Why is that?"

"I've seen what power can do," Marlene said quietly, picking imaginary lint from her clothing to avoid eye contact. She closed her eyes and inhaled deeply, then forced a smile at Cara as she opened here eyes. "You have, too."

"But I don't remember it." Cara frowned and shook her head, feeling like there was something right in front of her that she should know, but it was just out of her reach.

Marlene shook her head. "You don't have to. That's one of the benefits of history books. Remember we were talking about that before?"

Cara nodded.

"You can see what people did to manipulate others, and what you should and shouldn't do," Marlene continued. "Most of the great tragedies that occurred at the hands of humankind were done in the name of power."

"Some of them had nasty environmental impacts as well," Stephan said.

Cara's entire body felt like it was humming, and she sat down quickly, gripping the edge of the sofa cushion for support. Marlene and Stephan stayed where they were and watched her, both of them realizing that she needed to go through the process of remembering – or not – and nothing either of them could do would help her.

Finally, she opened her eyes, which seemed a deeper shade of blue, and her pupils were dark and huge in the centers. "That was weird," she said. "Did you hear the hum?"

They shook their heads. "Must have been meant for you," Stephan said.

"You said there were *environmental impacts*," Cara said, raising her chin and releasing her grip on the cushion. "And these were in the name of power? Ego?"

Marlene nodded. "We're seeing a lot more of it today, too," she said. "In the old days, dynasties existed for politics and religions. But now, with all the corporations, we have another whole realm that operates on the dynasty model, and we put people in positions of power who worship nothing but material wealth. They couldn't give a shit less about the well-being of the person in the next office, or the person who buys their product, much less the impact on the planet, on the universe as a whole. It's all very disconcerting."

"So what can we do about it?" Cara asked. "There must be a way to help them see that what they're doing is wrong."

Stephan and Marlene glanced at one another, a strange look passing between them. Cara watched Stephan's Adam's apple bob up and down in his throat, and he took a deep breath.

"That's the thing, sweetie," Marlene said. "When you try to influence someone else, it's your decision, not theirs. They make their mistakes, hopefully learn from them, and quit repeating the pattern at some point in the future."

"And if they don't learn?" Cara asked.

Marlene shrugged. "Then they keep repeating it until they advance beyond the bad. It's kind of like that movie *Groundhog Day*," she said, laughing.

Stephan shook his head as Marlene cackled at her own joke, and turned to face Cara. "My theory is that more of us are becoming aware of ourselves in order to influence people toward a better end," he said. "But in the end, the decision to change or not is completely up to the individual."

"We're overpopulated. We're sapping resources. Energies that should be used for good are being manipulated and causing harm," Marlene said. She reached up to rub her neck, as if to release something that had taken hold of her there. When she looked up again, her shoulders slumped slightly. "It's all just exhausting, really."

"But you said there are more people becoming aware of themselves – well, of their energy selves," Cara said. "That's a good thing, isn't it?"

"I suppose," Marlene said. "But again, if you look at history, there were entire populations of people who were aware, who recognized and understood the energy and its connection. Where are they now?"

"Their times passed," Stephan said, a little sharply. "Most of them have moved on."

Cara's head snapped up. "Passed? As in Nirvana? Moved on where?"

"Whoa. Slow down, sister! One question at a time!" Stephan

chuckled. "Like I said, sometimes, entire populations understood what was going on. But not everyone in that population practiced what was in the highest good for all. Some of them had to come back, while the rest of their contemporaries moved on to whatever is next. We call it Nirvana or Moksha or Salvation, among other things."

He paused to take a sip of his beer, frowning at the bitterness of it, as it was no longer cold. He swallowed, placed the bottle on the table and finished his thought. "The benefit those cultures have for us, though, is that they existed in a time close enough to ours that their lessons have not been lost."

"No. They've been bastardized, though," Marlene said. "Just like Christianity."

"Really?" Stephan said, crossing his arms and frowning at Marlene.

She nodded. "They're portrayed as naïve or quaint or delusional..."

"But people are looking into what they had to say, into what they believed, and they're realizing that it wasn't all *woo-woo*," Stephan said.

"So why do we send Christian missionaries in to *save* those people who adhere to those quaint, delusional beliefs?"

Stephen blew out his breath and looked up at the ceiling fan, his lips moving as if he were having a conversation with someone on the ceiling. Cara looked up to see if there was anyone or anything there, then, feeling foolish, began fiddling with the fringe on the edge of one of her pillows."

He ended his heart-to-heart with the ceiling fan and returned his attention to Cara and Marlene. "Look," he said quietly, "even the Christians have a lot of things right. They just tend to present the lessons with a little too much ego, is all. Well, most of them, anyway."

Cara felt as if the tennis match was resuming, and she closed her eyes and put her hands in the air. "What kinds of lessons?" she asked. "And why can't I learn them, too? If they're right there for whole cultures to see, why can't I just study them and move on with whatever it is I have to do next?"

He raised an eyebrow and shook his head. "You crack me up, Cara," he said. "Some of these cultures took thousands of years to hone their messages and recruit adherents. For some of them, we have written history, and those are easier than most for us to study and learn from – if you know the language or can get past the censorship in the translations."

"Some of it is verbal history, that has been translated by people who used and preferred the written word, so some of it isn't necessarily accurate," Marlene added.

Stephan nodded. "Right. Like we were talking about earlier. But some of it hasn't been translated, or parts of it have, but we don't know if we've got it right."

"You mean like the Egyptians? They used hieroglyphics to leave their stories on pyramid walls and stuff," Cara said. "It wasn't all word-of-mouth. The messages are right there, drawn out on stones and pyramid walls and cave walls for all the world to see."

"But who can read hieroglyphics today, honey?" Marlene asked.

"With accuracy, anyway," Stephan added. "I mean, there are people who theorize what's written..."

Cara was frowning, biting her lip. When her companions grew quiet, studying her, she shook her head and looked at them. "No. That's not right," she said.

"What's not right, Cara?" Stephan asked. He shivered, and realized she wasn't necessarily having a conversation with anyone they could see. He looked around, sensed a presence similar to the one he had been speaking with moments earlier, and smiled at Cara. She had come a long way tonight, he thought.

"The naïve, quaint peoples," Cara said. "They weren't – naïve or quaint, I mean. They were very advanced, as you know," she said. Her eyes had gone out of focus again, and she seemed to be concentrating on a spot on the floor between Marlene's and Stephan's feet.

Stephan's eyes followed her focus, searched the floor, but saw nothing, although he still felt the vibration of another energy in the room.

"Go on," Marlene said, nodding her encouragement.

220

"They didn't die off, either," Cara said. "They're still here." She nodded firmly at the floor, then raised her head and looked at her friends. "We can't see them, but they're still here, inhabiting the earth somehow."

Marlene frowned. "That's not what…"

Stephan moved his hand toward Marlene and she closed her mouth. So that was the energy Cara was channeling – Toltec or Mayan, or something even more ancient. The thought made his body fairly hum with recognition.

"Where are they, Cara?" Stephan asked. "Why can't we see them?"

She shrugged, her forehead wrinkling in concentration. "I'm not sure. They've figured something out somehow."

"Like in the *Celestine Prophecy*?" Marlene asked. She snorted and sat down heavily in her chair.

Stephan shot a look in her direction, but she ignored him. Marlene obviously didn't feel the presence in the room like he and Cara did, and she was getting frustrated. She wanted Cara to say something new.

"I think I read that," Cara said, nodding. "Yes, something like that. Although his message was a little too shoot-'em-up at the end for my taste."

"I kind of liked it," Stephan said. He picked up his beer bottle, frowned as he remembered how warm it was in the last sip, and put the bottle back down on the table. "It at least got people thinking."

Marlene frowned at him. "You liked it?" she muttered, and shook her head.

"What?" he asked, spreading his arms, beer bottle in one hand. "I did. Maybe it's a *guy* thing." He shrugged as Marlene made a face. "What? You were picking on us guys before, about males being power-hungry egomaniacs. I figured I'd just add a little flavor to the mix. We like guns and violence, too."

He went into the kitchen, dumped the warm beer into the sink and pitched the bottle into the bin, returning a moment later with a fresh bottle from the refrigerator – conspicuously missing the lime.

Cara cocked her head to one side, watching him stroll back to his seat. "You know that's not true, Steph," she said. "I'd be so disappointed to find out after all these years that you're just some macho idiot like my husband."

Stephan choked and sputtered on his sip of beer, wiping his mouth with the back of his hand. "Brandon? Macho? Please!"

Cara laughed. "I know, right?"

Marlene shook her head but said nothing.

"I never could figure out what you saw in that guy," Stephan said. "He is so totally not your type."

Cara frowned. "What do you mean? He looks like – and *acts* like – practically every guy I've dated since high school."

"She always did like having the upper hand, Steve," Marlene said, pronouncing his name wrong on purpose. "And she always has been drawn to warrior-types."

Stephan shot her a look and shook his head. Then he looked at Cara and shrugged. "I guess," he said.

"I did?" Cara asked. She threw up her hands. "I really hate being out of the loop, especially since it concerns my life! I feel like one of those amnesia patients on a soap opera: *'Don't you remember me and our children, Cara? We were so happy before your accident'*."

Stephan's eyes grew wide and his cheeks went slightly pale, but Marlene just laughed. "I can see how bad this must make you feel, honey," she said. "But believe me, that's not what we're trying to do." She put her wine glass on the side table and used both hands to raise herself from the armchair.

"You're not leaving, are you?" Cara asked.

Marlene shook her head. "Nope. Just going to take a lady-break," she said.

"Do you think I'll ever remember?" she asked Marlene as the older woman proceeded down the hallway. She was favoring one knee. Funny, Cara didn't usually think of her friend as *older*.

At Cara's question, she turned around, bracing herself with a hand on each wall of the hallway. "I think so, but I can't say for sure," she said. "That, of course, is up to you." She put her hands down and started to turn around, but paused and added, "stop rushing things."

Marlene closed the bathroom door and turned on the fan. Stephan blushed and scratched his nose with one finger, while still holding the beer in the same hand.

"What do you think?" Cara asked Stephan.

"About what?"

"Stephan. Really," she said.

He shrugged. "You almost seem like you do remember, Cara," he said. "Some of the things that come out of your mouth are so dead-on, but then you have no idea."

"Such as?" she prompted.

"Oh, I don't know." He thought for a moment, then let out his breath, as if making a decision he wasn't sure was the right one. "Like a minute ago, when you said you felt like a soap opera amnesiac."

"That was prophetic?" she asked.

"Not prophetic. More like, that *is* you."

"There was an accident?" she asked.

"Sort of..." He scratched his nose again, glancing over his shoulder toward the hallway bathroom door. The fan was still on, so he leaned forward and lowered his voice. "That's one version," he said.

He glanced back over his shoulder as he heard the water running and the toilet flush, and he sat back.

"You're not going to say anything else?" she asked.

He shook his head and reached for the beer, tilting it back as the fan switched off and the bathroom door opened.

Cara sighed heavily. "Do I have to remember, do you think? Or can I remain blissfully oblivious for my entire life?"

He shrugged. "I dunno. But the Mayans said the end of the world was coming, so I'd try to remember if I were you."

Chapter 8

Marlene returned to the living room and her eyes grew wide as she took in Cara's wide eyes and pale complexion. "What did you say to her, young man? She looks as if she's seen a monster!"

Cara was perched on the arm of the sofa, rocking back and forth, rubbing her arms with her hands. She looked up at Marlene. "You said we had all the time in the world," Cara said angrily. "But we don't, do we?"

Marlene frowned at Stephan and went to Cara's side. "Of course we do."

"The Mayans were pretty smart people," Cara said. "If they predicted the end of the world..."

Marlene closed her eyes and chuckled. "Everyone thinks the end of the world is going to be the Armageddon-like event at the end of the New Testament." She shook her head and smiled.

"Isn't it?"

Marlene opened her eyes. "I'm one of the non-conformists, I guess," she said. "Me? I think we're going to have some sort of reckoning, yes. But no blood spurting from people's eyes, no swarms of locusts, no great floods... Well, not on a global scale, anyway."

"What's that supposed to mean?" Cara turned quickly toward Marlene, fixing her friend with her wide eyes. "Do you know something you're not telling us?"

"Of course not," Marlene said, patting Cara's hand. "Things have to change. You said it yourself. The message Jesus tried to deliver was twisted around and it had long-term adverse effects on humankind. Lots of egomaniacs. Lots of nut-balls predicting the end of the world, acting like they know something."

"They don't?" Cara asked.

Marlene shook her head. "I don't think so. I mean, who can really say? But I do know that something has to happen to set things right again."

They all sat quietly, listening to the whirring of the ceiling fan, each lost in their own thoughts for the moment.

Cara set her shoulders and raised her chin to look directly at Marlene. "Is Jesus coming back? Like it says in the Bible?" she asked.

Marlene shrugged. "Who can say?"

"What *can* you say?" Cara asked, pounding her knees with her fists. "Dammit, Marlene! You know some of these things, and you're just not telling me! Is this one of the things the Christians got right, or isn't it?"

Stephan coughed and Marlene sighed. "Oh, they got it right, alright. He said he'd come back, he knew he'd come back. He wasn't finished yet," she said. "Of course, he has been back many times already, but he hasn't revealed himself as Jesus."

"He has?"

Marlene nodded. "Well, once or twice, anyway."

"If he said he was coming back, and he has come back, why won't he reveal himself?" Cara asked.

"You're kidding, right?" Marlene asked. "You know what happens to people who reveal what they know to the egos in power. They'd lock him up or medicate him to the point where he could do no good in this world."

"But there are so many believers waiting for that day..."

"Right. There's that, too," Marlene said. "The story about the end of the world coming when Jesus returns. There are too many people with too many opinions about what The Redeemer will look like when he returns. He could never satisfy every image. Would he be a peaceful man or a warrior? A man or a woman? Who can say?"

"Is he really The Redeemer, then?" Cara asked.

Marlene shrugged. "Again, who is to say? I suppose, if you came right down to it, anyone whose message could have a positive impact on the entire human population would be considered a redeemer, no?"

Cara frowned. "Could he have help this time? I mean, people who won't turn away from him when the authorities come around?"

Marlene shrugged again. "People will always turn away when things get hard," she said. "Who would have ever imagined that the chosen twelve would have done what they did – hidden, I mean?" She shook her head and sighed. "If you want to think of it in those terms, he did have help that time. Probably the other times, too, but he remembered and got smarter. He was quieter about it. I'm sure the crucifixion isn't something he wants to repeat, you know?"

Cara shivered and Stephan put his beer on the table. "Don't worry, Cara," he said. "I'm not one of those."

Marlene scowled.

"Those what?" Cara asked.

Stephan fixed his attention on Marlene as he spoke. "One of those who abandons their friends in times of trouble."

Cara frowned and looked at him, then at Marlene. "Really," she said. "So what are you saying, that I'm Jesus?" she laughed. "You're being ridiculous."

"Of course he is," Marlene said. "You were probably there, but you weren't one of the twelve." She glared at Stephan. "He wasn't either, I might add. Thank God!"

Stephan snorted.

"I should say, *Liris* wasn't one of them." Marlene said. She raised her wine glass to her lips and took a small sip, keeping her eyes on Stephan over the rim of her glass.

Cara looked up at him, then fixed her attention on Marlene. "What about... what's your name again? Keke?" Cara cocked her head to one side as she considered her two best friends. "Were you one of them?"

"No. Of course not," Marlene said quietly.

"The two of you just met," Cara said. "I really don't understand why you're at odds with one another."

"I didn't realize..." Marlene said, her voice rusty.

"Yes, you did," Stephan said. His cheeks were streaked with red.

"Okay, okay," Cara said, standing between the two of them with her palms facing her friends. "I don't want there to be any ugly feelings between you. I love you both. I'm trying to understand things that are, quite frankly, pretty hard to grasp. I don't need to worry about the two of you killing each other."

Marlene shivered and looked at Cara, her face white. "What did you say?"

Stephan forced a chuckle and returned to his seat. "Wow," he said. "See what I mean?" He inclined his head toward Marlene, who looked shaken. "Are you sure you don't remember anything?" he asked Cara.

"She even looks the same, now," Marlene said quietly.

"The same as what?" Cara asked.

"When you tried to break us up before," Marlene said. "It's what..."

Stephan leaned forward quickly and stopped Marlene from saying anything more. "Marlene and I weren't exactly friends... *before*," he said.

"But you said..."

Stephan closed his eyes. "No, no. You see, we were both *your* friends. But we weren't friends with each other." He glanced at Marlene, lifting his head as if he enjoyed being significantly taller than she was.

Cara rubbed the sides of her face with her hands. "I don't..."

"We have always loved you, honey," Marlene said, turning to look up at Stephan, then back at Cara. "Both of us. Always. But Liris and I tend to be on opposite ends of the spectrum when it comes to understanding our purpose. We've worked together..." she fixed an icy gaze on Stephan and added, "*many* times."

"Not because we liked each other, mind you," Stephan said. "We did it because we loved you. You kind of forced the issue." He spoke as if he were joking, but the tone of his voice betrayed him, and he cleared his throat and looked away to avoid Cara's gaze.

"But you said there wasn't really a purpose," Cara said. She looked at both of them. "You said we had all the time in the world. You told me there isn't some sort of grand scheme..."

"Not really," Stephan said. "But the Mayans..."

"Pishah!" Marlene interjected loudly, her hands waving. "The Mayans are living out a perfectly wonderful existence in a parallel universe somewhere. Their vibrations are so high at this point that they'd look at us like we're cockroaches or leeches or..."

"Says you," Stephan spat. "That's been your theory all along, hasn't it?"

"Stop it!" Cara said, standing between the two of them, her cheeks red, hands held out between them like a crossing guard. "This is ridiculous!" She looked at Stephan, then at Marlene, her breath coming in gasps as if she had been running. "Is there a purpose or grand scheme or isn't there?"

She continued to look at her two dearest friends, squaring off against one another, until Stephan finally dropped his head and returned to his seat. "No," he mumbled.

"No?" Cara looked at Marlene. "Really?"

Marlene's face bore twin patches of red as well, and her eyes were bright with emotion. She shook her head and retreated a few steps as well, although she remained standing.

"Okay. So why am I supposed to be waking up or whatever you want to call it? Why is it so important to the two of you that this happens right now? And why is my son involved?"

Marlene sighed and took her seat. "Ego, I suppose. Each of us has one."

Stephan snorted and raised an eyebrow, although he didn't look at either of them.

Cara frowned at him and turned back toward Marlene. "What do you mean? Whose ego?"

Marlene smiled. "Mine and his," she said, inclining her head toward Stephan without looking at him. "We all want to be mama's favorites, I suppose. Souls have those same shortcomings on an energetic level as we do in human form – or whatever form we take." She shrugged. "I suppose we both want to be the center of your attention."

"It's what got us into trouble before, lady," Stephan said, scowling. "We don't need a repeat performance."

"Repeat performance?" Cara asked.

"I'm not going there, Steve," Marlene said. "If Cara doesn't remember on her own, it's best that we don't force the issue."

"We've done this so many times..." Stephan said.

"And we've screwed it up more than once," Marlene told him. "I'm for just letting her do what feels right. She'll know. She's one smart cookie, our Ahriel." She smiled at Cara, whose stomach seemed to lurch at hearing her soul name said aloud in her living room.

"Ahriel," she said quietly to herself. She frowned. "How does a soul get its name?"

Stephan's shoulders raised slightly and he took a swallow of his beer, grimacing when it hit his throat, forgetting that it didn't have a lime in it. "I guess it's the one you choose when you first – I don't know – *manifest*?" He looked at Marlene. "What do you think?" His tone was still a little chilly, but he was trying to be conciliatory for Cara's sake.

Marlene pursed her lips. "I'm not sure. You have an identity. I mean, whether you recognize an actual name or not, your identity remains the same, regardless of whether you are energy bound or unbound." She made eye contact with Stephan. "I suppose that, for purposes of identity, that may be the way it happens, yes."

His eyes grew wide in surprise and Marlene forced a smile. "You're stubborn, but you've been around the block a few times. You do know what you're talking about – sometimes," she admitted.

He inhaled sharply. "I don't know if I can take much more of this. The world might fall apart."

Marlene snorted. "Or pigs might fly."

Stephan laughed at this, and the atmosphere in the room lightened considerably. Cara put her hands on her hips. "What is going on here? A minute ago, I thought the two of you were going to tear each other apart!"

"Mutual love and respect for you, honey," Marlene said.

"Maybe we have learned something after all," Stephan added.

"And what about my son?" she asked.

The two of them looked at each other and sighed simultaneously. "C'teus is probably your most devoted follower. You've been together more times than either of us can imagine. He's tied to you somehow, but he's different from us."

"Different? How?" Cara asked.

Stephan closed his eyes and smiled, then looked at Cara. "It's almost as if he is ego-less," he said. "It's a beautiful thing, really. It's what Jesus needed in at least one of his twelve."

Marlene nodded. "Hm," she said. "Yeah. You're right." She let out her breath and said, "he always puts you first, honey. C'teus would die for you without a second thought."

"Would?" Stephan asked.

Marlene scowled at him. "Let it go, *Steve*," she said. She turned to look at Cara and said, "He would... Again."

Cara felt her heart skip a beat as she let their words sink in. She shook her head and began gathering plates and empty glasses that were strewn around on various pieces of furniture, then carried them into the kitchen. Stephan and Marlene sat in silence, listening as Cara turned on the water, glasses and plates clinking together as she scrubbed them by hand.

"Can I help?" Marlene shouted.

"Nope," Cara replied, her tone still icy from the information she had been given just moments earlier.

Marlene sat back in her chair as if reprimanded, and Stephan laughed. "She always was like this," he said as quietly as he could, although he was sure Cara could hear everything if she chose to.

Marlene nodded. "Cleaning up everyone else's messes," she said, then closed her eyes and laughed softly at herself. "Both literally and figuratively," she added, gesturing with her chin toward the kitchen. "That's good and it's bad, you know."

"She's at least starting small this time," he said.

"Small consolation," Marlene said, rolling her eyes. "Dish soap versus explosives."

An exaggerated clinking of plates in the dish rack indicated Cara had heard that last comment, and Marlene covered her mouth with her fingers. "I don't want to say too much. Don't want to force painful memories."

Stephan nodded. "She *will* remember," he said. "If she hasn't already."

"I know that," Marlene told him. "But on her own terms. Don't you agree that's best?"

He nodded grudgingly and pushed himself up from his seat, ambling toward the kitchen to join Cara, leaving Marlene alone in the living room.

Cara turned off the faucet and turned to face him. "I agree with Marlene," she said. Her words surprised him. "I don't want anything or anyone to influence my memories, alright?" She shook her head, clutching the dish towel in her fists. "I'm not even sure that *memories* is the right way to refer to them. I'm so... *conflicted*. I'm not sure what I believe, what's real and what's my imagination." She closed her eyes, twisted the towel in her hands and exhaled, setting her jaw before opening her eyes and facing him. "But whatever it is, I don't want to have any ideas about what I did or didn't do, who I was or wasn't. I want to see for myself, when the time is right."

His lips stretched in a simulation of a smile, although she was certain he didn't agree with her – the expression didn't reach his eyes.

Tentatively, she reached out toward him. "Steph," she said quietly. "It's been just three months since I had that... whatever it was... *episode* on the beach. I'm confused. I'm not sure I'm not crazy, if you want to know the truth. I see things, I feel things, I know things, but I'm not sure how."

Marlene rounded the corner and leaned against the wall, arms folded across her chest.

"I want to live my life, *this* life, the way I'm supposed to. I want to raise my boys – and be devoted to *them*, not the other way around. I want to have my friends, and figure things out the way I need to." Cara shook out the towel and wiped a wet spot from the counter top near the sink, then she smiled at both of them. "I've listened to the messages of a woodpecker and a chipmunk, for heaven's sake. I'm realizing that all of these things I thought were dreams all these years were maybe memories, and I need time to sort that out. I appreciate both of you being here and helping me through it all. But I don't want to rush anything. I want to remember on my own."

"As it should be," Marlene said quietly as Stephan nodded. He turned and frowned but, seeing the expression on Marlene's face, his own features softened.

"We both love you and want what's best for you," Marlene said, her gaze moving from Stephan to Cara.

Stephan nodded again. "I guess I'm just afraid of losing you," he said. He stopped himself from adding *again.*

Cara sighed and smiled at him. "You won't. Don't worry," she said. "You've been my friend for my whole life. Both of you." She paused, tilted her head to one side and a strange smile stretched across her lips. "Apparently, for many of my lives."

She shook as a chill came over her, and her expression changed. "You have always looked out for me," she said. "And I haven't always listened. But it's okay. I'm different now."

"Humbler," Marlene said.

Stephan snorted again. "You can say that again!"

"So maybe we're all where we're supposed to be?" Cara suggested quietly. "And doing things differently might mean that we're learning something from our past... *indiscretions*, mistakes, whatever you want to call them."

He closed his eyes and shrugged, and Cara smiled. She folded the towel and put it on the counter, then went over to Stephan, took his hands and stood on her tiptoes, kissing him gently on the cheek. "You mean the world to me," she said. "All of them, actually."

He sighed and nodded. "It's usually you, but this time it's me who seems to be rushing things," he said. "You're right. No matter what happens here, we have all the time in the world." He chuckled. "*All* of them."

Marlene pushed herself away from the wall and clapped her hands together. "Well, sweetie," she said, "it looks like my work here is done. If it's all the same to you, I'm going to head home before it gets too late."

Cara nodded. "Sure," she said. "Here. Let me put the soup back..."

Marlene waved a hand at Cara. "Keep it," she said. "I have more at home, and I'll get the pot back from you next time I see you."

Stephan looked at Marlene, eyebrows raised. She closed her eyes and nodded.

Cara smiled. "Thanks. It was delicious."

Stephan nodded. "It was. I'm glad you ladies let me join you."

"Like we had a choice?" Marlene said, but there was humor in her voice. She glanced around until she found her purse and coat, folding the latter over her arm as she dug around the purse for her keys. She looked up at Cara once more. "Are you sure you're going to be okay tomorrow?"

Cara nodded. "Of course," she said. "I'm a big girl. I've got a little turkey breast and a whole bunch of movies to catch up on." She made a face and added, "the boys don't like chick flicks."

Stephan laughed. "I should say not!" Then he turned and retrieved his keys from the kitchen counter as well. "I guess I'd better go, too," he said, giving Cara a peck on the cheek. "Thanks again."

"You're both okay to drive?" she asked.

They turned and rolled their eyes simultaneously, and she laughed. "Just checking!" she said.

Stephan turned as he reached his car. "Is it okay if I stop by tomorrow to check on you? I'll have Liv with me."

She smiled. "Sure. But don't be surprised if I look a little disheveled. I don't plan on getting dressed tomorrow."

He laughed. "I'll keep that in mind."

Cara leaned on the door frame and watched both sets of headlights as they retreated down the driveway. She closed the door after the last glimpse of red tail lights disappeared behind the neighbor's shrubs, smiling to herself as she put the pot of soup into the refrigerator and turned off the kitchen light.

Epilogue

The house was empty but, for the first time since her divorce, Cara didn't feel alone as she went through the evening ritual of brushing her teeth and changing into her pajamas.

A warm glow spread from the lamp on the bedside table as she climbed into bed, the sheets chilly against her bare feet and ankles. She shivered and pulled the covers over her, trying to decide whether to read for a bit or turn out the light.

Smiling, she realized that there were no scritch-scratching sounds of the woodpecker outside her window. She yawned, relaxed and turned out the light.

Recalling the meditation methods Marlene had shared with her, she closed her eyes and concentrated on relaxing every inch of her body, starting with her toes. She hummed softly, imagining the stress of the day leaving her inch by inch, replaced by the energy that would fuel her night time journey.

When the relaxation exercise reached her shoulders, she noticed the traces of light at the edges of her consciousness – what would be her eyes if she were confined to the vessel she knew as Cara.

Excitement welled up within her, like champagne bubbles in her lungs, making her feel buoyant, like she could fly.

The idea became more of a suggestion, and she suddenly felt enormous and strong, although she was still light. She felt wings stretching on her back and she arched her body then launched skyward, exhilarated by the feeling of flight.

Glancing beneath her, she saw her feet – not her human feet, but great blue-gray claws with long, polished talons. Her great tail swished powerfully behind her like a rudder, keeping her enormous yet graceful body steady as she climbed ever higher into the clouds.

She turned eastward and instinctively knew where she needed to be. Traveling high above the earth, she saw the faint light of the sun creating a glow around the arc of the earth, drawing ever nearer with each flap of her powerful wings.

Although her flight pattern took her a great distance, and the sun was rising noticeably above the horizon in what would be east, it seemed as if the travel took no time at all. Crossing the expanse of water that she knew must be an ocean, she began her descent, searching below for her landing place. As the faint fingers of sunlight stretched across the land below, she spotted an island and felt the thrill of recognition.

She altered her direction, her long, sleek body gliding along effortlessly, her wings folding to allow for a steady but smooth descent. Out of the corner of one eye, she caught a reflection of the sunlight on her body, but she dared not look for long. She knew instinctively what she was, and a long perusal would not be possible mid-flight.

Laughter bubbled up inside her as she realized that she was flying of her own accord. She, who was frightened to death of traveling by airplane, felt buoyant, exhilarated. This was different, natural. She was free, not confined by the strap of a seatbelt, nor the metal skin of the mechanical beast that invaded the sky. Much like the clouds and birds in the world in which her body Cara inhabited, the body she inhabited here was a part of the sky. She belonged there.

As she flew closer to the island, she began to recognize hills and trees, landmarks that guided her toward her destination. She frowned, trying to remember what the place looked like, hoping she'd remember it when she saw it.

Flying low, she crossed a hill and smelled the ocean, then felt her heart swell with excitement as she spotted her destination. Below, her feet stretched out, the polished talons stretching wide in preparation for landing. She felt her body slow instinctively, and she arched her neck and settled gracefully on the sand, her wings flapping once, twice, then folding in a resting position along her back.

A stone circle, much older, more primitive than Stonehenge, stood before her as she flexed her feet on the ground, and the landscape hummed to her in greeting.

A gryffon emerged from behind one of the stones, its regal head perched upon a beautifully arched neck, its golden eyes soft with emotion. "Ahriel," the gryffon said, his voice a hum that made her heart race. "I knew you'd come."

Ahriel bowed her head, fighting back tears. When she raised her head, the circle was filled with creatures she recognized, if not by name, then by vibration. Their voices created a great hum, reminiscent of the sound that frightened Cara on the beach, but which now filled Ahriel with joy.

She took a breath, steadying herself, and smiled. "I'm home," she said at last. "I remember."

BOOK TWO TEASER
From *The Lightbearers: FOUND*

Chapter 1

Stephan stood in the dark with his hand on the light switch, changing his mind about flooding the room with light as his eyes adjusted to the pale glow from the street lamp at the end of the driveway. The polished wood appeared blue, and the glass reflected sparks of white and gold as he blinked his eyes or moved his head.

He smiled in spite of himself and shook his head, wondering why people were so quick to erase the darkness instead of embracing its beauty. He thought that the moments during a blackout, as the fear and surprise subsided, were the most magical of all, as people became aware of senses other than their sight.

He closed his eyes and inhaled deeply, smelling wood polish and the lingering scent of a beeswax candle that he had burned in his office before leaving for Cara's house a few hours earlier. There was a hum, also, of the electric appliances that occupied most of the rooms in his tiny house: the refrigerator just steps away in the kitchen, even the higher pitched hum of the clock on the microwave, and the almost whispering hum of the power cable to his computer.

Shivering, he realized he might need to add another hum – that of the furnace. It was already cold outside, and it was bound to get colder before the night was through. He was glad Olivia was with his parents tonight. He could keep the temperature a little lower than when she was in the house.

He held his hand out over the glass bowl on the wooden entry table and dropped his keys into it. They clattered against a collection of coins and other odds and ends he had emptied from his pockets recently, and he made a mental note to empty the bowl before his parents brought Olivia back tomorrow, then stepped forward carefully, his hands held out slightly in front to detect any furniture he may have inadvertently left pulled out or otherwise moved. He paused by the thermostat, but decided that he slept more soundly when it was cold. If the temperature dropped below sixty, the heat would kick on.

As he reached the kitchen, he felt for the drawer pull and withdrew a cardboard pack of matches. He removed one and struck it, the snap of ignition followed by the sharp smell of phosphorus. It flared blue, then blazed into a brilliant yellow-gold, which he stared at for a long moment before searching for the jar that contained one of the beeswax candles he and Olivia had made together. He tilted the jar toward him and extended the match inside, willing the wick to catch before his fingers did.

He shook his hand, extinguishing the match, then deposited the spent stick in the sink before wrapping both hands around the jar and carrying it through the kitchen and down the hall to his bedroom.

"No need for lights tonight," he said, his voice sounding odd in the silence as he set the candle on his bedside table.

He turned and peeled off his jacket, navigating the room by candlelight, and hung the garment on a hook inside his closet door, the metal buttons hitting wood a strange intrusion in the otherwise silent room.

Stephan removed his shoes and placed them carefully on wooden shelf in the closet, then rolled up his shirt sleeves and went into the bathroom to get ready for bed. Each whooshing, rustling, soft sound he made felt like he was disturbing the thousand tiny things that had already sought refuge in the dark, and he breathed an apology before deciding to forgo the light in the bathroom as well.

Almost instinctively he looked at the mirror, but saw only a vague blue outline of his head against the backdrop of the window curtain. The left side of his face was illuminated slightly by candlelight, and his eyes glittered, gold flecks sparking in his reflection.

He turned on the faucet and bent down, bracing himself against the cold water in the already chilly room. Reaching for the bar of soap, he inhaled its scent – some sort of pine-infused organic something that

Cara had given him for his birthday – then turned it over and over in his hands to create a lather. He washed and rinsed his face, then brushed his teeth in the dark, and stripped down to his boxers before climbing into bed, shivering against the chill of the cotton sheets.

The candle crackled and glowed on the table beside him and he glanced over at it. It seemed to be doing the sort of dance it would do in response to a draft or breeze, but there was none in the room. The soft floral scent of the candle tickled his nose and he frowned, then turned onto his side and propped himself up on his elbow to watch the show. The flame would shrink, shrink, shrink, then suddenly burst bright and sway back and forth, making comforting crackling sounds before the pattern began again.

As he stared into the flame, it grew brighter, more intense, and the blue glow became more pronounced. The crackling sound had a rhythm, like conversation but not the traditional kind – more like that of smoke signals used by Native Americans - and he frowned and leaned his head closer to listen, a soft smile pulling at his lips as he realized the candle sounded like waves crashing in the distance.

He moved closer and inhaled, intent on blowing the candle out, but was overcome by a feeling that someone needed the light – for comfort or guidance, he wasn't sure. Feeling foolish for a split second, he shrugged and lay on his side, pulling the covers closer to his chin, watching the candlelight dance grow farther and farther away as his eyelids drooped and he fell into a deep sleep.

CPSIA information can be obtained at www.ICGtesting.com
Printed in the USA
LVOW090413050712

288808LV00002B/4/P

9 781612 961200